THE BOOK OF FRED

THE BOOK OF FRED

ABBY BARDI

WASHINGTON SQUARE PRESS
PUBLISHED BY POCKET BOOKS
New York London Toronto Sydney Singapore

A WASHINGTON SQUARE PRESS *Original* Publication

A Washington Square Press Publication
POCKET BOOKS, a division of Simon & Schuster, Inc.
1230 Avenue of the Americas, New York, NY 10020

Library of Congress Cataloging-in-Publication Data

Bardi, Abby.
   The Book of Fred / Abby Bardi.
      p. cm.
   "A Washington Square Press original publication."
   ISBN 0-7434-1193-5
   1. Teenage girls—Fiction. 2. Suburban life—Fiction.
   3. Fundamentalism—Fiction. 4. Foster parents—Fiction. 5. Women
   librarians—Fiction. 6. Washington metropolitan area—Fiction.
   7. Eccentrics and eccentricities—Fiction. I. Title.

   PS3602.A79 B6 2001
   813'.6—dc21   2001034025

First Washington Square Press hardcover printing September 2001

10   9   8   7   6   5   4   3   2   1

For information regarding special discounts for bulk purchases, please
contact Simon & Schuster Special Sales at 1-800-456-6798 or
business@simonandschuster.com

Printed in the U.S.A.

for Tony, Andy, and Ariel

Acknowledgments

Many thanks to Jenny Bent; Eric Bond and the *Takoma Voice;* Lucy Childs; Paul Cirone; Dr. Wendy Cozen; Dr. Judith Friedman; Dana Hoffman; Sheri Holman; Jody Jaffe; Edward P. Jones; Billy Kemp; Joyce Kornblatt; Len Kruger; Rocco and Kathleen McGuffin; Nancy Miller; Howard Norman; Suzanne O'Neill; Beth Reynolds; Sandy Roemer, R.N.; Ben and Adele Rothblatt; Amy Rothblatt; David Rothblatt; Beth Schmais; Elizabeth Shah-Hosseini; Walter Teague; Christina Van Norman; and my colleagues and students at Prince George's Community College.

Special thanks to Rachel Carpenter, Molly Friedrich, Bob "Gamse" Pyle, Joe "G." Gannon, Greer Hendricks, and Gila Lewis.

Stars, scarves, and scooters to the Shrews: Vickie Bailey, Barbara Bass, and Andie DiMarco.

THE BOOK OF MARY FRED

When Little Freddie took sick, I knew things would change, and change fast. We sat next to his bed all day, laying our hands on him and saying the Beautiful Prayer, but he just got hotter to the touch and more shivery. His skin looked yellow, like he was turning into old paper. I laid my hand on his forehead and said "Get thee hence" a bunch of times, but it didn't help. That night I had a dream that the Archangel Willie came to me and said, "Lo, Mary Fred, thou wilt be traveling down the road. Thou wilt be somewheres else when the Big Cat comes. So look to yourself and say Ho."

When I woke up, I said Ho a bunch of times. Then I went to see Little Freddie, but he was already gone.

Mama and Papa wanted to take his body down to the Compound, but the people from the County came and said they needed to take him for an all topsy. I wish I could say I had never seen Papa so mad, but the truth is he had been that mad before. "My temper is my trial," he always used to say, but sometimes I thought he was right to get so steamed, especially the past year when the same thing happened down at

the Compound with my other brother, Fred. "My children be-
long to the One, not you people," he yelled at the man from
the Coroner's office as they took Fred away in a black bag.
We all stood there crying as they drove away with him. After
a few days, they brought him back and said we could bury
him, so we had a nice funeral in the Compound cemetery.
The Reverend Smith did the service and it sounded real
peaceful. I liked when he said Fred was up in the World
Beyond with all the angels dancing around him in a heavenly
circle. He made it sound so good I wanted to go there right
away.

So when Little Freddie went onward, I didn't feel as bad as
I might have. I was getting used to these things, and I figured
he'd be happier where he was. The only bad thing was we
couldn't bury him with Fred, we had to bury him up at the
Outpost, and not as many people were at the funeral, and the
Reverend Thigpen wasn't as jolly and nice as the Reverend
Smith. He talked about the mountains covered with snow, and
I wished Little Freddie had taken a coat with him because it
sounded mighty cold up there. After the service, we had some
sandwiches in the main hall, and then we went back to our
cabin to wait. Papa said he knew it would only be a matter of
time, and he was right.

It took two days for the County to come out to see us.
Mama had cleaned up the cabin as best as she could. She made
up Little Freddie's bed real nice, and the rest of us tidied up
our stuff so things looked neat. I swept out the kitchen and the
bathroom, which got a lot of spiders in them generally, and I
raked the leaves out front so the grass looked clean and orderly. I raked really hard because I knew something would
happen, and I was hoping to make it go as easy with all of us
as possible. The Book says that the One told us to sow lots of

grass, because grass is the word of the sower. That's why we planted so much, because it spread the Good News more quickly.

But it was a dry June, and the grass was dying all across the Outpost. That's how I knew.

The woman who drove me away said her name was Diane. She seemed like a nice enough lady, so I went with her without crying, or trying to run away, like my younger brothers and sisters were doing. We all went in different cars because we were going to different places, and all of them were hanging out the car windows yelling for Mama. By that time, Mama wasn't even there. They'd taken her and Papa away in a police van, but the little ones didn't know that. I kept them inside when she left. I was the only Big now, since Fred went home to the World Beyond, and sometimes it was hard being the only one who understood what was going on. I had been the middle one of the Bigs, between Fred and Little Freddie, and then there were the four Littles. Mama and Papa always said we were their stairsteps. There was a step missing between Little Freddie and me, a baby who had died.

Diane kept talking to me about stuff outside the window. She'd say things like "Look at the cows," and I'd look and say the cows were nice, though personally I liked pigs better because they were smarter. "Did you learn all about animals in school?" she asked me. I said of course not, I had learned about them from feeding them, and anyway, she probably knew I hadn't been to school in some time, not since we'd left the Compound. "Would you like to go to school?" she asked. She had a way of asking questions with this bright face that made you want to give her the right answer just to keep her from busting out crying. So I said yes, even though I didn't want to go to school. I wanted to go back to the Outpost, but since I knew Mama and Papa were going to be gone for a while, my second choice was the Compound. I knew that wasn't going to happen, so I decided to travel hopefully in the One.

I watched Diane as she drove. She had gray and black hair standing like wires all around her head, and red marks in the corners of her mouth. Her skin was spotty, and her eyes were squinting through her glasses while she watched the road. As we drove, the road got bigger and more full of cars and trucks, and things started to look more city-like on either side. I could see rows of little houses in lines, and all the green began to disappear. I thought of asking her where we were going, but it didn't matter that much to me. I knew that wherever it was, Mama and Papa wouldn't be there, and I would dwell among Lackers, like the Book said not to, and the Littles would be somewhere else, wondering where we all were and needing us. The thought made me want to cry, but I just stared really hard out the window and pretended I was running down one of the city streets, then flying up to the World Beyond, and in a while I felt a bit better.

After about an hour of driving, Diane got off at an exit and drove to a square building. We went up in an elevator. She asked if I wanted to push the button, and I did. When the doors opened, we went down a wide hallway to some glass doors that said County something or other. Only it was a different county from the one the Outpost was in. Both the Outpost and the Compound were in Frederick County, only they were two different Frederick Counties. The Reverend Smith always said that was no accident, that the counties had been waiting for the blessing of our Coming, and when we had come, we had fulfilled the prophecy of the county fathers.

This county was not a Frederick, but that didn't surprise me. I was ready to spend some time with Lackers. It had happened once before, when I was small. We got taken into custody because Papa was brought in for illegal possession of firearms, and it took a few weeks for us to get home to Mama. That was in Tennessee, before the Compound was located. We always say it was located, not found, because as far as we're concerned, the Compound was always there, we just didn't happen to be there with it.

I had been to school with Lackers, back at the Compound, and I didn't mind them. They left us alone and we left them alone, and most of the time we all got along just fine. Every so often one of them would beat up one of my brothers, or one of my brothers would beat up one of them—usually for saying something about our clothes. We always had to wear something brown, since brown is the color of prophecy, and sometimes people said mean things about that. But most of the time even the Lackers knew that the Big Cat was coming, and coming soon, and they seemed to want to stay on our good side just in case we turned out to be right about everything else.

I sat in a chair next to Diane's desk while she filled out forms. One form after another, she wrote and wrote, asking me questions every now and then. Did I wear glasses? No. How old would I be on my next birthday? Sixteen. Did I have any food allergies? No, but I didn't like beets. Had I ever had any serious illnesses? Chicken pox, measles, German measles, and mumps, and the One had seen me through all of them just fine, thank you for asking. What grade was I in? I would have been in tenth this year if we'd stayed at the Compound. Fred would have been in twelfth, and Little Freddie in seventh. She didn't ask me about them, but I thought that. I thought about them a lot and wondered how they liked it where they were.

"You'll have to stay at the shelter for a day or two, until this all gets processed," Diane said.

"Thank you, Miss Diane," I said. I was pretty good with my please-and-thank-yous. You never knew when you'd need them.

"Just call me Diane," she said.

"I don't think I can," I said. "Mama always says that adults are your olders and betters. I'd feel funny calling you just Diane."

"Try," she said.

"Okay. Diane. I'll do my best. Diane." It sounded odd to me, but then, I knew that a lot of things would be odd from now on.

The shelter was called the House of Ruth, which made me feel right at home since I know that Ruth was someone in the Old Book. We didn't read the Old Book, just the New, but still, I felt right at home with folks who were in it. I never did meet anyone named Ruth, but there were some nice enough women and kids in there. Some of them had brown skin, which took some getting used to, but we were always taught that brown was a gift from Above, so we didn't mind it.

They gave me a stuffed dog to sleep with the first night there. We had never had any toys like that, since Papa said they were craven images, but when I tried to go to sleep, I found myself petting the dog and thinking about Little Freddie. I'd close my eyes and see him playing hopscotch with my sisters, and throwing stones at cans in the woods. The hair at the back of his head wouldn't lay flat, and we were always licking our hands and patting his head to get it to stay down. His hair was soft and straight, and he smelled like boys do, of sweat and dirt and the air. I felt the smell of him, and as I breathed in, something caught in my chest, and I put my arms around the stuffed dog and held him while I tried to sleep. All night long, I dreamed I was home, at the dinner table with my whole family, but then sometimes when I'd look at Fred, or

Little Freddie, they would seem to be disappearing, turning all filmy and see-through like veils. I'd try to call out to them, but the words would stick in my throat, and once I woke myself up trying to shout. It was hard to get back to sleep after that, but finally I did.

That morning, the sun shone in the window and woke me, and I knew it was the light of the One telling me to get up and get cracking. I jumped up and put on my clothes. Some of the little kids in the room were still sleeping, so I dressed real quietly, then went downstairs to wait for Diane. One of the volunteers made me some oatmeal, and I ate it, though I don't like oatmeal in summer and it was already hot out, not really an oatmeal kind of day. By the time Diane came at ten o'clock, the little kids were up and watching TV, and one of them was jumping up and down on the sofa but nobody seemed to mind. Diane came and filled out some paperwork while I tried to shush everyone, and then we got back into her car and drove some more. I was just as glad to get away from the children, since being with them was making me think about the Littles and wonder where they were and if they were sad like I was.

It felt weird to be in Diane's car, since we didn't ride in cars at all back at the Compound, though at the Outpost we did it a lot more since stuff was more spread out and the town was nearby. I liked looking out the window, so I watched the road as it got wider and busier still, and then we turned off the highway onto a street and went past a bunch of apartments. Kids were playing outside, and though they were brown, mostly, they reminded me of Little Freddie. Everywhere I looked, I saw little boys playing with their sisters, throwing balls to them, chasing them down the street and laughing.

After a while, the streets got more winding and narrow, and they were lined with houses, the kind of houses with porches and flowers climbing up the side of them. Some of the flowers were big and bushy, with wild purple blossoms, as if no one had ever trimmed them. The houses weren't the new kind you see all over the county, but old, with funny angles and peeling paint. I knew that the Book said something about flowers, but I couldn't think of what it was. "The flower falleth, but the proverbs of Fred endureth forever." Something like that. It worried me that I had forgotten.

We pulled up in front of a pink house with purple trim that looked like it had just been painted. The pink was the color of rare meat, and looking at it made me a little queasy. As we were driving, Diane had explained to me that I was going to stay with a foster family, the Cullisons, for a while, and that I would like it there. She said they were a nice family and that they would take good care of me. I asked if all my brothers and sisters were going to nice foster families too, and she said yes. So I tried to make myself feel relieved about that, but I didn't—I felt jittery and out of sorts.

We walked through a wooden gate in the front. When we swung it open, it leaned sideways on its hinges. Papa would have hammered a few nails in it right away, but he wasn't there, of course, so we just walked right in and up some steps. The steps had been newly painted purple too, and they were a little bit sticky. The front door was heavy and wooden, and it had a piece of glass in it with little diamond-shapes around the edges. Through the glass, I could see someone approaching. Her eyes seemed to widen, and then she threw the door open and stood there smiling at me but in a nervous kind of way, like someone seeing a skunk on the path on their way back from the well.

"Mary Fred, this is Alice Cullison. She's going to be taking care of you for a while."

"Pleased to meet you, Mrs. Cullison."

"Oh," Alice Cullison said. She had straggly graying brown hair, pulled back in a ponytail, and very pale skin, and her eyes were light gray-blue. Her cheeks got a little bit red, and she said, "Oh, not Mrs., dear. Could you just call me Alice, please?"

I knew better than to argue, having gone that round with Diane. "Sure, Alice." I felt all smart-alecky saying it, and I grinned a little.

"Come in, come in," Alice said, smacking herself on the side of the head with her hand like she'd forgotten something. "It's so hot out already today, isn't it? I'm sorry we don't have air-conditioning, Mary Fred, but it's cool in your room. I put a fan in there, and it works pretty well. It sort of sucks the air in from the window and stirs things up."

We walked into a small, dark sitting room with some old faded sofas in it. The sofas had blankets thrown over them but you could still see that their arms were worn out. Alice went on chatting with us as if she hadn't seen another living soul in a week. "Would you like some lemonade? It's just Country Time but I made a whole pitcher of it. Of course, it has aspartame in it and—Mary Fred, you don't have a seizure disorder or anything, do you? I hate aspartame, but Heather likes it so I always—Diane, can I get you something? Mary Fred?"

"Yes, ma'am, I'd like a lemonade please, and thank you."

Alice gave Diane a funny look, like she was panicking and needed help in the kitchen, but Diane sat down on the sofa and motioned for me to do the same. "Do you have any questions for me, Mary Fred?"

"No, ma'am. Diane."

"Don't you want to know something about the Cullisons?"

"Not really, ma'am. I'm sure I'll find out soon enough." The truth was, I knew the Cullisons were Lackers—I could tell the minute I walked in there and saw no brown in sight, nor an ark, nor the Holy Books. All Lackers were pretty much the same to me. Some were nice and some weren't, and it didn't matter because where I was going, none of them were going to be there anyway, and the time was coming for the Big Cat, and coming soon. It was already 1999, and the signs were manifold. That was what Papa always said, "manifold," which was also part of a car engine, he said. I could tell Diane wanted me to ask a question, though, so I said, "Well, Diane, how long do you think I'll be here?"

"It's hard to say, Mary Fred." Diane looked at me like this was not the question she was hoping for. "It depends."

"What does it depend on?" I asked in spite of myself, though we were always taught that it's not polite to ask adults questions, especially not two in a row.

"Well, there's the trial. Both trials, actually. And then after that, it's impossible to say."

"To say what?" I couldn't believe my impertinence, asking her a third question. The Reverend Thigpen would have said that I was being presumptive and told Mama and Papa about it, then I would have gotten a beating. But Diane didn't seem to think it was odd, though I could tell she didn't like this question any better than the last one.

"It's hard to say if they'll be convicted and if so, how much time they'll have to serve."

"Well, our lives are service," I said cheerfully.

"I mean, in jail," Diane said, biting her lip. "It depends on what the judge says."

"I know," I said, trying to make it easier for Diane, though I was getting a knot in my stomach. "So how long do you think it will be?"

"I don't know," Diane said, looking at me. Her eyes looked so sad behind her glasses that I wanted to say something to comfort her.

"I'm sure I'll like it here," I said. "I'm sure it will be just fine."

"Here's your lemonade." Alice came through the kitchen door carrying a tray with three different-sized glasses on it. "The big one is for you, Mary Fred," she said, stooping in front of me. I had never seen an adult serve a child before, and certainly not from a tray, and I felt funny taking the big glass, but I did. I waited for her to give Diane her lemonade and to sit down, and then I took a sip of mine. It tasted like old sweat, but I drank it all down fast so I didn't notice it. I decided to get me a bunch of lemons and some sugar sometime soon and show the Cullisons what real lemonade was. It looked like I'd be here for a while, so I figured I'd get a chance.

"Alice, why don't you tell Mary Fred something about your family?" Diane said, waving her hand in the air like she was trying to swat a fly.

"Oh, okay!" Alice brightened up and pressed the palms of her hands together. "Well, Mary Fred, it's me, and my daughter Heather, and my brother Roy. We've lived in this house for about thirteen years, since Heather was two."

"Heather is just your age," Diane added, in case I couldn't do the arithmetic for myself.

"I work in the library at the college near here. Heather just finished the tenth grade, and she'll be going into eleventh next year."

I waited for her to tell me what Roy did, but she didn't. I also wondered where Heather's father was, and how you could call one woman, her brother, and her daughter a family. I thought about my own family, the seven of us kids, and Mama and Papa at the dinner table, all of us saying the Beautiful

Prayer together. But of course two places at the table were empty when I tried to imagine it, and that just made me feel worse and more confused. For a moment I felt like crying, and I wished I'd been able to bring the stuffed dog with me from the shelter. I'd gotten kind of attached to him.

"Would you like to see your room, Mary Fred?" Diane asked. It seemed like Diane was the only one who knew what to do. Alice jumped to her feet like she was about to dance, and started up the stairs. I followed her. The stairs were made of scuffed wood, and they twisted up onto a small, dark landing. Alice flipped a light on and I could see five wooden doorways. One had a flowered name tag on it that said "Heather" and stood open just a crack. I could see an unmade bed, a bunch of stuffed animals, and a lot of clothes on the floor. Two doors were closed, but the third was open, and I could see a bathroom. Alice opened the fifth door wide so I could look in. There was a bed with a flowered bedspread and a big piece of the same flowered fabric across the window. It didn't look like any curtains I had ever seen.

"This is your room, Mary Fred," Alice said, waving me in. "It used to be the guest room, but I fixed it up a little and tried to make it look more, well, feminine." Diane gave her a disapproving look that I pretended not to notice. We went into the room. It was all nice and neat, and a little fan was blowing as hard as it could next to the open window. Through the window, framed by the flowery fabric, I could see a big oak tree. It was a spready oak, the kind in the Book, and I made a plan to stand under it for a while in case the One wanted to send me a prophecy, or maybe just some idea of what was going to happen now.

"It's very nice," I said to Alice, who smiled and looked pleased altogether. "It's a fancy room." It was just the kind of fanciness Lackers seemed to like, so I figured I ought to say that.

"You can put your things down, Mary Fred," Diane said. I was carrying my overnight bag. I put it down on the bed.

"Why don't you get unpacked, and maybe you'd like to wash up," Diane said.

I knew it would only take me about two minutes to unpack, but I said I would, and they left me there. I opened my suitcase and started taking things out. I had brought my two best dresses, in case we went to church, though last time I'd been with Lackers that hadn't happened. I looked for somewhere to hang them up and sure enough, there were a bunch of plastic hangers in the closet. The closet was big enough for another twenty dresses or so, but needless to say I didn't have them. I had a pair of brown dungarees for working in the garden, in case there was a garden, and I folded those up and put them in a drawer in the dresser next to my bed, along with five pairs of cotton underpants. Next to them, I put my stripy yellow and brown shirt, the one that Fred used to say made me look like a skinny little bumblebee. "A bee in the body of a lion," Mama would add, smacking Fred for making fun of me. I would make a loud buzzing sound and swoop down on all the Littles like I was going to sting them, and they would scream and run away, laughing. It would be a hot day, like this one, and we'd all be out in the yard raking and watering, chasing each other with the hose. I put my hands over my ears because all I could hear was laughing in my mind and then the terrible silence of this house, with nothing but the fan humming.

I sat there for a moment, still holding my ears and shaking my head to get the fan sound out of it. Then I made myself get up and close the dresser drawer, and I looked for somewhere to put the toiletries that I had in a small plastic bag. I didn't want to leave them in the bathroom in case they were in anybody's way, so I put them down on the nightstand. I put *The*

Book of Fred right down next to them, but that seemed kind of disrespectful, so I put the plastic bag on the floor. Then I noticed a little bookshelf next to the window, so I put my book there, squeezed in between a bunch of what looked like picture books. On top of the bookshelf was a plastic pony with long, braided, wavy pink hair. What will they think of next, I thought to myself. We used to braid our horses' manes sometimes, but of course they were never pink. I had to admit, though, that the plastic pony looked awfully pretty that way.

When I had unpacked everything, I slid my overnight bag under the bed and sat down on the comforter for a while with my hands in my lap. I figured that Diane and Alice might have needed to talk about me some, so I gave them a little time. Then I went out on the landing and found the bathroom, and I splashed some cold water on my face and washed my hands. I said to myself, "The water of life is bright as crystal," and then, "Blessed is the one who keepeth the words of the prophecy of the Book." I looked at myself in the mirror and said, "Amen." I wasn't used to mirrors, since Mama didn't believe in them, and my face always looked like a stranger's. But I said hello to the girl in the mirror anyway, and gave her a little wink.

Diane and Alice were sitting on the sofas talking when I came downstairs. I was sure they had been talking about me before, but now they were on the weather and how hot it was, and Alice was saying that she really wished she could afford air-conditioning but it was just one of the many things, something or other, and she mentioned some man's name and looked sad. Diane looked bristly, and her wiry hair seemed to pick up an electrical charge and quiver, but she didn't say anything, just shook her head and stood up. "Mary Fred, I'll be leaving now. Is there anything you need to ask us?"

I thought for a minute. "What are my chores?"

Diane and Alice both laughed, like this was funny. "Oh, Mary Fred," Alice said, touching me lightly on the arm, "it's not like we want you to be our servant or anything. We want you to feel like you're part of the family."

I said I figured that anyone who was part of a family had chores. They laughed some more, so I gave up and asked about school. Diane told me that school was just about over so I didn't have to worry about it until fall, but that they would try to get a tutor for me over the summer so I could catch up with my grade. "Heather can help you," Alice said, though Diane looked at her funny, like she thought that wasn't likely.

"Is Heather at school right now?" I asked.

"I hope so," Alice said. "I mean, yes."

"Well, Mary Fred, I'd better be off. Welcome to your new home. I know you'll like it here." Diane gave me a little pat on the arm, and then handed me a card. "Call me if you have any more questions, or if you just need someone to talk to."

"I will, ma'am," I said, putting the card in the pocket of my dress. Diane smiled at me and said, "I'll talk to you later," to Alice. She went out the door, pulling it shut behind her. The air whooshed around us as the door closed. Alice turned to me, smiled brightly, and said, "Are you hungry?"

"Not really, ma'am. Alice. But thank you."

"Would you like to go lie down for a while?"

"No thanks. I'm not really tired."

"Would you like to watch some TV?"

"Oh, no, ma'am." I didn't want to explain that only Lackers watched television, that we would never, ever poison our brains like that. That would have been a rude thing to say, so I just said, "I don't care for TV, thank you."

Alice looked like she had no idea what to do with me, so to bail her out I said, "Why don't I bake something for dinnertime?"

"You mean like cookies?"

"Yes, ma'am. Alice. I can do cookies, or a cake if you'd rather."

"Do you like to cook?"

"I like it fine. That's what I'd be doing right now. If I was at home. So I figure since this is home for a while, I ought to do what I'd be doing. At home."

"Oh, of course, honey. Well, let's go see what ingredients we've got. It's awfully hot for baking, isn't it?"

"Well, yes, I guess it is. In the summer, we generally do it in the morning when the day is still cool. Mama says the heat is just a little reminder for us of what it would be like to go to the other place. She says baking concentrates the mind because of that."

Alice opened her mouth as if she was about to say something, then closed it again. We went into the kitchen and she started pulling open cabinets and peering into them. There were a lot of cabinets, but they were full of things all jumbled together, not in lines or rows or anything. In one of them she found a bag of flour, but when she looked inside, she made a tsking sound with her mouth and threw it away. There was another bag of flour in another cabinet, and that one had never been opened, so she handed it to me. She found a can of baking powder and gave me that too. I checked the date on the bottom—it had expired, but it would probably still work. She found sugar in a large canister and some walnuts in the freezer.

"Do you have any vanilla?" I asked. She gave me a bottle of extract with the cap kind of stuck on and gooey. "Any ginger?" She handed me a little jar with a red cap. "How about butter?" She found me some on a shelf in the fridge. The fridge gave off a sour smell when she opened it, so she shut it back up quick. "Cookie sheet?" Alice was smiling now, like we were having our own little game, and I have to say I was kind of enjoying it too. It felt good to do something normal, something I was used to. When everything I needed was piled up on the counter, I asked if she had some matches to light the oven. She said the oven lighted by itself and just to turn it on. I had a feeling Alice wasn't really interested in baking at all, just in entertaining me, so I said that if she had other chores she needed to do, I would be happy to do the baking all on my own. She said that actually, she had brought some work home and needed to see to it, so I thanked her and she left. I found some mixing bowls in a cabinet under the counter and got to work.

When I had put the cookies in the oven, I went back out into the living room. It was dark and a lot cooler than the kitchen. I listened for Alice but didn't hear her, so I sat down on one of the sofas. It was dark green and kind of prickly underneath a blanket with moons and stars on it. All around me were tall shelves crammed full of all kinds of books. I looked at some of their titles but I had never heard of any of them. We never read books by Lackers, or as Mama says, not by anybody unless they had heard the trumpet sound. A television was next to me, staring at me with its big blank eye.

I had been sitting there for a while, not doing much of anything, when the front door opened and a girl came in. She looked surprised to see me, but then seemed to realize who I was. "Oh, hi," she said, throwing a huge book bag down on the sofa opposite me. "I'm Heather." The way she said her name it sounded like it had a thousand Rs at the end of it.

"Hi, I'm Mary Fred," I said, looking at her. She was tall, with wavy hair like Alice's only darker brown, with a few streaks of orange and even a bit of what looked like blue but couldn't have been, since hair is never blue. Where Alice was thin and wispy, Heather was more solid-looking, and her face was tan, though she seemed to have some kind of white makeup all over it. She had a lot of dark stuff on her eyes that had smudged. I stood up and went over to her in case she wanted to shake hands, but she just waved and threw herself into a big armchair.

"So you're, like, going to live with us for a while?"

"It looks that way."

I stood above where she was flopped in the chair, her arms and legs sticking out in all directions, and neither of us said anything. I started to wonder if Heather was happy about getting a new family member. She didn't look all that happy.

Alice came down the stairs that moment and said, "Puffin, what are you doing home?"

"Half-day," Heather said. "We had a final."

"Really? Already? What was it in?"

"Bio." Warming to the topic a little, Heather said, "It was *so horrible*. I thought I was going to *die* right in the middle. One kid actually started crying."

"Really? Who?"

"Oh, it was Danny Fox. That dork."

I wasn't sure what a dork was but it definitely didn't sound good. I expected to hear Alice tell Heather that we are all creatures of the earth and none of us are dorks, but she just said, "Mary Fred is baking cookies. Smell? Mmmn, Mary Fred, they smell great."

"Oh, cookies," Heather said in a miserable-sounding voice. "Just what I need."

She didn't sound happy at all about the cookies, so I wasn't sure why she thought she needed them. Alice went into the kitchen and returned with two glasses of lemonade. She handed one to each of us and I knew I'd have to guzzle mine down just to be polite. Heather swallowed hers in one gulp and put the empty glass down on a wooden end table, and Alice picked it up, saying, "Not on the wood, Puff, you'll leave a ring." She took it into the kitchen, then went upstairs. Heather picked up a plastic thing and pushed a button on it, and the television came on. "Do you watch *All My Children?*" she asked. I had no idea what she was talking about, but I said no. On the screen, a man and a woman were in a bed, the man on top of the woman. It looked like they didn't have any clothes on, but when the police came into the room and the picture got bigger, you could see the woman was wearing black underwear. The man stood up—he was wearing pants—and the policeman put handcuffs on him and led him away. Then a woman came on and talked about vitamins. I finished my lemonade and brought it into the kitchen. I had washed all my dishes from baking, and I rinsed the glass out and put it on a wooden rack next to the sink. There were only a few minutes left till the cookies would be ready, so I decided to wait by the oven, since I figured the half-naked people would be back on the television pretty soon, and I knew Mama wouldn't want me to be anywhere near them.

When the cookies were ready, I put them on a plate and brought it into the living room. Heather took one and said, "I'm trying to lose weight. I'm only going to have one. How do you stay so thin, Mary Fred, if you bake cookies all the time?"

"I'm just made this way I guess. My brothers always say if I turn sideways I'll disappear. They say the crows will see me and fly away as fast as they can." There, I had done it again—I had said it as if they were still alive and were going to come in the door any minute and tease me about my skinniness. In spite of myself, I felt tears come into my eyes, but I blinked them away before Heather saw. I wouldn't want her to pity me, though I wasn't sure she was the pitying type anyway.

"I'd give anything to have your body," Heather said, taking a second cookie. "You look like a model."

"A model what?" I asked, but Heather just laughed and didn't answer.

I sat with Heather for a while in front of the television, doing my best to ignore what was on it. I was going to have to remember to leave the Book in the sitting room in case I got stuck here a lot and needed something to do. I hoped no one would think it was rude if I read to myself instead of participating in the family activities, whatever they turned out to be. I was a tiny bit curious about what was going to happen to the man on the television, but I didn't let myself look up because I could just about feel Mama smacking me on my hand and saying, "Mary Fred, now you know better." So I sat staring at the carpet, which was one of those round knotted ones, faded and flattened in spots, and tried to think about all the nice things there would be about living here for a while. I would have my own room. I would have an opportunity to experience something new. And maybe if I was here long enough, I could share the Word of the Book with the Cullisons. That was a good thing, I thought, and I said "Amen!" to myself, though I knew that in actual fact, Lackers would never hear the word, not in a million Sundays.

I sat on the sofa most of the afternoon with Heather, trying not to pay any attention to whatever she was watching on the television. Whenever Alice would come into the room, I would look up at her and wait for her to tell us to get on with our chores, or for Heather to do her homework or something, but she would just pass through the room with a look on her face like she was thinking and disappear for a while. Heather sat with her leg over the side of the armchair, flipping the channels back and forth on the television. A bunch of the channels had people talking to large audiences about the strange things they had done, such as courting their sisters' husbands and stuff like that. I figured that nobody would ever do anything that terrible, and I couldn't understand how Heather could waste a whole day watching them as if they were real. Heather looked pretty bored too, and every so often she would say something to me about the people's clothes, or their hair, but apart from that, we just kept quiet, which was fine with me.

At about five o'clock, a man came in the front door. "Hi, Puff," he said to Heather. I guessed that they called her Puff for some reason. He looked at me like he wasn't expecting to see anyone else, then said, "Oh, you must be—" He stopped, like he didn't know what my name was supposed to be.

"I'm Mary Fred," I said, walking over to him and shaking his hand.

"This is my uncle Roy," Heather said, waving her hand toward him but not looking up.

"Hi, Uncle Roy," I said. I figured that was what I should call him too.

Uncle Roy was carrying a big plastic bag. He put it down on the floor and looked at me, like he was trying to see if I was someone he would like or not. He wasn't much taller than me, with sandy, wavy hair like Alice's, and a scraggly little beard. His hair was thinning in patches on top, like he'd been tearing it out. He had one big, dark eyebrow and dark eyes. "So, Mary Fred, tell us about yourself," he said, walking into the room and sitting on the sofa across from the television.

"There's not much to tell. I guess I'll be here for a while. You probably know all the rest."

"More or less." I expected him to say his condolences like most people did, but he didn't. "Are you going to be a good influence on our Puffin here?"

"I don't know, Uncle Roy. I hope I'm always an influence for good."

"Roy," Alice said in a sharp voice, as she swung through the kitchen door, "are you already giving Mary Fred a hard time?"

"Not yet," Roy said. "I was just working up to it. I hadn't even gotten started yet."

"Give it a rest, Roy," Alice said, sounding snappish. "Just take the day off from being you. Mary Fred, how would you like to help me in the kitchen?"

"I'd love to." I jumped to my feet, relieved to have something to do besides not watch the stupid television shows or talk to Uncle Roy.

"Did you see that, Puffin?" Roy said to Heather. "That's how it's done. When someone asks you to do something, you respond in the affirmative. You don't just continue to sit like a lump with a hearing impairment, or scream like someone is disemboweling you."

Heather seemed not to have noticed that Roy had even spoken. She was still flipping channels as I ran out of the room with Alice.

It turned out that Alice didn't really have any particular chores in mind for me, but I managed to find plenty to do. After I had washed the remaining cookie sheets, I sorted through the fridge and threw out some old food that was making it smell bad, while Alice poked around, looking for something to make for dinner. "I'm sorry, Mary Fred, I meant to go to the store and make you a special meal for your first night, but I just didn't have time. I brought work home today so I could be here for you, but it took longer than I thought, and I—"

"It's perfectly all right, ma'am," I said, though I felt a little sad about not getting a special welcome dinner. Then I decided well, I'll help make dinner special for all of us one way or another.

"What do you like to eat?" Alice asked me. "Is there anything you don't like? Do you have any dietary restrictions?"

"No, I'll eat anything, ma'am. Though we tend to eat a lot of fish. Like the proverb says, If the child asks for a fish, give him a fish."

"I'd never heard that," Alice said. "I'll get some fish tomorrow, I promise. Let's see, what do we have for tonight?" She started rummaging around in the freezer and pulled out a bunch of plastic containers and old boxes until she found a big package of frozen lasagna. We put that in the oven and then I found a bunch of carrots in the fridge and grated them for a salad. I put a little yogurt on them and some honey and raisins, and I scooped the salad into a pretty flowered bowl I found in a low cabinet. Next I went into the dining room to set the table. There were stacks of books on it, so I had to move them first, but I managed to find all the right plates and silverware and some paper napkins, and pretty soon it looked nice. The lasagna had to cook for an hour, so I found a bunch of little things to do before dinner. I put all the clean dishes away, and I rearranged a couple of cabinets. I mopped part of the floor that had some sticky stuff on it, and I cleaned all the counters.

When we sat down to dinner, Heather said, "Why is everything so fancy?" She sounded grumpy.

"Puffin would rather eat out of a trough," Roy said. "It's more efficient."

"Mary Fred made everything nice," Alice said. She smiled, and I could see that she was glad about how nice things were. She seemed like the kind of person who liked things to be calm and sweet and pretty, but from the looks of it, nothing in her life was like that. I resolved to try to make things a little better for Alice, as part of my stay here.

"Great lasagna," Roy said, digging in. "My compliments to the chef at Le Club de Price."

"Try the carrot salad," Alice said, pushing the flowered bowl toward him. "Mary Fred made that." She smiled at me, and I felt almost happy for a second.

When I came downstairs the next morning, I was expecting to see everybody at the table already, since it was nearly eight when I finally got up. I'd been dreaming I was at the Compound and I was trying to feed the chickens, but every time I looked in the big cabinet in the barn where we kept their food, bats would fly out at me, or birds, or giant bees, and I don't think I ever did find the chickenfeed. The whole floor of the barn was mud, and as I walked across it, trying to get back to the big house, my feet stuck to the ground and I couldn't pull them up. I tried yelling for Papa but I knew nobody could hear me, and when I woke up, I was making little *P* sounds with my mouth, like I'd started to say Papa but hadn't quite finished.

But nobody was in the dining room when I got there, and when I looked in the kitchen, it was empty too. I opened the fridge to look for something to cook, but there weren't any eggs, and all the breakfast things I knew how to make had eggs in them. Finally, I went back out into the sitting room and sat down on the sofa to wait for Alice to get up. I watched the clock as I sat there, humming to myself. I hummed "Holy Sanctuary" and "Where Is the Word to Be Found." I hummed until my throat started to hurt, and then I just sat there, thinking the music instead. At about ten, Alice came downstairs in a flowered bathrobe. Her eyes looked sleepy and her hair was standing up all around her head like she'd had a bad dream.

"Oh, Mary Fred," she said when she saw me, like she had totally forgotten I would be there.

"Good morning, ma'am," I said.

"Did you help yourself to something to eat?" Alice asked. "I'm sorry, I forgot to show you where everything is."

"I was waiting for everybody else," I said.

"We never eat in the mornings," Alice said. "I'm so sorry, Mary Fred, I should have said something last night. Let me get you some cereal."

She stood there kind of twisting her hands together, like she felt really guilty for forgetting, so I said, "I never eat in the mornings either. It makes me kind of bilious."

This seemed to make her feel better, and she stopped twisting her hands and said, "Are you sure I can't get you some cereal?"

"Not till at least ten o'clock," I said. "I never eat before that."

"I think it's ten o'clock right now," Alice said, turning to look at the clock behind her. It was a big wooden clock, like the top half of a grandfather. "This clock is always ten minutes slow. It's really ten past ten."

"Well then, I guess I should have something to eat," I said, jumping up and following Alice into the kitchen. She showed me some boxes of cereal on a high shelf in the pantry. When I opened the first one, a moth flew out, so I went for the second one, which was something called Tropical Muesli. It tasted kind of strange, like it had perfume in it, but it was okay. Alice asked if I wanted any coffee. I said no, that I had never had coffee before and didn't know if it would agree with me, so she made herself some. She sat across from me at the dining room table drinking it while I ate my cereal. She looked too tired to talk, so I didn't try to make conversation with her, but she kept thinking of things to say like she was afraid of my getting too bored.

"Do you need to go shopping?" Alice asked. "Do you need anything? Socks, underwear? They give me a little allowance for you so I want to make sure you get everything you need."

I didn't think I ought to discuss underwear with someone I had just met, but then again, she was supposed to be my family for a while, so I said, "I brought five pairs of underpants, and we generally do the laundry every other day so they ought to do just fine." Then I thought maybe Alice didn't have a washing machine in her house, and that I had just said something rude, so I said, "Of course, I can wash them out in the sink," but then I thought, well maybe people don't want people washing their dirty underwear out in sinks, where the germs might sit and wait for them, so I was about to say that I could change them every other day if necessary, but then I didn't want Alice to think I was dirty, so I just opened and closed my mouth a couple of times like a fish.

"Well, let me know if you need anything," Alice said. "We can go shopping any time you want to. Clothes, makeup, whatever you need. . . ."

I had never worn makeup in my life, but I just said thanks.

After we finished breakfast, Alice went outside and got the newspaper from the front lawn, and she asked me if I wanted part of it. We had always made a point of never reading the newspaper, since it was all lies, but I didn't want to say that to Alice, so I looked at some of it. I read the comics and then a thing called a horoscope that seemed to be telling everybody what to do. Papa would say that that was how the government controlled people's minds, but it didn't sound like the horoscope was asking anyone to do anything bad. The advice for Aries was to wear mauve and green. I figured I'd watch all day for someone wearing mauve and green and then ask them if they were Aries.

"What's Aries?" I asked Alice, so I'd know.

"That's someone born anywhere from March 21 to April 20 or so. What sign are you, Mary Fred?"

"Sign?"

"When's your birthday?"

"December 14."

"That makes you a Sagittarius. That's what I am too. Mine's December 10."

"Well, then I guess we should look beyond the immediate and gain an overall view. Stress ability to make friend of one from foreign land. Question concerning marriage will loom large. Pisces plays dominant role."

"Roy's a Pisces," Alice said.

"Does this mean that when a person's birthday is tells them what they ought to do?"

"Sort of. Maybe. I don't know if it really means anything, Mary Fred, but some people believe in it."

"Do you?"

"Not really. Maybe a little. I basically think we're responsible for our own destinies."

Now, I knew better than to argue with this, because of course we're all in the hands of the One, but I understood that Lackers often thought that they were deciding things for themselves. Part of me wanted to try to convince Alice to follow the One and come with me into the Hereafter when the Big Cat came, but I had had enough experience with Lackers to know that they weren't going to listen, and that alls that would happen is they would want to discuss things. And Papa always said those things were best left alone. Lackers would hear when the lame walked and the blind received their sight, Papa said, and meanwhile, it was no use sowing a seed on barren ground. So I asked why they had the horoscopes in the newspaper. Alice said they were for entertainment. "Anyway," she said, "you're too young for marriage to loom large."

"Maybe it's someone else's marriage, though," I said.

Alice shook her head and looked kind of sad.

"Maybe I'm the friend from a foreign land," I said.

She looked at me and smiled. "I don't think Frederick County is a foreign land, do you?"

I smiled and said no, but the fact was, this place did seem like a foreign land to me, in fact, like a whole new planet.

We'd been sitting there for a while, reading the paper and not saying anything, when Heather came down. Her eyes were still almost closed, and she moved unsteadily, like she was sleepwalking. I had seen someone sleepwalking once at the Compound one night and he almost fell into the lake. The men had to holler and wake him. Heather waved a hand and lurched herself into a chair, looking at me like she was trying to remember who I was.

"Good morning, Heather," I said. Heather made a little grunting sound, and Alice told her to say good morning back to me, so she did. I waited for Alice to jump up and ask Heather to help her get some breakfast, but she went on reading the paper. After a while, Heather picked herself out of the chair, went into the kitchen, and came back with a bag of potato chips.

"Don't eat potato chips for breakfast," Alice said, glancing at Heather and then looking back at the paper.

I wasn't at all surprised when Heather went right on eating the potato chips as if her mother hadn't said anything. I was getting the hang of things.

It was just past noon when Roy came down the stairs. He was wearing a green T-shirt and blue jeans with holes in them, and he didn't look very clean. His hair was all messy and his beard looked even more scraggly than before. We were still sitting at the table. I had gone and taken a shower and then cleaned up some in the kitchen until Alice had made me stop. "It makes me feel guilty," she said. "Just relax." Of course I was used to relaxing, but we did it on Sunday afternoon after church. Papa always used to say, "Humankind is made for the Sabbath, not the Sabbath for humankind."

"I left you some coffee," Alice said as Roy went into the kitchen. The big wooden door swung closed behind him and then swung back open a minute later with him carrying a big clay mug that looked like it had been made by someone in kindergarten.

By this time, I knew he wasn't going to say good morning or anything, but I thought I'd have some fun with him so I said, "Good morning, Uncle Roy, did you sleep well?"

Roy nodded and took a big guzzle of coffee.

"I guess you're a morning person," Alice said to me, smiling like the very thought of being a morning person made her feel tired all over again.

"I'm an all-day-long kind of person," I said.

"Like the Energizer Bunny," Heather said. It was the first thing she'd said so far today.

"The who?"

Heather looked at me sadly. "Mary Fred," she said, "you're going to have to watch more TV."

By midafternoon, I had already cleaned the kitchen, vacuumed the sitting room rug, which Heather would only let me do during commercials, and cleaned and rearranged the closet in my room. Alice was puttering around, watering plants (there were *lots* of plants everywhere, most of them brown and wilting), and stopping at the dining table to rest every so often. I thought about dusting, but Alice said she didn't have a feather duster, and some of the little stuff she had everywhere was too delicate for a rag, so I decided I would use some of the allowance she got for me to buy a feather duster when we went shopping.

"Mary Fred," Alice said finally as I was beating the hearthrug on the back porch, "really, you don't have to do any chores. We didn't have you come here so you could work."

"I feel better when I keep busy," I said.

"Oh," Alice said, as if she suddenly remembered all about me. "I'm *so* sorry, Mary Fred. Of course you do. After all, you've been through so much. I should have thought of some kind of structured activity for you to do. I'm so used to Heather. She just kind of sits around all the time, so it didn't occur to me that you might need something more—" She broke off in the middle of a sentence and stood with her hand on her chin, like she was trying to think of something for me to do. Then she waved both hands in the air and said, "Don't worry, we'll think of something."

"Until we do," I said, "is it okay if I clean things?"

"Sure, Mary Fred. Of course. It's great, in fact, I really appreciate it."

I had just finished scrubbing the bathroom floor when Alice asked if I wanted to go to the grocery store with her. I said sure, and we went to a store that was so big, you could have fit the Compound's general store into it about twenty-five times and still had room left over for all of the Apostles to do cartwheels. They had a gigantic fish counter, full of all kinds of big fish with the heads still on them, so Alice bought one for dinner. We bought some rice, and some green beans, and a lot of strange things that Alice said Heather liked—pink breakfast cereals, and rolls of tape that were made of fruit, and some frozen things with jelly and icing that were supposed to be strudel but didn't look like any strudel I'd ever seen.

"Is there anything I can buy you?" Alice asked me, her voice almost pleading. "Anything at all?"

"No, ma'am, I think I've got everything I need." We had picked up the feather duster. "Maybe a can of Campbell's Cream of Mushroom soup to go with the green beans."

"Okay. Anything else?"

"No'm. I think that's it."

"Oh, Mary Fred," Alice said, looking like she was going to burst into tears. "I just feel so inadequate. I don't know what to do, or how to help you. I want to do a good job at this, but I don't think I know how. What was I thinking? I'm such a terrible mother anyway, and now—"

I put my arm around her and patted her on the shoulder. "It's fine, ma'am. Alice. Really, I'm happy as can be." We were standing near the express checkout line, since we had fewer than fifteen items, and on the shelf next to it were some long pink plastic tubes with little multicolored beads in them. I didn't know what they were, but I said, "Oh, Alice, can I have one of these?" I picked one up and showed it to her.

"Of course you can, Mary Fred," she said, wiping one eye and looking at me like I had just done something really nice for her instead of the other way around.

I asked if we could get one for Heather too, and she said sure, so I grabbed another one. That meant we had sixteen items, but Alice took us through the express line anyway and the woman at the cash register never said a thing about it.

Heather seemed to like the little beads—she ate them right up before dinner—and everyone liked the green beans with mushroom soup. It felt funny sitting around the dinner table and eating the same food I'd be eating at home, but without saying the Beautiful Prayer first, and without my real family. Uncle Roy made some comment about sitting there that made me think that they didn't always eat together, or even at the table.

Still, it was a nice dinner, and I think they liked it. They were all kind of smiley afterward, even Heather, who didn't smile much in general. I had folded up the paper napkins into little swans, and after dinner she wanted me to show her how to do it, so I did. Then Alice made her come help us in the kitchen, while Roy took out the garbage, because it was getting kind of smelly with the fish and all, and Heather showed me where all the dishes belonged and helped me wipe them. While we were working, she talked about her school. She said her French test last Friday hadn't been too bad, the only bad part was that she was concentrating so hard while she was taking it that her foot fell asleep, so when she stood up to go turn the test in, she fell over sideways and couldn't manage to stand upright, and everybody laughed at her. "It was *so embarrassing,*" she said.

"But it wasn't your fault," I said. "I mean, a person can't help if their foot goes to sleep."

"Mary Fred's right, Puffin," Alice said. "It's not like you did it on purpose."

"I don't care, I just looked like the biggest dork in the world," Heather said, rolling her eyes. "And stop calling me Puffin."

"How come everybody calls you Puffin?" I asked her.

"They *shouldn't,*" she said, giving Alice a dark look. "They *know* not to call me Puffin. But they do it anyway."

"I don't know," Alice said. "Roy, why do we call Puffin Puffin?"

"It's because when she was born, she was all puffy," Roy said, coming back through the kitchen with the garbage can and putting it down beside the sink. "Her face was all red and bloated, like a walrus's."

"That's not why," Heather said, punching Roy on the arm,

which kind of shocked me in spite of myself. "It's because when I was born, I looked like a bird. A puffin. That's what Dad always says."

"Does he?" Alice asked. She stopped wiping the dish she was holding and stood staring at Heather like this was some really interesting information. "Is that what he says?"

"He says I had this cute little beak," Heather went on, looking pleased with herself. "And I made these little tweeting noises, like a puffin."

"I don't think your father is up on his ornithology," Roy said. "I don't think puffins tweet."

"They *do* tweet," Heather said. "And they're really cute. That's what he says."

"You were a cute baby," Alice said. "You had such tiny little hands." She reached for one of Heather's big hands with her soapy, wet one, and Heather let her hold it for about a second, then snatched it away. Alice turned to me, as if to be fair, and said, "Do you have a nickname in your family, Mary Fred?"

"Sometimes everyone calls me M.F.," I said. "We have a lot of Fred names in my family so sometimes we use initials to keep from getting confused."

"M.F.?" Roy sort of smirked.

"That's nice," Alice said. "So other people in your family are named Fred too? Is that a family name?"

"No, ma'am," I said. I had explained this to many Lackers before in the past, but still, I always felt surprised when people asked me this. "It's our religion. People tend to be named after Fred."

"Oh, so your whole family is, um, named after Fred?"

"Well, not Mama and Papa, but all my brothers and sisters."

"What are their names?" Alice asked.

"Well, there are the little ones. Fredericka, we call her

Rickie, then Bobby Fred, then Billy Fred, but we call him Biffles, then Boo, who is really Susie Fred, then—" My voice got stuck when I came to Little Freddie, and I just stopped there.

"Who's Fred?" Heather asked.

"Fred is our founder," I said, staring down at the floor while my eyes watered. "Fred was the man who founded us and found us and brought us into the light. That's how we say it, usually. He brought us into the light."

"How exactly did he do this?" Roy asked. I looked up at him and saw that he had a little smile on his face.

"With his Prophecy. And his Holy Book."

"So your family met this Fred person and followed him to— where were you living?"

"Virginia, at first. Then we moved up to Maryland. But we never met him."

"No?"

"No, he lived a long time ago. He died in 1947."

"But his ideas lived on?"

"That's right." Although he sounded polite enough, I had a feeling Uncle Roy thought there was something funny about this, and since I didn't, I resolved to just clam up. This was how things went with Lackers, and while of course I wasn't angry, since as Papa always said, there was no point in being angry with Lackers, it was like being mad at the rain for ruining your picnic, still, I was getting this feeling in my stomach like someone had stuck a knife in it and was giving it a good twist. I decided to try not to talk about my family with anyone, especially not Roy, and it probably wasn't a very good idea to talk about the Book either, since I might as well have been speaking Chinese to them anyway.

The next morning was Sunday, and when I got up, at first I thought I had better get ready for church, but then when I thought more about it, I was absolutely positive that no one would be going to church. I went downstairs and sure enough, none of them were there—everyone was still asleep. I brought the Book down with me and just sat reading it for a while, though I kept daydreaming in the middle of the page, so then I felt bad, like my mind was going to start Lacking if I didn't watch out. What I kept imagining were my brothers and sisters in their church clothes, and Mama and Papa leading us down the path to the Chapel at the Compound, past the wild raspberry bushes and the honeysuckle that grew all over everything. I could see Fred and Little Freddie running after Boo, trying to tickle her, and how they'd pick her up and whirl her around, and how she would scream and laugh and yell at them to stop but they knew that what Boo really liked best was to be swung in the air. When I started to feel sad like this, I would pick up the Book and find some comfort in it, like I would read about the Sabbath and how we should keep it holy and not do any work, and rest like the Lord rested. I tried to have the feeling of Sunday all by myself, but things kept getting in the way of it—the sounds of cars outside, and the big TV that sat looking at me with its square blank face. I read the part in the Book about the Imminence, but it just didn't make me feel any more holy, since all I could think about was how I was sitting in some Lackers' living room, and it was Sunday, and no one was going to church, or anywhere else for that matter. After a while I just put the Book down and went into the kitchen and made myself some toast. I wondered where Mama and Papa were right now and whether they were getting enough to eat, and where the Littles were, and if they were living with Lackers too, and watching television, and forgetting the holy Word. I imagined Rickie and Boo wearing fancy dresses and saying a bunch of cuss words, and then I tried to stop myself

from picturing that. I knew Rickie would never behave like
that, though to be honest, I had some doubts about Boo. She
was six and had a dramatic way with her, at least that's what
Mama and Papa always said. I wondered what they were doing
right now, and it seemed so strange to think they were all out
there somewhere and I didn't even know where. Then I wondered why I was feeling so bad suddenly, like I had fallen down
and bruised myself all over on the inside.

I went back into the sitting room with my toast on a plate.
Back home, we'd never be allowed to eat in the sitting room,
but I had seen Heather break this rule several times yesterday
so I figured it was okay. I stared at the blank TV while I ate,
feeling bored and angry. Here it was, Sunday morning, and I
was lounging in front of a TV in my gardening trousers instead
of in the family pew at the Compound, and I hadn't heard a
sermon in nearly three weeks, and if I wasn't careful I was
going to start Lacking, I was going to let Evil into my heart,
and before I knew it, I'd be wearing a golden gown and feathers like some hootchie-kootchie woman. That was what the
Reverend Thigpen said sometimes. And meanwhile, I didn't
have any idea where the Littles were, and I only hoped that
wherever it was—I guessed they had all gone to different families—they weren't going to start Lacking, and they weren't
lonely and afraid and crying for Mama and me.

I picked up the remote from the sofa where Heather had
thrown it and flicked on the TV. I flipped the channels around
past a bunch of cartoon bears and some ugly puppets until I
found a channel that had a church on it. For a moment I felt relieved, like I was going to be okay, because I could spend my
Sundays at the TV church and not fall away from the News, but
after I listened to the man for a few minutes, I shut the TV off
again. He was talking about the same Words we talked about,

but I could see that deep down, he was really a Lacker. He was talking about the God of Peace and Kindness, and it was the kind of thing that the Reverend Thigpen warned us was really just Evil talking in a pearly guise. That's what he said. "If Evil cast out Evil, then Evil is divided against itself," the Book said. I felt divided against myself, like I wasn't sure anymore exactly what Evil was. I just hoped none of it had found its way into me and tried to make a home there like someone camping in a ditch.

By the time everyone got up, it was nearly noon, and I was feeling even worse. I'd been sitting there for hours, I was bored, and I felt restless, like I was all shivery and twitchy inside and needed a good run, or maybe a horseback ride. Alice got up first and said good morning to me in her ghostly way, making a beeline for the coffeepot like she was dying of thirst. Then Heather came down and mumbled something, grabbing a bag of cookies and flinging herself down with them on the sofa. I could see crumbs spraying from her mouth in a fine mist. Finally, Roy got up, looking grim and grubby, without so much as a word to anyone. I just sat there, watching everyone waste a perfectly beautiful Sunday morning when they could have been out serving someone somehow.

"Don't you get tired of just sitting?" I asked Heather.

She looked at me like I had said something ridiculous. "I get tired if I don't sit," she said. "So then I sit some more and I feel rested. That's how it works."

"But don't you feel like the whole world is just waiting for you to get up and do something? Like there's this really important thing out there that you could be doing, and you're just sitting here instead, and the important thing is going to pass right by you and you'll never even know what it was?"

Heather seemed to think for a minute. Then she said, "No."

*   *   *

I will say that Alice made us a nice lunch, with cream of tomato soup and some bread that she took out of the freezer and then put in the oven and it came out like fresh bread. She had put some onions and some wilted leaves from the fridge into the tomato soup so it tasted strange, but I kind of liked it that way. I didn't say much during lunch—I had a lumpy feeling in my throat, and it was too hard to get food past it and talk at the same time. When we had finished, Roy got up and went out without even clearing his plate, and Heather went back to the sofa, and Alice and me cleared up the table and did the dishes. Alice was talking to me about Heather's father and how he was going to take Heather to France for two weeks, and how she didn't really want Heather to go to France but she didn't see any way out of it. I said that from what I understood, all the people in France just drank wine all the time and got into mischief because of it, and that the women didn't wear underwear, and I could understand if she didn't want Heather in a place like that.

"It's not that, really," Alice said, staring at a stack of dishes like she'd forgotten what they were. "I just don't want her to be away for her birthday, and for such a long time. And I don't like the idea of her taking a plane. What if something happened—I just couldn't deal with it."

I thought of telling her that something *was* going to happen anyway, the Big Cat was coming, and coming soon, but that would just have made her feel worse, plus being a Lacker, there was nothing she could do about it anyway, so why tell her. So I said, "I'm sure everything will be fine. Those planes are really safe. They're big and powerful, so if they run into any trouble they can just fly away from it real fast. And when they land, they've got all kinds of emergency landing gear so if one set of gear doesn't work, the extra ones open right up, no problem."

"I'm sure you're right, Mary Fred. It's just that she's never been that far away from me. Usually he just takes her to Florida or the Caribbean. I don't like the idea of her being across a whole ocean, especially on her birthday."

"It's hard being separated from your people," I said. "But sometimes you just have to make the best of it."

"Oh, Mary Fred," she said. "I'm sorry. I hadn't thought."

"It's okay," I said.

"No, really, I'm sorry. It's so selfish of me to think of worrying about a little two-week vacation, when you're—really, I'm so—"

"It's okay," I said in a voice that sounded surprisingly hard to me. "I'm grown up enough to know that whatever the Will has set forth for me, well, that's the path I have to take, and sometimes it's a path I don't much like, sometimes it's a hard path, like when the One decides to just take both of my brothers, it's hard, Alice, but when you truly have faith, then you know, why, you just know that it's—"

"It's so hard, I know," Alice said, like I hadn't said anything about faith or the One at all. "I know."

"You couldn't possibly know," I said, my voice a little rasp like Evil was starting to possess me and make itself heard. "You just couldn't possibly imagine." Alice started toward me but I held up my hand, palm outward, to ward her off. "It's my own burden, ma'am, not yours. My yoke is easy and my burden is light."

"It's not easy, Mary Fred," Alice said, stopping about a foot from me and looking at me with sad eyes. "I understand that. I wish there was something I could do to help."

"There's nothing you can do," I said, taking a step backward. "There's nothing any Lacker could possibly do. It's just the way things are."

"Let me know, Mary Fred, if there's anything—" Alice held

out her hands, palms outward, almost in a shrug, like she just
had no idea what to say to me.

"I apologize, ma'am," I said. "I don't know what came over
me. I just lost the discipline of my tongue for a minute there."
I said I was sorry, and Alice said it was okay, and we finished
the dishes without mentioning anything else about it. The
truth was, though, I didn't really feel sorry; I felt stiff and un-
kind inside, like someone had starched me.

We were going to work in the garden in the afternoon, but
right after lunch it started to rain. I wasn't even surprised,
since I felt all rainy myself, but it meant we were going to sit in
the sitting room all afternoon while Heather changed the channels every couple of seconds. Roy had gone back upstairs.
Alice sat at the dining room table with a pile of catalogues. I
looked at them for a while with her—some had books in them
and some had movies, and none of them had to do with anything that interested me. She said the fiscal year was ending at
work and she needed to order a bunch of stuff for the library
by June 30, otherwise the money would just go to waste. I
could hear Papa saying in my mind that there was only One
Book and One Word, and he didn't approve of movies at all
anyway. The Reverend Thigpen said they were all just a bunch
of undulating flesh. Every so often Heather would pass a
movie on the TV, and she would leave it on for a few minutes
and before I knew it, I was wondering what happened to the
people on the speeding bus, or the people being chased by di-
nosaurs, but luckily she'd flip to a new channel before I got
too interested, and sometimes she would say, "Boring," like it
was two words, Bo and Ring. I began to picture Bo and Ring
as two clowns who danced around in the living room, trying to
entertain Heather. It was not easy and I felt sorry for them.

"Heather, do you want to come work in the garden with

me?" I said after a while when I noticed that the rain had let up a little.

"It's raining," Heather said.

"No, it's stopped. Look, the sun is coming out."

"But it's all wet out there."

"It's summer. It's a nice, warm wetness. The ground will smell nice."

"The ground will smell like cat poop," Heather said. "Trust me."

"Heather, go on out with Mary Fred," Alice called from the dining room. "It'll do you good."

"You're crazy if you think I'm going out there and getting soaked," Heather said. Whenever she talked to her mother, she raised her voice to a little screech. "You're totally nuts."

I stood up and said, "Well, I'm going to go out and do some weeding." As I walked past Alice, she looked up and said, "If you need to, Mary Fred, it's okay, but I don't want you to—"

"I need—" I stopped in the middle of the sentence, not exactly sure what I was saying. Then suddenly, I wasn't even sure where I was. It seemed like I had landed somewhere strange where I didn't recognize anything. The room looked small and fake, like I was watching everything on a television. "I need—"

At that moment, Roy came down the stairs. His eyes were all slitty, like he'd been sleeping. "What do you need, Mary Fred?" His voice was raspy, like he had a frog in his throat, or maybe a big dog.

I looked at him and said, "I don't know." I ran into the kitchen and out the back door into the yard, past the spready oak and over to the toolshed, which was made of metal and kind of leaned to one side, like it was tired. A bunch of stuff was crammed inside, and it took a lot of hunting through it but

I finally found a trowel. I kneeled down in a bed of nasty yellow flowers and started digging up the ground between them. It was all overgrown with weeds, and the flowers were being strangled. I could see their sad little faces just gasping for breath. I was used to taking gardening very seriously, partly because we grew all our own food at the Compound, and a lot of it at the Outpost, but also because we believed that the World Beyond was a garden, and we needed to know how to live there. The Reverend Smith had always said we had to develop all our skills in this world because we were going to need them, but that everything would be easier there, flowers would jump from the ground and reach up overhead in praise, and the fruits and vegetables would just bust out all over like fireworks. The cows would beg us to make them into hamburger meat, and the sheep would lay down his life for us, and our table would overfloweth. When the Reverend Smith said this, I pictured a huge table with a white tablecloth, and all my family sitting there, and our friends from the Compound, the ones that had died in the fire and the ones who were in prison, and my brothers would be at the head of the table, and we'd be eating these great big tomatoes the size of watermelons and saying Hallelujah.

When I looked up, I noticed that it had started raining again and that I had been kneeling in the dirt, crying, for some time.

It was strange how all this time I hadn't really cried at all, just a little here and there, because Mama had said not to cry, but there was something about the garden in the World Beyond that must have gotten to me. How beautiful it was, and how when I opened my eyes back up again, I was in a pile of weeds in front of Alice's toolshed. That was the worst part about waiting, I always thought, that though this world was pretty enough sometimes, at least some of it was, the next was going to be so much prettier that I could hardly stand how long it would take to get there. There were things about life on earth that I had liked—Sunday dinners, and playing soldiers in the woods with Fred, Little Freddie, and Rickie, and riding our horses across the fields. But now it seemed like the happy things about this world were gone, and there was nothing to do but wait for the next. I looked up at the spready oak, and it seemed to lead all the way up to the places that mattered.

When I went back in the house, Alice was standing in the kitchen, talking to Roy. They stopped talking when I came in and then Alice said, "Roy, it's getting late and we have nothing for dinner. Could you go out and pick something up?"

Of course, what I was thinking was that Alice seemed surprised that here it was almost evening and we were going to have to eat again, as if she didn't realize that we were all going to have to eat today, and tomorrow, and every day after that. We had been in the grocery store just yesterday, but she had only bought enough for one day, like she was thinking that she never knew for sure if the next day was going to happen or not. I could have told her that she was right about that, because the Big Cat was coming, and coming soon, but I didn't see the point of mentioning it.

Roy was saying that he had stuff to do and he didn't see how he was going to have time to go pick up dinner, but Alice just handed him two new-looking twenty-dollar bills and gave him a firm, mean look, at least it was mean for Alice. Bad as I still felt, I almost laughed at the way she knitted her eyebrows together and took in her breath like she was about to start yelling at him, though we all knew that she was never going to yell at anyone. Roy took the money, wadded it up, and stuffed it in his pocket, but then he sat down in a chair next to Heather in the living room, like he was too tired to go anywhere just yet.

"Mary Fred, you're soaking wet," Alice said, looking at me. "Let me get you a towel."

"I'm okay," I said, though she was right, I was soaked to the skin.

Alice went upstairs and came back with a long stripy towel. She wrapped it around my shoulders and started rubbing me dry.

I found myself pushing her arms away and taking a few steps backward. Alice handed me the towel, like she hadn't noticed how rude I'd just been. I took it, draped it over me, and began to dry my hair. The towel got all wet and smelled like rain, and I held it in front of my nose, just breathing, in and out, taking in the smell of the water. I stopped drying myself and stood there, just smelling, and pretty soon my shoulders started to shake. I felt myself drop down to my knees, onto the hard floor, and lay my forehead down against it, still in the towel. I was making this howling sound, like wolves had gotten into me somehow.

"Mary Fred?" I felt Alice's hand on my head.

I shook my head underneath the towel and kept on howling.

"Mary Fred? What can I do for you? Tell me."

I didn't say anything.

"Puffin, go make Mary Fred some chamomile tea. Mary Fred, come here, I'm going to help you over to the couch." I felt Alice's arms lift me up and walk me over to the sofa next to where Puffin had been. I felt myself sit down, and Alice's arms go around me. I let her keep them there for a moment, but when she peeled the towel away from my face, I pushed her arms away. I saw her face, puzzled and concerned, her graying hair all in a frazzle and the glasses that she wore sometimes on the end of her nose a little bit crooked, and I just shook my head again.

"What can I do for you, Mary Fred?"

"Nothing. There's nothing anyone can do. The One will

wipe away every tear from mine eyes and guide me to the water of life."

"You want some tea?" Heather asked. She was holding a steaming cup out to me.

"No, thank you," I said. My voice was sounding so evil again that it scared me. I looked at the three of them. I was amazed that Heather had actually done something her mother asked her to do and gone and made me tea. Alice was sitting next to me, staring miserably at me like she was waiting for me to snap out of it. Roy was standing a few feet away from me, looking more awake than I'd ever seen him. "There's nothing I want from any of you Lackers," I went on. "I just have to wait for the Imminence, and then I'll be in the garden and everything will be fine. The Big Cat is coming, and coming soon, and I'll be leaving you all behind anyway. You'll all be down here broiling in the lake of fire, and I'll be at the white table with my brethren, feasting on the feast of true foods, while the flowers reach around me like the hands of the Apostles, and fruits fall from the sky like holy rain. Yea, then it will rain and rain true—fire for you, holy water for me. I'll be in the kingdom of the Eternal One for all eternity. It won't be long now, no, it won't be long." By now, a mixed-up bunch of the Reverend Thigpen's words and the Words of the Book were pouring from me like hailstones. I shut my mouth to stop them.

There was a moment of silence, and then Roy said, "What brought this on, Mary Fred?" The stupid look had gone from his face and he just looked worried and confused. "Is it because it's Sunday?"

I felt my eyes fill with more tears.

"You miss your family worse on a Sunday, don't you?" he said.

I didn't say anything.

Roy took a few steps backward, nodding the whole time like he'd just made a brilliant discovery. He looked at Alice, who shook her head like she was too tired to know how to speak, and then he went out the front door. When he had gone, I let Alice put her arm around me. Heather went back into the kitchen and I could hear running water, like she was doing dishes or something. After a while, I felt so limp and tired that I just laid my head down on Alice's shoulder. Her shoulder smelled funny, like her shirt had been in a closet for a long time, and the skin underneath it smelled a little sweaty, but it was a comforting smell. I hid my face in the towel again and we just sat there like that for a while.

When I was done crying, Alice held both of my hands and looked into my face. "Mary Fred, this is hard, I know, but we'll get through it somehow."

"How long will I have to be here?" I asked, still sniveling.

"I don't know. The court has given us custody of you indefinitely. It all depends on—on what happens. It's hard to adjust, I know—everything is so different. . . ."

"*So* different," I said.

"And we must seem strange to you. But you know, you're strange to us too. We're just all different, that's all. Everybody's different."

"I know that," I said, sounding grumpy like Heather. But the truth was, I had never liked anyone who was different. Or rather, no, it wasn't that I hadn't liked them, but I had just felt sorry for them, for all the suffering they were going to have that I was going to miss out on, and it didn't make me want to know anybody like that very well. There was too much pitying involved.

"Come on," Alice said, standing up, still holding my hands. "Let's set the table. Do you have Sunday dinner at home?"

"Of course."

"Let's make it fancy. Can you make those swans out of napkins for me now?"

"I guess."

"I'll get the dishes." Alice went into a wooden cabinet and took out a bunch of flowered plates with gold rims that I hadn't seen before, and some glasses with stems. She went into a drawer and drug out some silverware that looked all old and tarnishy. I sat down at the table with a stack of napkins and started making swans, though every so often I'd have to use one to dry my eyes or blow my nose. When I had finished the swans, I went upstairs to the bathroom and washed my hands. I looked at myself in the mirror. My eyes were all red and the lashes were stuck together, and my cheeks were pale but with pink spots in them. I splashed cold water on my face until it was all reddish, and then I patted myself dry with a dirty little hand towel. When I came downstairs again, the table was set, and Alice had put yellow candles in big brass candlesticks right in the center and lit them. She had lowered the lights in the room so that the candles lit most of it, and the TV had been turned off and music with violins was playing.

The front door swung open and Roy walked in, carrying three big paper bags that said "Chicken A Go-Go" on the side. He took them into the kitchen, and before long, he and Alice came back out carrying plates full of food and laid them down in the center of the table. We all sat down. Roy was about to start eating, but Alice asked, "Do you have a prayer you want to say?"

At first I just sat for a minute, not saying anything. I could hear the sound of my breaths as they passed in and out of my body. But then I said the Beautiful Prayer, and we ate.

THE BOOK OF ALICE

"You're crazy," Roy said to me. "I mean, Alice, what are you thinking?"

"She needs somewhere to live," I said.

"Alice, you're insane."

"I just think it would be kind of nice. It would be good for Puffin to have a foster sister."

"Puffin doesn't get enough attention as it is."

"Oh, thanks, now you're saying I'm a bad mother."

"I don't think you're a bad mother, Al, but face it, we're not exactly Ozzie and Harriet here."

"Look, Roy, I told Diane we would do it, and now it's too late to back out."

"Let Diane do it."

"Diane can't do it, Roy."

"Why can't Diane do it?"

"You know why."

"Why?"

"She's a lesbian."

"So?"

"She doesn't think this girl could handle living with a lesbian couple. I mean, she's from some kind of religious cult, and they're born again, or something like that, and—"

"She's *what?*"

"She's in this group up in Frederick County and they—"

"You're having some kind of Moonie kid move in with us?"

"I think they're some sort of Christians, actually."

"Alice, *please,* think about this, use your brain here."

"I *am* using my brain, Roy." I was nearly screaming at him by this time. Of course, Roy says that when I scream, I sound like a lamb bleating, but I felt about ready to punch him. "I've already done the paperwork, we've been approved by the court, and the decision has been made. *Legally.* So that's really the end of the discussion." And it was. It had been more than a year since Roy had paid me any rent, and though he knew I would never throw that in his face, it always hovered between us like a dark cloud. Roy opened his mouth as if he were about to say something else, but then he closed it, shook his head, and started out the front door. I ran after him and caught his arm. "Look, Roy, I'm sorry, but it's just something I feel I need to do. When Diane told me about her, I thought we ought to try to help. I had a gut feeling about it. And Diane was having trouble finding her a family."

"A family," Roy said, shaking his head.

"Come on, Roy." I touched his cheek with my hand and smiled at him. He was my baby brother, and sometimes I still thought of him as little Binky, his cheeks smeared with peanut butter, jelly, tears. "We're a nice family. It'll be fine. It'll do us all good."

Roy shook his head again, though at least by now he was smiling a little, and said, "You're nuts, Al."

I said, "I know."

I had thought Puffin might not take the news too well either, but it wasn't as bad as I'd feared. Sometimes Puffin could be a bit histrionic, but she remained fairly calm while we had our little talk. Her main concern seemed to be that her new foster sister not impinge upon her space. "She's not going to sleep in my room, right?"

"We'll put her in the guest room."

"And she won't need to use any of my stuff. Like, she'll have her own stuff."

"I'm sure she will."

"And I'll still be in charge of the TV."

"I guess so." She went on for a while with her list of demands, all of which I agreed to, as usual. When it seemed we were finished, I said, "So, are you okay with this, Puff?"

"What*ever*," she said, adding, "You're so weird."

I spent the next few days cleaning out the guest room— we called it that, though we rarely had guests in it. My mother came up from Florida for a week every spring, spending the whole time playing canasta with her old cronies, but apart from that, we mostly used the room to throw things in when we were finished with them. It was full of Puffin's old books, and Roy's tennis racket, which he never used anymore, and a StairMaster I had bought and then given up on. I took a bunch of the stuff I knew we would never need again to a yard sale that one of our neighbors was having, but that didn't seem to help much. The room still looked cluttered, but eventually it was a neat sort of clutter, and I had made room in the closet by taking out a bunch of my father's old suits that I had ended up with somehow when he died. My mother hadn't wanted them and had made me take them when she moved to Florida, and I just couldn't bear to throw them away, since they were all anyone had left of my father. But I needed the space, and I made myself take them to Good Will. When I came home, the guest room seemed lighter, airier, as if it had been reborn as someone else's room.

The rest of our house, meanwhile, was in the process of falling into ruin. No one but me ever cleaned, and Puffin and Roy left things in piles all over the house. When Puffin came home from school, she would throw her book bag on the floor and scatter papers everywhere, leaving notes for me to sign, empty Oreo packets, and pencil shavings all over the dining-room table. Most days, the table was so heaped with people's junk that we just ate in the living room in front of the TV. I hired a painter to touch up the front of the house, which had been quietly peeling off, and I tackled the inside. When I finished with the guest room (I had bought a bedspread and some matching window treatments at JCPenney), I started in on the rest of the house, sweeping piles of debris into boxes and carting them up to Roy's and Puffin's rooms; I opened their doors and just shoved everything in, then closed them again. Doing this made me feel that in some small way I had triumphed for a moment over the chaos that always hovered around me, threatening to close in.

When I actually saw Mary Fred for the first time, I felt disappointed. I don't know what I'd been expecting—someone younger, maybe, though I knew how old she would be, or someone cuter. Mary Fred was not cute—she was a little too tall and gangly, with dark blond stringy hair, and her front teeth stuck out in a way you don't see much anymore, since everyone gets braces now. Her eyes were just a little too small, and her nose was just a little too long, but that wasn't it. I guess what kept her from being cute, and what scared me, was that she looked all grown up already, like there was nothing I could do to help her.

Her manner was off-putting too. I was used to Puffin and her friends, and I had never met a child that polite. When she thanked me for everything, and called me "ma'am," I knew this was meant to sound respectful, but it just made me feel ancient. Even more difficult for me was the fact that she didn't seem to need anything. I was used to people who did, and I didn't know what to do with Mary Fred at first. She was cool, calm, self-sufficient—of course, I'd been expecting a trauma victim (though soon it became clear that she was much more upset than she let herself show, or even than she knew). Within hours of her arrival, she had cleaned my entire house more thoroughly than I had since the days when Peter lived there. Even the bottles of cleaning sprays under my sink now stood in rows that had been arranged with military precision, as if they were only waiting for my orders to spring into action.

I just wasn't used to people like this. And then there was her religion. Although Roy and I grew up pretty much confused about that kind of thing, I did know people who went to church or temple, and they seemed normal enough, though the idea of getting all dressed up and actually leaving the house on a Sunday morning or worse, a Saturday, seemed strange and pointless. But Mary Fred had clearly never taken a breath in her life that did not have to do with the doctrines of her religion, whatever it was. I never quite understood it. Everything she said seemed to have something to do with their beliefs, and she seemed so sure of them. All my life I had struggled—in college, staying up late arguing about philosophy, about whether physics proved that there was a God or that there wasn't, about ethics, personal and societal, weighing, wishing there were something I could come to that we could all decide was Truth—and there never was. But here was Mary Fred with this calm certainty about everything, and even cheer about this event she called the Big Cat, though when I found out what it was, I began to see her cheer in a different light.

The first few days were hard. I kept trying to think of ways I could help her, but there seemed to be none. She just kept thanking me. Still, and this was a surprise, Roy and Puffin seemed to respond to her somewhat. That first Saturday night when we had dinner together, it felt like we were having a little party, and they were on their best behavior. No one yelled and said they hated me (Puffin) or went to their room alone and sulked (Roy). I felt glad and relieved, like maybe everything was going to be all right.

When Mary Fred finally had her meltdown that Sunday, that too was kind of a relief to me. I had been unable to see how anyone could go through what she'd gone through, which was so tragic, and still seem perky and jolly, whereas here I, who had after all gone through so much less, was having trouble just getting up in the morning—I now see when I look back on it—and was clawing my way through every day, hoping to simply get through it. I'd go to a workshop on our new CD-ROM databases, which seemed destined never to function properly, or enter data about the library's new acquisitions into our new online catalogue, which was also always on the blink, and all I could think about was that I wanted to lie down on the floor behind the circulation desk where no one could see me and take a nap, or maybe cry. Mary Fred's sobs, however heartbreaking they sounded in one way, comforted me, as if they revealed a secret self she hadn't known about, a childish self I felt I could reach, and help. When she finally sank her head onto my shoulder, she felt like a kid, which is what I'd been expecting and even hoping for.

The next day, she was up and already tidying things when I came downstairs. When I told her I was going to work, she seemed disappointed, and I stood there frozen, just kicking myself for not having thought this through better. I had said this to Diane when she first mentioned to me that she thought I'd do a wonderful job as a foster mother. "All the resources you have," she said, "and all those people out there in need." Diane had a way of making a person feel guilty about the most ordinary things. If you went to a restaurant with her, she'd talk about the people who were starving; if you said you'd been dancing, she'd talk about the people whose legs had been shot off by military dictatorships; if you said you'd been listening to music, she'd say that the people in prison in Central America heard only the sounds of their own screams.

"But I have to work all the time, Diane," I pointed out. "What kind of supervision is that for a child?"

"You'd need an older child, of course," she said. I didn't realize it at the time, but she already knew about Mary Fred and was trying to place her. "But Alice, surely you're not suggesting that women shouldn't work. I mean, I hope we've progressed some in the struggle since the days of—"

"Of course, Diane, I only meant—"

"These children need positive female role models," Diane said, picking up one of my chicken bones and sucking on it, though she always claimed to be a vegetarian. We were in Delices, a local eatery; Diane had ordered the tofu *au vin*. "Strong women. Women of courage. Women at work."

At that point, I had agreed with Diane in the abstract, and

before I knew it, I was filling out all the necessary paperwork. But then there I was, leaving the house, leaving Mary
Fred home with Puffin in front of the TV. Diane said she was
arranging for a Board of Education tutor to come work with
Mary Fred, but apparently, they were short-staffed, and so
far there was no sign of one. I had encouraged Puffin to find
a job, since she was now old enough, or to do her community
service (she needed to volunteer seventy-five hours to graduate, and she hadn't completed any of it yet), but Puffin said
no one was hiring anywhere, she had tried. I knew she was
lying, since there were Now Hiring signs on every gas station and grocery store in the neighborhood, but I didn't push
it. I remembered all my teenage summers, how hard we'd
had to work after our father died, and I didn't wish that
on her.

I guess that was one of the reasons I'd thought it would be
a good thing to have Mary Fred around—she could keep
Puffin company and, presumably, keep her out of trouble
while I worked. When I saw Mary Fred, I knew that at the very
least, Puffin was not going to be able to be a bad influence on
her, though she might try. Mary Fred did not look the least bit
likely to want to get her belly button pierced or dye her hair
blue, both of which Puffin had done, though she had had to let
the piercing close up when her navel got infected—and the
blue hair dye always grew out eventually. I thought she was
probably doing these things to freak out her father, but Peter
was not easily freaked and seemed proud of his oldest daughter's eccentricities. Though he was a very successful lawyer
now, Peter had had hair halfway down his back when I met
him, and maybe Puffin was somehow keeping the flame of hip-
ness alive for him. Especially as he now had almost no hair
at all.

Anyway, I had to leave them at home. Of course, Roy was there too, but he seldom got up until at least eleven, and then he went out and did whatever it was he did, I was never sure. Sometimes I saw him at the coffee shop in town, sitting at the counter with a bunch of other messy, sleepy-looking men. He'd generally be home already by the time I returned from work, and if I cooked, he would have something with us in front of the TV and then go back up to his room. Diane said he was clearly suffering from clinical depression and that I ought to put some Prozac in his coffee, but I think she just didn't like him.

I could tell that Mary Fred had never seen much TV because she kept making comments about the commercials, whose purpose she did not quite seem to understand, as she sat watching *Judge Judy* every day with Puffin. As I listened to them talking, I could see she didn't realize which of the shows were fictitious and which weren't. In fact, the whole concept of fiction seemed alien to her. I had suggested that she might want to read some of the books that were in her room, old books of Puffin's mostly, and she said she only ever read two books, the Bible, by which she meant the New Testament, and something called *The Book of Fred.* She said they were the only books that had ever been written that had any truth in them, and that there wasn't any point in reading anything that didn't. I felt myself sighing and again thinking how nice it must be to feel so sure about things. Every day, she sat in the living room with *The Book of Fred* by her side, but though she had the book open and seemed to be trying to read, her eyes increasingly kept drifting to the TV.

When she was in the bathroom one evening, I picked the book up and looked at it. It was 741 pages long, including the index, and it had chapter titles like "Persecution," "Evil Spirits," and "The Prophecies." The index had entries like "Incarnations of Satan" and "Evil, final extermination of." I put it down quickly when I heard her step on the top stair, which creaked, and laid it back as she had had it, open to a page on the history of the Crusades. I went into the kitchen to stick a chicken in the oven—I had bought a Perdue roaster. I washed it first, which I hated doing because it felt like a fat naked baby, and closing the oven door on it felt barbaric. I had basically tried to be a vegetarian for most of my adult life, but I had kept on eating meat because Peter had liked it, and Roy seemed to need a lot of protein or he looked even more pale and listless than usual. As for Puffin, she wouldn't eat anything unless it came directly from a bag or a box.

As I entered the living room, I overheard Puffin trying to explain to Mary Fred that Judge Judy was not only a real judge but a great heroine for our times. Let them fight it out, I thought to myself. After a while, it appeared that Puffin had won—Mary Fred was cheering and saying, "She's *so* right about these people, they just need to pull themselves together and start acting like grown-ups." By the time dinner was ready, they were watching *Friends,* an episode Puffin had already seen forty times, and I had to practically drag them to the table. "But do they ever find the baby?" Mary Fred asked, sounding really worried. Puffin assured her that they did.

The whole first week went on basically the same way. I would leave in the morning and Mary Fred would already be up and dressed. She always wore brown, and eventually when I asked her about it she told me that brown was the holiest color, which was why when the original Fred had come to earth and been incarnated as a modern prophet, he had been given the last name of Brown. "So you're saying this man's name was Fred Brown?" I asked her. She said yes, and she made a little motion with her hand, as if she were drawing the letters *F* and *B* with her fingertip. I found out later that that was what she did whenever anyone said the name Fred Brown, and when Roy found that out he used to say the name just to watch her make this motion. He seemed to get a big kick out of this.

So I'd go out the door, telling Mary Fred good-bye. It was nice to have someone to say good-bye to, since Puffin and Roy were always still asleep when I left, and unlike Puffin, she let me kiss her on the cheek after a few days, and though she didn't kiss back, she would smile. Mary Fred had the sweetest smile—a little lopsided, because of her wide mouth and crooked teeth, but big and cheerful. It was so nice to see her looking happy that I found myself trying anything I could to get that smile out of her. When I brought home some more of those pink beads she had asked for in the Safeway, she seemed glad that I had thought of it, though it seemed to me that she didn't much care about the beads. (Whereas Puffin sucked them right down. They were pure sugar.) I began to suspect that what she really liked was the color pink, so I started buying pink cupcakes to see if they would make her smile too, and they did.

When I came home from work that first week, they would be sitting silently together in front of the TV, Puffin sprawled in the armchair, Mary Fred sitting primly on the couch with her weird book propped in her lap, trying to read. But by the second week, I'd find Mary Fred riveted to the screen, and the two of them chattering about the transsexuals on *Jenny Jones* or the incestuous lesbian sisters on *Jerry Springer.* "Are you saying that woman was really a *man?*" Mary Fred would be squealing. "But if he was born a man, I don't see why he'd want to wear a dress."

"Sometimes they *have things cut off,*" Puffin would say darkly, and Mary Fred would squeal some more.

Some days I'd get the two of them to help me with dinner, just to pry them away from Jerry Springer. I had never had much luck getting Puffin to help me in the past, but now that Mary Fred was here, she pitched in when I suggested it without her usual yelling, as if she didn't want her new foster sister to know how uncooperative she normally was. But other days, I just left them where they were, since it was nice to hear them talking and sometimes laughing. Puffin had always been a quiet girl when she wasn't shrieking, at least since her father and I had split up, and I liked hearing ordinary noises, instead of the sounds of yelling or whining, coming from her.

The second Sunday that Mary Fred was with us, I decided to get up early and take her to church. Diane had given me the name of the church she belonged to, though she and Sandy would be away that weekend at their beach house and wouldn't be there for moral support. I didn't much like Sandy anyway; she seemed to disapprove of me, maybe because I was heterosexual, or because she knew I was still hung up on my ex-husband, or just because I had known Diane longer than she had (we had met in college).

I told Mary Fred on Saturday that I would be taking her to church the following morning. I had pried her and Puffin away from the TV and had taken them shopping. Puffin dragged us through a bunch of cheap teen stores at the mall, somehow talking me into buying her a see-through black shirt that she said looked cool. I wasn't sure whether she meant literally or figuratively cool, but I let her get it since it was on sale. Mary Fred walked through all the stores, fingering the fabric and drawing her hand back as if she had never felt synthetics before. Maybe she was looking for something brown. There was no brown, though there was a lot of black. At one point, she stopped in front of a rack of pink hair clips, and I offered to buy her one but she declined, though she glanced back at them with what looked like wistfulness.

She seemed excited about the idea of going to church, and when I got up the next morning, she was sitting in the living room in a brown dress, reading *The Book of Fred* again. "Aren't Heather and Uncle Roy coming?" she asked as we pulled out of the driveway. I told her they were still sleeping and she said, "Many of those who sleep shall awake to everlasting shame." I told her I thought that was quite likely.

It wasn't hard to find the church, and we got there just in time. I ran into a few people I knew in the lobby and said good morning, and we made our way to a pew in the back. There was a program on the seat and I picked it up and read it as the congregation sang a song I had never heard before about world peace. There was a brochure in the program asking for donations for the Cows for Kids program. I knew all about this because Diane had been one of its leading lights. She and a bunch of other people had raised money to buy a herd of cows for a group of people in Nicaragua. Diane had often handed me pamphlets with a black and white splotchy cow-ish pattern on their covers.

After the song, a bunch of people stood up one by one and made positive wishes for people who were sick, or refugees, and occasionally for ailing pets. I looked over at Mary Fred and she was smiling as if she was having a nice time. The wishes took about forty-five minutes—it seemed that everyone had something to wish for, but when it was finally over, a woman in a plain black suit stood up and talked for twenty minutes about the situation in Kosovo. I guessed from the program that she was the presiding lay person; there was no minister. There was another song, and then everyone held hands and gave the person next to them a kiss of peace, and the service was over. People were serving bagels in the lobby, but I thought we had better head home and see if Puffin was awake yet. When we got in the car, I looked over at Mary Fred and asked her if she had enjoyed the service. She looked out the window and said, "Oh yes, Alice, it was very nice."

"What did you like best about it?"

"Oh. . . ." She seemed to be thinking. "Some of the songs were nice. I liked that one about the woman named Sibyl."

"Sibyl? Oh, the one about civil rights."

"Was that it? I thought her last name was Wright." Mary Fred continued to look out the window, though there wasn't anything interesting out there, just a bunch of small suburban houses and the occasional strip mall.

"Was it like your church, Mary Fred? I mean, I know it was different, but did they have anything in common at all?" I turned to glance at her and saw that her shoulders were shaking, and I thought she was crying. We stopped at a stoplight, and I leaned over to put my arm around her, but when she turned to face me I saw that she was laughing uncontrollably.

"Oh, Alice," she said, gasping for breath, "I don't know what that was, but it sure wasn't church." She started to laugh some more, and something about her laughter was so infectious that I started giggling too as she went over some parts of the service that she had found particularly striking. "And when that lady said she wanted her dog Snuffles to get over his dia—his dia—" She was laughing too hard to say the word "diarrhea." We drove down the street in hysterics and didn't stop until we were back home, and then Mary Fred tried to explain it all to Puffin, who was sitting groggily in the living room, flipping channels, but like all funny things, it was impossible to explain and after a while she gave up.

The next few weeks went on basically the same way. I didn't try taking Mary Fred to church again, since she said she was afraid she would start giggling and not be able to stop, and she didn't want to offend anyone. She explained to me that there were no churches anywhere but the ones in the Frederick counties that were the right kind; it seemed that everyone else was really a Lacker in disguise, so there was no point in bothering about them. I thought about taking her up to the one in Frederick County, but Diane had warned me to keep Mary Fred away from her previous life, since we wanted her to make a good adjustment. Every morning I'd go to work and find her awake already, dusting the furniture or sometimes doing dishes that Roy had left there in the middle of the night, or reading her book. During the day, while I was at work, I suppose she and Puffin spent most of their time in front of the TV, though when I got home, the house always looked nicer than it had when I left, and I could tell Mary Fred had been cleaning, though I had urged her not to. I have to admit that when I came home and found things tidy, orderly, shiny, it gave me a feeling of tremendous relief, even peace. I would bring my groceries into the kitchen and Mary Fred would help me put things away, talking to me the whole time about things Judge Judy had said, or about Jerry Springer's concluding message, and occasionally she would quote something to me from *The Book of Fred*. Her quotations always sounded sort of biblical, but garbled, like someone had not quite gotten it right. Of course, I had only ever read the Bible when I had been stuck in motel rooms with nothing else to do, so I had no idea if Fred Brown had bastardized it or not. When I thought of the name "Fred Brown," it made me want to draw a little F and B in my mind. Mary Fred was definitely getting to me.

Mary Fred always helped me with dinner, and she often came up with great ideas for what to do with things like cauliflower or frozen peas. We ate a lot of fish, since she seemed to like it, and she knew how long to cook every variety, and whether to bake it, fry it, or broil it. (She got me to boil haddock once and I can't say I liked it much, but she did.) We ate at the dinner table instead of in front of the TV, and Roy almost always joined us, which surprised me. I had never had much luck with getting him to sit at the table. Puffin and Mary Fred would chatter on about things they had seen on TV, and Mary Fred would ask Roy and me how our days had been. It seemed odd to hear so much talking in the evening. Sometimes I ended up telling them about things that had happened to me at work, and though Puffin still looked completely bored by anything that did not have to do with, well, Puffin, Mary Fred would listen avidly, like she really wanted to know what had happened when our whole network went down. Roy never said much.

After dinner, Mary Fred would help me clear up, and we would do the dishes. Sometimes she was able to get Puffin to

dry them or even to put them away. Her technique was to lure
Puffin into the kitchen with a discussion of an interesting
court case and then to go on talking to her, handing her a dish-
towel without comment. Puffin would start wiping without
even seeming to realize that what she was doing was technically work, so she never got a chance to scream her usual
protest that she was being exploited, that she was nothing but
a chattel, which was one of her SAT words, and that the work-
ers of the world had to rise up and take over (I think she got
that from Diane).

For three weeks, my house just kept on getting cleaner,
and things proceeded smoothly until about the middle of
July, when Puffin had to go to France with Peter. I'd been
dreading this, and I can't say Puffin seemed to be looking forward to it much either. Peter was taking his wife and their
five-year-old twins, Samantha and Kate, and though Puffin
seemed fond of her little half sisters in a way, I knew she
would have rather been alone with her dad. She got along
fairly well with Peter's wife, Jemma, and I was careful to tell
her that that was okay with me, that I didn't view it as a be-
trayal. Though the truth is, I did; in my heart of hearts, I felt
that Puffin should simply refuse to talk to Jemma and should
stay home on principle, but of course, I never said anything
to her about this because I knew it was completely unfair of
me. I knew that the idea of traveling with them *en famille*
was hard for her, and that she would have preferred to spend
her sixteenth birthday at home. On the other hand, she really
wanted to go to France, since she had been studying French
for years, though her accent sounded closer to Baltimore
than Versailles.

In any case, she was going, and I didn't even try to talk her
out of it. A little voice in my head, a voice that had had a lot

of therapy since the divorce, said that maybe I had decided to
foster Mary Fred so I wouldn't have to deal with being alone.
I neither confirmed nor denied this. I told the voice that I
was not alone, that I had Roy, but the voice just laughed at
this.

When it was finally time for Puffin to leave, Mary Fred and
I stood on the porch waiting for Peter's car. When I saw his
Saab coming up the street, I wished her a quick bon voyage
and darted back into the house. I could see Mary Fred through
the porch window, still waving long after the car had pulled
away.

I think things were tougher for Mary Fred while Puffin was
away, and I know they were harder for me. I had already felt
inadequate when dealing with Mary Fred, but now I felt down-
right incompetent; I had *no* idea what she needed or what I
ought to be doing for her. Ever since childhood, I had often
felt that everyone else in the world had attended classes on
how to do all the ordinary things in life, but I had somehow
skipped them. It was the ordinary things that Mary Fred
seemed to need—food, guidance, nurturing, companionship—
but easy as those things seemed to be for most people, they
were the hardest ones for me. In the evenings, the TV was
strangely silent now—I suppose she couldn't bring herself to
watch it unless under duress—and when I came home from
work, I found her reading to herself most days. I called Diane
a number of times about getting Mary Fred a tutor, but she
said the program's funds had been cut, though she was still
working on it. The house just kept getting cleaner than ever,
and I felt terribly guilty about it, but I told myself that at least
poor Mary Fred had something to do. When I was home, I sat
and talked to her, and she seemed to like that well enough.
Whenever I asked her questions about her family or her past,

she seemed to clam up, but she was always ready to talk about religion.

"What is a Lacker?" I asked her one night. I had heard her use the word a few times since her outburst that first weekend.

"Well, ma'am," she said, pausing as if trying to decide how to put it. She hadn't called me "ma'am" in a while. "It's pretty hard to explain. I'll put it the simple way. A Lacker is someone who is lacking in what we call Soti."

"What is Soti?"

"It means a sense of the Imminence."

"Oh, it's an acronym." I thought she had said the word "immanence," but later I found out she meant imminence with an *i.* "The in-dwelling spirit?"

"No, the Imminence means—we call it the soon-ness."

"Of God?"

"Of the One. See, we'll be there soon, in the garden."

"Whereas Lackers—"

"Yes." She looked sad. "That's the thing. Lackers don't have Soti, and without Soti, well, you just don't know how to prepare. You have to be prepared in mind and body."

"Prepared for what? The Big Cat?"

Mary Fred pressed her thin lips together like she was afraid that too much information was going to escape. "Papa says it's no use talking about it."

"With Lackers, you mean?"

"Well, ma'am, I'm sorry. That doesn't sound very polite, does it?"

"Is the Big Cat some kind of animal?"

Mary Fred let out a peal of laughter. "Oh, no, Alice, good heavens. You thought it was some kind of big pussycat that was coming to catch us all like mice?" She laughed till her eyes teared. Then she didn't seem to want to say any more about it.

On the weekends, I took her to the mall and tried to find her things she might like. We looked for brown clothes, and after a lot of searching, we actually found a few shirts, though they were nylon and Mary Fred said they felt strange. I guess she had never worn anything but cotton. We went into shoe stores, and it wasn't hard to find her some nice plain brown sandals. I was so used to trying to talk Puffin out of huge tottering heels that it was refreshing to buy a pair of flats without a struggle. We went into the accessories store and looked for brown hair clips. There weren't any, but there were a lot of pink ones, and when Mary Fred wasn't looking, I bought her one, hoping I was not somehow corrupting her. Then we went to the food court for lunch. I had stir-fried vegetables and Mary Fred had a fish sandwich.

When we got home, I gave her the pink hair clip. She opened the bag, and when she saw it, she took in her breath really sharply and looked at me with rapt eyes. I helped her put it in her hair. Her hair was thin and very straight, and it slipped out of the clip after a few minutes, but she put it right back and then kept looking at her reflection in the mirror over the mantel and smiling at herself. When she smiled, she was a very pretty girl, and it was nice to see her in pink after all that unremitting brown. With her hair up, she had a swan-like neck, and looked very graceful. "Oh, Alice," she said. "I look like one of those movie stars."

"Yeah, like Arnold Schwarzenegger," Roy said as he drifted past us.

Mary Fred seemed to know who Arnold Schwarzenegger was, and she threw back her head and laughed like Roy was just the funniest person on earth.

*   *   *

Some nights when Mary Fred had gone to bed, I sat up alone in the living room, trying to read in the armchair. I could never seem to get my mind to focus; it kept drifting away, usually to Peter. I had not taken the divorce well, in fact there had been times when I was not sure I would ever be able to function again, but it had been years now and I was basically okay, unless something set me off. Right now it was anything to do with France. It seemed as if every book I opened had some reference to it—the author would talk about someone's *je ne sais quoi,* or about Napoleon, or if it was a novel, the characters would start eating camembert, or brioche, and I would picture Peter on the Boulevard St. Michel with his new family, his beautiful children and his calm, solid-looking wife, the edges of my vision all fuzzy, all of them skipping along, flowers sprouting up behind them like in a soft-focus ad for allergy medication. Peter and I had been to Paris when we were young and had always planned to return, but like so many of the things I had counted on, it had never happened. I sat in the armchair and willed the vision to go away, but it wouldn't, and sometimes I found myself mentally dumping Jemma into the Seine and taking her place, and I could see myself skipping along with them, my hair, no longer gray, floating on the breeze, my face happy again.

By the time Puffin got back, Mary Fred and I had developed one of those wordless relationships where you stand in the kitchen together, one person washing and the other drying the dishes, without saying much beyond remarking on how light out it still was, or how you saw a cardinal this morning in the rhododendrons. We would go from washing the dishes to putting them away like synchronized swimmers, and then we would move into the dining room, wiping the table with a rag and putting the good silverware, which we had started using routinely, back in the sideboard. Roy was often still sitting in the living room when we got done, and we would tidy up around him, fluffing the pillows on the couch, straightening the throws I had laid there to hide the stains and holes. Roy would never help us, though he'd sometimes jokingly call out directions—"You missed a spot," he'd say when we were dusting, or "I'd like my slippers, please." One time, Mary Fred went and found a pair of slippers for him and brought them downstairs, and he looked really embarrassed and said he'd been kidding.

"Don't joke with me, Uncle Roy, I always take people seriously," she said.

He looked even more embarrassed at this, and he put the slippers on.

A few days before Puffin came home, Mary Fred spent about forty-eight hours painting a huge sign to hang on the front door. She had made me go to Kmart and buy a long roll of paper and some poster paints. The sign said "Bienvenue Chez Vous, Mademoiselle Heather" and had about forty exclamation points after it. I could tell Roy had given her all the high school French he remembered. Above the words, she had painted little things she thought were French: the Eiffel Tower, a beret, a poodle. Roy suggested she paint some French fries, but she could tell from his tone that he was joking again.

We all sat in the living room, waiting for Puffin—even Roy—and finally, about an hour later than we expected, she came bursting in the door, smiling, and kissed us all on both cheeks. "It's so clean in here," she said, looking around.

"Well?" Mary Fred said when Puffin had settled in a bit. "Tell us all about it. We want to know *everything*. Can you speak French now?"

"*Où se trouve le Métro?*" Puffin said, and Mary Fred clapped her hands.

"What was your favorite place?" Mary Fred asked.

"It's hard to say. It was all just so—*splendide.*" Puffin went over to her suitcase, which she had flung down on the couch, and rummaged around in it, pulling out several bags. "*J'ai les cadeaux,*" she said with no trace of a French accent, and she handed a flat bag to me, a small round bag to Roy, and a large box to Mary Fred. Roy reached into his bag and pulled out a snowstorm with the Eiffel Tower in it. "Wow, thanks, Puff," he said, sounding genuinely pleased.

"*Pas de quoi,*" she said. "Mom, you go next."

I reached into my bag and pulled out a small print of my favorite Renoir painting, *La Moulin de la Galette.* "Oh, Puff, how did you know?"

"Dad told me," Puffin said, not quite meeting my eyes.

I put my arms around her and said, "*Merci,* sweetheart." I felt like running up to my room, throwing myself down on the bed, and sobbing, but I managed to just stand there.

"It's from Jeu de Paume," she explained. I told her I knew. "Mary Fred's turn," she said, pointing to the large white box.

"Really?" Mary Fred looked all excited. "Oh, Heather, what could it be?" She pulled the top off the box carefully, drew out something pink and slinky, and held it up so we all could see. "Oh, my goodness!" she said with a little squeal. "Is this for me?"

"*Oui, pour toi,*" Puffin said. "*Essayer*—um, try it on."

"Should I?"

"Go on, Mary Fred," Roy said. "Let's see what you'd look like if you were French."

Mary Fred ran upstairs and came back down with the shirt on. She was still wearing her plain brown skirt, which looked strange below the shirt—it was tight, with a low neckline, and had little gathers on it with embroidered flowers. I was sure it had cost Puffin a fair amount of money. "Oh, honey," I said, "you look beautiful."

"Do I?" Mary Fred looked at herself in the mirror and let out a little gasp.

"Ooh la la," Puffin said. *"Tu est trés belle."*

It was true; Mary Fred looked incredible. I was so used to seeing her in brown cotton that I hadn't realized how blue her eyes were, or how sweet and heart-shaped her face was. Even her freckles, which had made her seem kind of homely before, seemed stylish and flattering, and her hair, pulled back in the pink clip, fell loosely around her face and framed it. I watched her in the mirror as she tilted her head to one side and smiled at herself.

"Voilà," Puffin said. "Le makeover."

I looked over at Roy. He was watching her too but not saying anything.

We had dinner—Mary Fred had insisted we make something French, so that afternoon I had thrown a bottle of burgundy into a pot roast, which shocked her. She hadn't known people cooked with wine, though I assured her that all the alcohol burned off when you did it. "Boeuf bourgignon," I said when I took it out of the oven. It smelled of thyme, and the smell made me terribly sad. When Peter and I were in France, though we had been graduate students and very poor, we had had some incredible meals. When we got home, I tried to copy everything we had eaten, and he often said I had exactly duplicated the recipe for whatever it was, but to me nothing ever tasted quite right.

Mary Fred had set the table with the paper napkins folded into swans again as well as some cloth napkins we had gotten at Pier 1, which she had folded and fanned in our wineglasses. We had picked some flowers from the garden and she had arranged them in the center of the table, a weird combination of dahlias, zinnias, and yarrow. Puffin looked happy to be home. She was smiling and chattering away about the Champs-Elysées and how expensive everything had been, but how her dad had bought her a really nice shirt there anyway. She looked up at me when she said it, and I guessed that she was making sure I didn't mind. She knew I hated it when she talked about things Peter had bought her, things I couldn't afford.

"Did you go to the Left Bank?" I asked her. That was where Peter and I had stayed, in a cheap hotel next to a crêpe stand. We had only been married a year at that time, and it was still new and exciting to sleep together, and in a new place. We could lean out our hotel window and see the lights up and down the street start to blink on. When my thoughts started to drift to things like this, I was in the habit of snapping myself out of it, giving myself a little mental slap before I ended up daydreaming about Peter. But since Puffin had gone to France with him, the slap didn't seem to do much good; I kept seeing myself in bed with him, naked, him gazing at me adoringly as if I were a treasure. I wondered if he looked at Jemma like that.

When I looked up, I realized that Mary Fred was examining my face quizzically. I wondered what my expression had been—had I been frowning, or had I looked like I was about to cry? "How were the twins, Puffin?" I asked in as neutral a voice as I could muster.

"Oh, they were brats," Puffin said. "They cried on the plane, both ways. We had to keep giving them ice cream to shut them up. I forget how to say 'ice cream' in French. I think it's 'glass' or something. Anyway, we went to the most amazing toy store, it was totally awesome, and they wanted everything in there. There was a stuffed bear about twice my size, and they kept crying because they wanted Dad to buy it for them. He kept telling them he'd have to buy it a seat on the airplane but they said they didn't care. Samantha actually lay on the ground and started kicking her feet. It was *so* embarrassing."

"I know the feeling," Roy said. "That's how I feel most of the time. Hey, Al, remember how when I was six, we stopped at a Howard Johnson's and I found a stuffed dog in the gift shop and I just had to have it?"

"No," I said.

"Oh, come on, you've got to remember. I just stood there crying until Mom dragged me out of there, and I screamed all the way to Pittsburgh."

"No, doesn't ring a bell."

"Geeze, Al, it was the most traumatic experience of my life, and you don't even remember it?"

"Nope. Sorry."

"What kind of stuffed dog was it?" Mary Fred asked.

"I still remember it perfectly," Roy said, stroking his shaggy chin whiskers, which suddenly seemed so odd to me, thinking of his six-year-old self. "It was a brown dog with a white stomach and these big cute brown eyes. I had already named it Brownie in my mind. We kept on driving, and I kept screaming 'I want Brownie, I want Brownie,' till I felt like I was going to throw up. Finally Dad pulled the car over to the side of the road and said he was going to smack me if

I didn't shut up. Come on, Al, tell me you don't remember this."

"Honest, Roy, I wish I did. It's just that it probably happened a million times. You only remember the once."

"No, Al, that was the only time that mattered. My heart was broken. I was never the same boy after that."

"Was that what your problem was?" It was true that at some point, Roy had gone from being a bubbly little elf to a droopy, sad creature. "It was all because of Brownie?"

"Sure," Roy said. "That was it."

"Poor little Roy," Mary Fred said. "I can just see you there, crying your little heart out." She gave him a look of utmost compassion. He stared down at his plate, as if he suddenly felt silly for telling us his sad story.

"Poor little Roy," I said. "Would you like some more beef?"

"*Boeuf,*" Puffin corrected me.

"*Oui, où est la boeuf?*" Roy said.

"*La boeuf est ici,*" Puffin said, actually passing it to him instead of just sitting there waiting for someone else to do it.

We all ate some more, then Mary Fred and I brought out a chocolate cake that she had made and we sang "Happy Birthday" to Puffin and gave her some presents, which she seemed to like, even though they weren't French. When she had finished opening everything and sat in a large mess of crumpled wrapping paper, she leaned back in her chair and smiled, which made me feel warm and relieved, at least for a moment. Then Mary Fred and I went into the kitchen and did all the dishes while Roy sat in the living room, listening to jazz, and Puffin came into the kitchen every few minutes and stood leaning against the wall, watching us work, then went out again to go look at her presents. Though I was very relieved now that she was back home, I kept feeling waves of such sadness that at times I had to lean against the sink to keep from just collapsing onto the floor. Mary Fred was scampering around, putting the clean plates away, and every so often Puffin would come help halfheartedly (Puffin always put everything in the wrong place so I had to move it all again when she was done), and they were chattering about a pair of shoes Puffin had seen a few weeks ago at Nine West. She said to Mary Fred that she just had to have these shoes, they were awesome, and Mary Fred said they sounded like really nice shoes. As Puffin went on describing them in copious detail, I felt worse and worse because I knew that I couldn't afford them, and that Peter would probably buy them for her, or maybe even Jemma.

When the dishes were finished, I excused myself, gave Puffin a Happy Birthday kiss (she let me without protesting), and went up to bed. I lay down and propped the print she had given me against my knees. As I looked at it, I tried to just dissolve into the painting, into its colors. I could see Peter and me in Jeu de Paume, the museum next to the Louvre, where we had spent most of three days with bags of bread and cheese, which we ate while the guards weren't looking. I had stood in front of this Renoir and refused to leave; there was something about it that made me feel incredibly happy, like if life could be the way it looked in the painting, with its sea of dancing couples, clearly Peter and I were destined for heights of ecstasy that were beyond the possibilities of ordinary life. I could hear our voices. "Look, Peter, look at the color in their faces. That's the color of happiness."

"Kind of a pink," Peter said, "like they're wearing too much makeup." He put his arms around me and we kissed in front of the painting. I closed my eyes and tried to make the image go away, but it wouldn't; instead, we stood there entwined in the midst of all the Renoirs and Monets, the room full of colors and light. I noticed that I was crying, though I wasn't making any sound, but tears were streaming out of the corners of my eyes.

I still had the postcard he had bought me that day when we finally left the museum, somewhere, along with his letters to me, letters that had promised undying love and faithfulness.

When I finally fell asleep, I could see the colors of the Renoir painting behind my eyelids.

Puffin spoke fractured French to us for a few days and seemed to feel that our house wasn't quite exotic enough for her, and she reset her clock to European time and made me buy croissants, then complained that the American ones weren't any good. She and Mary Fred appeared to be glad enough to go right back to their intensive TV-watching schedule, but after a week or so they both seemed bored. "We can't keep doing this," I heard Puffin saying one afternoon when I had just come home from work. "If I see *Real World* one more time, I'll go insane."

"Well, let's think of something else to do," Mary Fred said. I wondered if she had sat there patiently by the TV all these weeks just waiting for Puffin to grow restless. "Why don't we go for a walk?"

"Geeze, M.F., it's about a million degrees out there."

"How about a swim? Is there a lake around here?"

"A *lake?* No, there's no lake. Not even a puddle. Nothing but suburbs."

"There's the community pool," I chipped in, though I probably wasn't supposed to be listening.

"Oh, *God,* Mom, it's so *gross* there. The entire top of the water is covered with dead bugs. And I'm sure I saw a boy pee-ing in there. The whole pool is practically yellow. What about shopping?" They both looked hopefully over at me.

"I'm sorry, girls, not tonight. I'll take you somewhere on Saturday, I promise."

I went into the kitchen and started dinner. Because it was so hot, I was broiling salmon filet and making a big salad. Roy had said the other day that since Mary Fred had been here, he had eaten enough fish to stock the National Aquarium. "The entire ocean has been denuded," he said.

"I don't think you can denude an ocean," Puffin said. "That was one of our SAT words."

"And the vegetables," he said. "I think I'm turning green."

"Vegetables are good for you," Mary Fred said.

"That's the problem," Roy said. "I hate things that are good for me."

"It's true," I said. "When we were growing up, Roy refused to eat anything but pizza. Our mother used to carry a can of tomato paste and a bag of mozzarella wherever we went."

"She'd put it on everything to get me to eat it," Roy said. "Toast. Steak. Ice cream."

"Ice cream?" Mary Fred said, sounding appalled, then she said, "Oh, you're kidding again, aren't you, Uncle Roy?" and let out a little shriek of laughter.

"It was so clever of us to find ourselves a new family member who would laugh at my jokes," Roy said, taking two sticks of celery and inserting them in his mouth like fangs. Mary Fred laughed again. "I don't know why, M.F., but Al and Puffin don't think I'm funny."

"Of course you're funny," Puffin said, and she and I both said, "Funny-*looking.*"

Mary Fred laughed at this too. When she laughed, she looked like she was having the time of her life.

When I came back out into the dining room, carrying the salad in a huge wooden bowl that someone had given Peter and me as a wedding present, I could hear the girls talking. "Okay, it's all settled then," Mary Fred said. "Oh, Alice, I'm sorry, can we help? Come on, Heather." They jumped up and brought everything else out from the kitchen for me.

"What's settled? Have you figured out something to do with the rest of your summer?"

"Mary Fred thought of something," Puffin said, sounding less than thrilled about it.

"What is it?"

"Community service," Mary Fred said, bringing two candles over to the table and lighting them. "Heather told me she needs to do seventy-five hours before she graduates, and I thought heck, this is the perfect time to do it. I told her I'd do it with her."

"And she agreed?" I looked over at Puffin, who nodded, though she did give a little trademark Puffin eye roll.

"So, what are you girls going to do?" Roy asked over dinner. "Will you volunteer at NASA to help them plan their routes to the moon?"

"We thought we might be able to find a day-care center," Puffin explained, chewing. "That doesn't sound too bad. Not as bad as, like, old folks."

"I'll ask Diane," I said. "She knows all about that sort of thing."

"Yeah, Diane will hook you up," Roy said. "She knows how you can serve the community. She probably knows a day-care center for lesbian three-year-olds."

I tried to kick him under the table, but missed and hit the

table leg instead. "It's nice of Mary Fred to offer to do it with you," I said to Puffin. "Thanks, Mary Fred."

"It's not like she's got anything better to do," Puffin said. "Plus, if she stays at Mount Pleasant for the next two years, she'll have to have seventy-five hours too."

"Two years?" Mary Fred's face froze, and she turned to me. "Alice, you don't think I'll be here two years, do you?" She looked absolutely horrified.

"Oh, no, I'm sure you'll be home way before then," I said, though I wasn't sure of this at all. Later, when I was going to bed, staring at my Renoir print again, I thought about Mary Fred and how bright and cheerful she always seemed, though inside, something entirely different had to be going on. It was hard to imagine just how divided she must feel. Then I thought of myself at work, and how I sat at the desk in the reference area talking to people all day, smiling and helping them use the databases, and no one ever knew that I had lain awake the night before, staring into a copy of an old painting, wondering how I had ended up like this.

On the weekend, the temperature fell below ninety, so I decided to do some gardening. I took the girls to Kmart and we bought a bunch of annuals on sale. It was so late in the season that they were all pot-bound and overgrown, but Mary Fred and Puffin found lots of wilted impatiens, petunias, and nicotiana and put them all in my cart, plus a tray of plastic Popsicle makers, two pink beach chairs for when they wanted to sit in the yard (I think that was Mary Fred's idea), a citronella torch (ditto), two pairs of Martha Stewart–brand gardening gloves, in case they wanted to help me garden, and more of those pink sugar beads that they liked. They went and looked at clothes for a while, but Puffin told Mary Fred in no uncertain terms that it was not cool to buy clothes at Kmart, or even to be seen in the clothes section there—after all, what if someone they knew came in? Mary Fred pointed out that she didn't actually know anyone but Puffin, and that Puffin was already there. Puffin said it was the principle of the thing. I stood near them, pretending not to listen, laughing to myself.

When we got home, I went out in the backyard. I hadn't been out there all summer, and the grass was almost a foot high. I dragged the lawn mower out of the shed and managed to start it up after a few tries. Puffin and Mary Fred put on their new gardening gloves and pulled out a bunch of dandelions, leaving the roots behind. Mary Fred showed Puffin how to make floral chains, which they put in their hair; then they danced around the yard in them. When I had finished mowing, which took over an hour, I dug a little trench beside the fence and the girls put the new flowers into the ground, where they sagged, listing to the side, their leaves drooping. I got the hose out of the shed, hooked it up, and handed it to Mary Fred, and the two of them took turns watering the flowers and squirting each other.

"Let me guess—*The Patty Duke Show*," said a voice from the other side of the fence. It was my neighbor, Paula. "What's wrong with Puffin? Is she sick? I've never seen her outdoors before. And who's the farm girl?"

"That's Mary Fred," I said.

I explained the situation to Paula, who nodded and said, "Oh, Alice, you're so *good.*" She gave a little shudder. "You'll have to let me do her chart. What is she, Libra?"

"No, Sagittarius."

"Like you? Oh la la—too much sincerity for one house. I'd go mad."

"I think she's a good influence on Puffin," I said, lowering my voice.

"Evidently. Look at her, she seems to be having fun. How odd."

Paula asked me all about how Mary Fred had ended up with us, and I told her about how Diane had sort of talked me into it—she knew Diane, and didn't like her. Paula looked thoughtful the whole time I was speaking. Finally, she said, "Alice, I think I saw all this on *Dateline.*" She looked over at Mary Fred again, squinting as if trying to remember her face. "Was that her family?"

"It might have been. What did they say?"

"Were they called the Something-ians?"

"I think so. I'm not even sure. Diane didn't give me too many details. She just said the parents were in jail."

"And you don't know why?"

"I sort of know why. She said they were being accused of child neglect or something."

"Child neglect?" Paula gave a little snort and shook her hair, which fell in tight brown curls around her face. She was short and stocky, and was wearing a little crocheted cap to cover the fact that her hair was thin on the top. At one time, before I met her, Paula had been a man. "Hardly. They're being tried for second-degree murder."

"They're what?"

"Apparently the D.A. is holding them responsible for the deaths of their two sons."

"Mary Fred's brothers? I knew they had died, but I didn't realize . . . How did they die?"

"Evidently, the Whatever-it-is-ians don't believe in medical treatment. I remember now—they were living down in Virginia on some big farm—"

"The Compound. Go on."

"And one of the boys got sick. Just appendicitis or something. They wouldn't let him get medical treatment, just stood by the bed praying for about a week. Then his appendix ruptured and peritonitis set in." Paula was a nurse. "The authorities in Virginia were just starting to investigate, so they all moved up to Maryland, right near Frederick."

"The Outpost."

"What?"

"That's what they call it."

"So you do know some of this."

"Just smatterings. Go on."

"Then the other boy got sick. Pneumonia or something—again, something that could easily have been cured. More praying, and then boom, he dies too. The DA in Frederick County was a lot quicker to act than the one in Virginia."

"Apparently they lived in Frederick County, Virginia, too," I said.

"That was it. The Fredians. Named after the counties?"

"No, I think they must be named after some guy named Fred. Fred Brown. That's why they wear so much brown. I guess. That's all I know about it."

"Alice, you really don't pay much attention to details, do you?"

"I guess not. I don't know, it didn't seem to matter. All I knew was she was a child who needed help."

"Oh, *Al*ice. Please, I'll be sick." Paula looked over at the lawn where Mary Fred and Puffin were still squirting each other with water and laughing. They were both drenched, and Puffin's hair was lying flat across her face in a way I knew she hated. "Well, I hope you know what you're doing. She's a cute girl, in a sort of Pippi Longstocking way. Listen, if you need some guidance, I'd be happy to do your cards for you. I'll use the Osho deck."

"Thanks, Paula. Maybe next week some time—we're pretty busy."

"I can see that. Okay, I'd better run—massage appointment. Tell the girls to come by if they'd like a facial. It's on me."

"Oh, Paula, that's sweet. Thanks, I'll bet they would."

"I've got a new cream I think they'll really like."

"I'll tell them."

Paula started back toward her house, then turned around, said, "White light, honey," and went away.

The girls did go to Paula's for facials the next day. That's what I had started to call them, "the girls," as if they had become an entity. When Roy and I were growing up, our parents had called us "the kids," and on some level I knew both of us still thought of ourselves that way—no matter how old we got, we would always be the kids. Roy had been nine when our father died, I was twelve, and sometimes it felt to me as if we had just frozen at that age. My mother had been so bewildered at first, and then so resentful, and we had not been able to figure out what to do to cheer her up. She took a job she hated and went to a crummy law school at night, and she walked around the house snarling and smoking Kents for what seemed like an eternity. So Roy and I entered a little world of our own at that time, and sometimes I had the feeling that's where we still were. Our mother had finally finished school, gotten a better job, started making money and having what she felt was a glamorous life, but it was too late, we were already stuck in our weird other world, as if we lived, forever young, on the opposite side of an invisible panel and could see her through it, reading legal briefs and smoking (though she finally quit when she turned sixty), but we never really talked to her again.

Since the day she finished law school, my mother had always had her hair done in a perfectly dyed helmet, and her makeup was always a little too heavy. Sometimes I was afraid Puffin was going to turn out like her; the two of them were so conscious of their appearances, so vain, really, that it always shocked me. Now Puffin came prancing back into the house with her hair piled up on top of her head. She looked like a waitress from the fifties, but I told her it looked magnificent. If I said anything less than glowing about the way she looked, she would begin to shout at me, so I was always sure to praise her. "How's my skin?" she asked.

"Breathtaking," said Roy, who was sitting in the living room watching golf. That was about as athletic as Roy got.

"Very nice," I said, though actually it was a little spotty. "And Mary Fred, yours is nice too."

"Alice, is it true what Heather says about Paula?"

"What did she say?"

"I told her that Paula's a transsexual," Puffin said, looking at herself in the mirror above the mantelpiece and sucking in her cheeks.

"I mean, I've seen that on *Jerry*, but I didn't know people really did it." Mary Fred looked at me hopefully.

"They really do everything, Mary Fred," Roy said. "There's nothing people don't do. That's what a strange and wonderful world we live in."

"Then it's true?"

"Yes, it's true," I said. I expected Mary Fred to make a face or something, but she just said "Oh," and went over to where Puffin was standing and said, "Okay, you win the bet. I owe you fifty cents."

"Lucky you won, Puff," Roy said. "Puffin doesn't have fifty cents, Mary Fred. Plus, she's a welsher."

"What's a welsher?"

"Someone from Wales?" Roy said, looking at me to see if I was scowling at him, which I was.

"Oh, Uncle Roy, you're so funny," Mary Fred said, walking over to Roy and tapping him on the arm. He winced, as if the tap had hurt him. I don't know why, but my attention suddenly zoomed in on Roy's face. He didn't look well. His skin was pasty, and there were dark circles under his eyes. He never combed his hair anyway, but it looked particularly unkempt today, and his beige Mexican cotton shirt was wrinkled and grubby. I looked over at the girls—Mary Fred had gone back over to Puffin and the two of them were looking at themselves in the mirror. Paula had put some eye makeup on both of them, and because of the heat it had already started to run, so Puffin looked like a raccoon, a look she seemed to favor. But the startling thing was that in the mirror, she looked so much older than I pictured her. She had just turned sixteen, but when I thought of her, or when she appeared in my dreams, she was considerably younger, sometimes only about eight, the age she was when Peter and I got divorced. It was clear that while I was not paying attention, things constantly changed around me.

The girls turned to each other and high-fived, which Puffin had evidently taught Mary Fred to do. "We're divas," Puffin said, and the two of them clumped away up the stairs. Puffin had always made a lot of noise going upstairs, and for a second I was able to pretend she was just eight again, but then I remembered her face in the mirror.

"Roy, do I just go through life not looking at anything?"

Roy glanced up from the news. Another mass grave had

been discovered in Kosovo, and there were piles of bodies on the TV screen. "Al, you didn't know this about yourself?"

"Know what?"

"Oh, Al." Roy gave me a kind look, not exactly a smile but a faint dimpling of his cheeks. "Don't ever change."

"Change from what? What am I like?"

"I don't know, Al. What can I tell you. You're a little bit— foggy."

"Foggy?"

"You move in mysterious ways. Ways known only to you. You see what you want to see."

"Oh, I do, do I?" I felt myself getting a bit annoyed. "Like what?"

"Like what, she wants to know. Please, Al. Don't make me say any more."

"Go on, Roy, say it. What's the matter with me?"

"I don't know, Al. You're—"

"What?"

"Well, okay. Take Peter, for example."

"What about Peter?"

"I can't stand it, Alice. The guy has a new wife, new kids, you've been divorced for how long is it? And you still drift around like he's going to change his mind and come back."

"Roy, that's not true. I know he's never—I mean I don't think—"

"Maybe not consciously, Alice, but can you explain why you haven't slept with anyone but Peter in seven years?"

"Roy, please. That's kind of personal, isn't it?"

"The guy dumps you for your best friend, and you're just waiting around for him like some demented high school chick."

"Jemma was not my best friend."

"Okay, whatever. Even if she was just an acquaintance, or your hairdresser, or the queen of Belgium—it just sucks, Alice. And you're—you're better than that. You deserve more."

"Oh, Roy."

"Really, Al. You're a beautiful woman. You're smart, you're nice, you have a charming brother. But you're—languishing. And you don't see any of it."

"We're back to seeing now."

"Seeing, Alice. You need to just see things. As they are."

"Oh, God, Roy," I said, sitting down on the arm of his chair and putting my hand on his shoulder. I looked at the piles of bodies that still covered the TV screen. "Oh, God. I just don't want to see any of it."

Roy reached for my hand, patted it, and said, "I know."

It took the girls a few weeks to figure out where to do their community service. Puffin was adamant about avoiding old people—she said they smelled bad and were boring. I tried telling her that she too would be old someday, and that she would be glad then if some nice young girls came and got to know her. She said she'd rather be dead.

"Live fast," Roy said to her. "Die young. That's my advice."

"Oh, Roy, for God's sake," I said.

"It's okay, Mom," Puffin said. "I never pay attention to advice. In fact, I'm likely to do the opposite. I'm a rebellious teen."

"Yeah, right," Roy said. "You're about as rebellious as our aunt Tootsie." Tootsie was our mother's sister, who lived in New Jersey.

"Whatever," Puffin said, glaring at him, then turned to

Mary Fred and said, "Positively no old people. What about day care?"

"Well," Mary Fred said. "That one we visited—it made me sad, Heather. That one little guy reminded me—"

"Okay," Puffin said. "Well then, I guess it's the soup kitchen."

"Oh, that's wonderful, girls," I said.

"And the benefits are great," Roy said. "You get a lot of soup there."

"I'm not sure they really serve soup," Puffin said. "I think it's mostly stew."

"Sounds great," Roy said. "When do we eat?"

"Oh, Uncle Roy," Mary Fred said. "You can't eat there. You have to be poor."

"I'm poor," Roy said.

"Yeah, he doesn't have a job or anything," Puffin said. "Don't worry, Roy, we'll give you some stew."

The girls started work at the soup kitchen the next afternoon, and when they came home, they were talking excitedly about recipes. Mary Fred said she knew how to make a great fruit bread and that the people there would certainly like it, especially the little kids. They went into the kitchen and baked five loaves of bread using a bunch of rotting peaches and what was left of our flour, and the next day they brought them to the kitchen.

"We taught them the Beautiful Prayer," Puffin said when they came home the next day.

"You did?"

"Yeah. M.F. said it would be nice for everyone if they had a prayer to say before eating, so we taught it to them."

We had been saying the Beautiful Prayer, or as Mary Fred sometimes called it, the B.P., since Mary Fred had been with us. I had never liked the idea of praying before meals, or of praying in general, since I had no idea who I was praying to. Roy had told me once that his conception of God was a big tattooed bearded guy in a sleeveless undershirt with mustard stains on it, and I had a hard time shaking that image from my mind. But Mary Fred seemed to love doing the B.P., and we all liked doing anything that made her happy. Sometimes I could see from her face that she was sad, and I could tell she was thinking about her other family. When we all said the B.P. together, it seemed, at least for the moment, like we were approximating for her what a family should be.

In general, though I grew to kind of like the B.P., I had a lot of trouble with what I could discern of Mary Fred's religion. Ever since Paula had told me about the story behind Mary Fred's brothers' deaths, I had found the whole picture increasingly sinister. I never really asked her much about her beliefs, or the structure of the religion itself, since I guess I was afraid of what her answers might be—I didn't want to get into a disagreement with her, so I just kept silent when she came out with her strange proverbs. When she talked about lambs, lepers, dragons, and angels, which she occasionally did, I never asked her to elaborate. One good thing about her religion was that it was evidently not evangelical; in fact, it seemed quite the reverse, like only a select few were able to participate. I was glad about that, and I'm sure Roy was too.

The soup kitchen kept the girls occupied for the rest of the summer, and it cut their TV watching way down, which I was also glad about. Every summer, I had despaired of poor old Puffin, who always started out reasonably perky, as perky as Puffin ever got, but grew increasingly miserable with each day. All her friends went on European vacations with their parents, or to camp, but even if I could have afforded to send Puffin to camp without Peter's help (and I never liked to ask him for extra money—in fact, I hated taking his child support payments as it was), she flatly refused to go. She had gone to camp the first summer after Peter and I had separated, and had been so unhappy there that finally in the middle of the second week, I had brought her back to our house, which had suddenly seemed terribly empty, dark, and sad. I had persuaded Roy to move in with us the following year so the house would not be so alarmingly still, and while Roy was not the most ebullient person in the world, he was company. I never tried making Puffin go to camp again, but neither of us could ever think of anything else for her to do during the summer.

So this was the first summer that Puffin had done something constructive to occupy her time, and even after the first couple days of the soup kitchen, she seemed less edgy, even fairly cheerful. Mary Fred seemed more comfortable too, as if she had gotten into the habit of serving others and preferred to keep doing that. I loved to see the two of them sitting on the couch with the TV off, talking about their day, about how the old man with the eyepatch had had two helpings of their potato salad, and how they had showed some of the new volunteers where all the serving spoons were. They went to the soup kitchen every day for lunch, stayed till midafternoon, and then went back again for dinner. We all ate together when they got home and they would recount their adventures to us. Roy said they ought to write a book called *Girls on Stew*. After dinner, they would help me clean the kitchen—I didn't even have to beg Puffin anymore—and then we would go sit on the front porch. The girls would sit in the swing, and I would sit in an old wicker chair, watching the fireflies in the trees as it got dark. When I was a child, I had always wanted to live in a house like this, with a porch. We had lived outside Baltimore in an apartment that got unbearably hot and airless in the summer, and it always felt to me like there was some perfect life outside, on some other street, that other people were living, the kind of ordinary life that I would never be entitled to. When Peter and I found this house, bought it, fixed it up, I was reaching for that perfection, that ordinariness, and there had been times years ago when I thought I had found it. Now when I sat on the porch with the girls, I had brief moments of it again, glimmers of ecstasy that glowed and instantly dissolved again like the light from fireflies.

July turned into August. It got hotter and more humid, and the cicadas came. We sat on the porch practically shouting over their constant chirping. One weekend, the temperature reached one hundred degrees, so I decided to take the girls down to the beach. We rented a room in Ocean City in the cheapest hotel we could find and spent three days on the boardwalk, eating shaved ice and crabs. Mary Fred seemed to love all the crummy little stores that sold T-shirts, hermit crabs, temporary tattoos. She especially liked the amusement park at the south end of the boardwalk, and we spent a lot of time on the Ferris wheel there. Whenever we got to the top, she would shriek that you could see the whole coastline and that the people looked like ants. Another of her favorite things to do was to have her fortune told by a mechanical woman named Esmerelda, a life-sized doll in a glass case. Heather's fortune would say that she would be rich and famous, and Mary Fred's that she would travel and find romance, and then they would put more money in and their fortunes would be exchanged, and their lucky numbers shifted so by the time we left they had ended up with all of them. They would roll their eyes (Puffin) or giggle (Mary Fred) at each fortune, and Mary Fred would speculate about precisely how she would become

rich, or famous, as if she took these predictions absolutely seriously. One day, Mary Fred's fortune said that she would have
an enormous trial but would emerge triumphant. She said this
was exactly what *The Book of Fred* predicted, so it had to be
true.

On Monday, just before we left, I got a fortune that said I
would have a strange visitor, so I wasn't too surprised when I
came home and found a scrawled note from Roy saying that
Diane had called and that she needed to come over for the
eight-week interview. I wasn't too worried about this, since
Diane had more or less pressured me into fostering Mary Fred
in the first place, but I found that I was a tad nervous when I
called her back. Roy always said I was just too darn eager to
please, and I found myself wanting Diane's approval. Diane
sounded brusque on the phone, but then she always sounded
brusque—she was always in a hurry, or her feet hurt (she had
fallen arches), or she'd just had a big fight with Sandy. I invited her to come the following day and to stay for dinner, and
she said that would be fine, and hung up. Diane had a way of
hanging up while you were in the middle of a sentence, but I
had known her long enough that it didn't bother me.

The next day, I left work early so I could stop at the store,
and by the time Diane arrived at six, I had arranged a big salad
in a blue ceramic bowl and was marinating the tilapia filet.
The girls were still at the soup kitchen but were expected back
any minute. I figured this would give Diane and me a chance
to talk privately.

When I opened the front door, she came partway in and
then stood in the entrance, looking around the living room as
if checking for land mines. "What happened here?" she asked,
taking a step forward rather gingerly.

"What do you mean?"

"It's so clean."

"Is it?"

"Yes, it's amazing. Everything's sparkling."

I was afraid Diane was thinking that I had forced Mary Fred into some kind of slave labor, but she just said, "Excellent," and wrote something on the clipboard she was carrying.

"Come on in, Diane. Can I get you something? Some juice?"

Diane said she wouldn't mind some juice, so I went into the kitchen and poured some in one of my crystal glasses. We had taken to using the wedding crystal for ordinary occasions, since Mary Fred had pointed out that it was just going to waste otherwise. When I came back out, Diane was standing there, still writing on the clipboard as if she were taking inventory of the room.

We sat down on the couch. "How are things going?" she asked. She had a slight New York accent, though she hadn't lived there in twenty years, and it always made her tone sound clipped and sarcastic.

"Well, Diane, actually, things are going really well. Mary Fred is a great girl, and we all get along famously. She and Puffin are out at the soup kitchen now, and they've been volunteering there every day."

"Good, good," Diane said, looking very serious and writing some more.

"Yes, things are just fine."

"Really? No conflicts?"

"Well, every now and then she gets upset about—things. Her family, you know. The situation. You know, Diane, I wish you had told me the whole story. I didn't know any of it— about her brothers dying, and her parents being tried for second-degree murder."

"I thought it was felony child abuse."

"Not according to Paula. She said she saw it on *Dateline*."

"Paula," Diane sniffed. She did not like Paula any better than Paula liked her. Though she would have denied it if I'd asked, I think there was something about transsexuality that she found unsettling, as if she felt it should be more difficult to become female than that. "Well, Alice, would it have made a difference if you had known?"

"I don't know, Diane. I just wish I'd had all the information."

"Why?" Diane had an intimidating way of looking at a person. She had small brown eyes that were slightly too close together, and they seemed to bore into you. Her face was small, framed by her frizzy gray-black hair. Roy said she looked like a rabid mouse with feathers.

"I just like to know things." Of course, the minute these words were out of my mouth, they felt like a lie. Roy would say that I didn't really want to know anything at all, that I'd sooner not be told.

"We didn't have all the details at the time," Diane said, as if that put an end to that discussion. "How's her health?"

I told her that Mary Fred's health was good, her hygiene was excellent, and that she seemed happy. At that moment, Mary Fred and Puffin burst through the front door, both crying hysterically. When I was able to get them to speak coherently, they explained that one of their favorite soup kitchen people, an old man named Buddy, had died in his sleep the night before and they had just found out about it. They threw themselves down on the couch, still sobbing, and through their tears, they talked about Buddy for a while, and about how he had always thanked them for his dinner and given them each a quarter, which they had tried and failed to refuse. The whole time they were talking, Diane was taking notes.

"Girls, could you go put the fish in the oven?" I asked, and they scurried away, still sobbing, into the kitchen.

Diane stared after them. "I can't believe it," she said.

"Oh, Diane, she's not usually like this, she's just upset—"

"No, I mean Puffin. What's happened to her?"

"What do you mean, Diane? Doesn't she seem—"

"She went right into the kitchen when you asked her to."

"Does that seem odd?"

"It seems odd for Puffin."

"Does it?"

"Of course it does, Alice." Diane sighed and put the cap back on her pen. "Does she do this all the time?"

"Puffin? I guess so. I hadn't really thought about it."

"Would you say that Mary Fred has had a positive effect on her?"

"Well, now that you mention it."

"I notice her hair is all one color now."

"True."

"Do they have any conflicts?"

I thought about it for a minute. "Actually, no. Not really. I think Puffin is a little jealous of Mary Fred's figure, but apart from that—" I stopped myself, realizing that Diane would think it was highly politically incorrect of Puffin not to embrace her own body image.

"And would you say Mary Fred is happy here?"

I thought about this too. The truth was, she seemed happy enough, but I could see shadows pass over her sometimes. I knew how that felt, how you could be scouring a pot at the sink when suddenly you were transported into your memory, and light began to stream through the kitchen window and give everything in the past a golden glow, like at sunset, and you would feel warm and safe, and then just as abruptly, you would snap back into the present and everything would be blanched and empty, and you'd have a weird sense of dislocation just before color returned, as if you'd been kidnapped by aliens for a minute or so and then dumped back on Earth. "Yes, she's very happy here," I said to Diane.

"Does she miss her family?"

"Of course she does." Sometimes when we walked around the neighborhood, Mary Fred would see small children playing, and her eyes would well up, but she never said anything about it. "Naturally. But I think she's made a good adjustment to being here."

"So everything is totally rosy." Diane went on scribbling on her clipboard.

"That's right. I mean, except for poor Buddy."

"Buddy?"

"The man from the shelter. The one who died."

"Oh, right." Diane did not look the least bit interested in Buddy. "Okay, Alice. I'll turn in a positive report. Even glowing."

Though I hadn't been consciously worried about it, I felt relief flood me. I guess in some dark part of my mind, I'd been afraid that Diane would take Mary Fred away.

By the time dinner was ready, the girls had sufficiently recovered from their grief to regale Diane with stories about the soup kitchen—how difficult it was to plan meals because you never knew who was coming, and how funny and sweet some of the clientele were, though some of them were obviously drunk or on drugs. They took turns talking, and it was like listening to one long sentence. Diane just kept nodding and looking at me every so often as if to suggest that something one of the girls had said had some kind of special significance. I went in and out of the kitchen, bringing food, while they chattered on. (Roy wasn't there. He had excused himself, since he preferred to avoid Diane when possible.)

Diane looked a little uncomfortable during the B.P.—despite her church membership, I knew she was a devout atheist. When we finished, she asked Mary Fred how she had liked going to church. Mary Fred said diplomatically that it had been a very nice church, though not exactly what she was used to. Diane seemed to accept this without question, and I was relieved that she didn't ask me if I had taken Mary Fred to any other churches. I wasn't sure what would make Diane the happiest, if I hadn't or if I had.

"Oh, Diane," Puffin said, her mouth full of fish. "How are the cows?"

"The cows?"

"Mary Fred told me about how you were on that committee to send cows to Nicaragua. Cows for Kids?"

Diane wiped her mouth with a napkin, which was a good thing, since she had broccoli on her upper lip, and cleared her throat. "We had a little problem with the cows."

"Really? What kind of problem?" Mary Fred asked. "We had a lot of trouble with our cows too. Sometimes they just colic for no reason at all. I've spent many a night with a sick cow. Did your cows get sick?"

"Well, not exactly." Diane looked very uncomfortable. Her little eyes darted around as if looking for an exit.

"Have some more fish, Diane," I said, passing her the platter on which I had arranged the pieces of tilapia and some sprigs of thyme from the garden. Mary Fred had weeded the herb patch and it was now growing so rapidly that we put herbs in almost everything we ate.

"Thank you," Diane said, taking the plate and busying herself with selecting a piece of fish. I found myself hoping that its oil would clear up her skin, which was always blotchy and acne-scarred. Eating fish several times a week had been very good for our complexions.

There was a small silence while Diane put a chunk of tilapia in her mouth and chewed slowly, and then Puffin said, "So what happened to the cows?"

Diane looked down at her plate and said, "The cows aren't doing very well."

"What happened?"

"There was a problem with their food, apparently." Diane coughed.

"Oh, no!" Mary Fred clapped her hands together. "We had a cow that had a terrible allergy once. We finally had to give it oatmeal—that was all it could eat. Was it something like that?"

"Well, evidently the problem was not with the food, per se. The problem was with the lack of food. Evidently, no one knew how to take care of cows down there. You see, in a small third-world village, people lack the fundamental agricultural skills that we take for granted," Diane said in a didactic voice that I remembered from college.

"So the people didn't know how to take care of the cows?" Mary Fred asked.

"That's right. They didn't have the requisite knowledge base."

"So the cows all got sick?" Puffin asked, putting her hand over her mouth.

"Yes," Diane said. "They got sick."

"Are they all better now?"

"Well . . ." Diane cleared her throat again and looked intently at her salad. "Actually, they died."

"They died?" Mary Fred looked at her in horror. "How?"

"They starved to death."

"Oh, my goodness gracious!" Mary Fred said. It was the most extravagant exclamation I had heard from her yet.

When Diane had gone, we went and sat out on the porch. I think all of us felt relieved that she was gone, though I'm not sure the girls knew why she'd been visiting. I poured us some fresh lemonade that Mary Fred had squeezed for us and put mint from the garden in it.

"Alice, I don't think I understand about the cows," Mary Fred said. "Why did they send the cows down there if the people didn't know how to take care of them?"

"I don't know, Mary Fred. I guess they were trying to do the right thing. It's not always easy to know how to do that, though."

"But didn't they realize that the cows would need to eat?"

"I'm not sure they thought it through all the way."

"But they had all those pamphlets. With the cow patterns on them. It looked like they knew what they were doing."

"I guess people don't always know when they don't know what they're doing. That's what life is like, you just kind of stab around in the dark until you find out, I guess."

"It's horrible," Mary Fred said. "Those poor cows."

"It *is* horrible," Puffin said, "but it's also just so incredibly—" She started to laugh, and before we knew it, Mary Fred and I were laughing too. "The poor c-c-cows," Puffin gasped, tears rolling down her cheeks.

"What's all this?" Roy came up the steps and looked at the

three of us. "You ladies are insane." Mary Fred and Puffin tried to explain to him about the cows, but they were still laughing too hard to talk, and finally he just shook his head and went indoors.

After we had calmed down, we just sat there for a while without saying anything, looking out at the street whenever anyone walked by, usually someone with a dog. The girls rocked back and forth on the porch swing, kicking their feet in the air. Finally Puffin said she was going to go take a shower— she always showered at night and then put her hair up in a lit- tle ponytail to sleep, to keep it from frizzing. She had been doing it since she was old enough to bathe alone, and the ponytail still seemed to transform her into little Puffin, the lit- tle Puffin I still often thought of her as.

"Alice," Mary Fred said when Puffin had gone. "How long will I be here?"

"I don't know, honey. I guess until things get—back to nor- mal. With your family." I looked at her. She was chewing a strand of her hair, and her face looked strained, as if she were anxious. "Are you okay with that, Mary Fred?"

"Well—seeing Diane reminded me. . . ." Her eyes started to fill up with tears. I reached over to grab her hand, but the swing went backward as I reached and I just grasped the air.

"Aren't you happy here? You seem so well adjusted. And we just love having you here, you know that."

"I know. I mean, it's great and all, Alice, I really like being with you—at least, part of me does, in fact part of me *really* likes it, and sometimes I feel bad about that. Like I don't even know who I am anymore. Puffin and I get along great, and I love everyone at the soup kitchen, and you're so good to me, ma'am, Alice, but—"

"I know. It's hard. You miss your family."

"Alice, here's the thing. It's not just that. Oh, I miss them really bad sometimes, so bad it makes my heart just hurt. But I know there's nothing I can do about it. The only thing I can do is just wait and travel in the One. I know the Littles must be all right, wherever they are, and Mama and Papa will be fine too, because the One will see all of us through all our trials. . . ." Her voice trailed off, as if she had said this so many times that it was hardly necessary to finish the thought.

"Yes, I'm sure they're all fine." Actually, I wasn't sure at all about this, and I felt bad saying something I didn't believe, but she seemed to accept it. "Does it worry you to be away from your, um, people?"

She swung back and forth, not looking at me. "It's not just that I'm with Lackers and watching television and all that kind of thing. That's bad enough. And I haven't been reading the Book nearly as often as I should—we've just been too busy in the soup kitchen, and cooking dinner and stuff like that."

"I know."

"But I'm worried about something, and I might as well tell you right out." She took a deep breath and let it out slowly. "See, Alice, there's this thing that's going to happen. And happen soon."

"Do you mean the Big Cat?"

"How'd you know that?" She looked startled.

"You've mentioned it a few times." Though I already knew that I didn't want to hear the answer, I asked, "Mary Fred, what is the Big Cat?"

"Well, I told you it's not a cat." She put her feet on the floor to stop her swinging and looked at me. "Cat is sort of a nickname. We have names for things."

"I know. What does it mean?"

"I guess it's short for cataclysm. Or catastrophe. I'm not even sure. But you see, the Book has predicted it. And it's supposed to happen at the end of the century."

"I see. And here we are—the century is almost over. But you're stuck with us."

"Well, stuck isn't quite the right word." She smiled at me, but her smile looked pained. "But that's the problem, see. All my life, we've been planning for this year. We've waited for the time, knowing it's going to come—for a time, and times, and half a time. And it's coming, and coming soon, Alice, and I don't know what to do."

"What are you supposed to do when the Big Cat comes?"

"Well, first of all, we have to be at the Compound. We had buses at the Outpost ready to take us there. We had to go where we'd be safe, and alone, I mean without Lackers, and there we would wait for the—oh Alice, I'm not supposed to say what will happen."

"That's okay, Mary Fred. You don't have to tell me."

She dropped her voice to a whisper and said, "The Imminence."

"I see. Is it a sort of second coming?"

She looked away and said, "We think it's a third coming. But yes, and there we will be at the foot of the mountain, waiting for the Glory, all of us together, and we will be translated— that's the word he uses in the Book, translated—into the light."

"And what happens to all the Lackers?"

Mary Fred's face crumpled and she began to sob. I went and sat down next to her on the swing and put my arms around her. When she had cried for a while, she lifted her face up and said, "Ma'am, that's the terrible thing. I realize now that I never cared before. I never minded that all the Lackers were going to be turned into dust, and were going to go to seven and seven hells and stay there. I mean, I thought it was too bad, but I didn't—"

"I understand," I said, stroking her hair, which was soft and kind of sticky from sweat. "You care about us. I know."

"It just hurts so much. All of it. Everything that happened, Fred and Little Freddie, and Mama and Papa, I never felt all the hurt of it, not at first. I was always protected by the idea of the light. But now not even that is a comfort to me—it's all just dust and ashes, Alice, just dust and ashes."

She cried some more and I let her. After a while, I dried her eyes and said, "Okay, Mary Fred, let's be practical. When exactly is this Big Cat supposed to come?"

"In the new year, on the seventh day." She took a breath, and her shoulders shook a little.

"January seventh?" She nodded so I said, "All right, Mary Fred. I'll make sure we can take you to the Compound that day, somehow. So you'll be there."

"You mean you'll drive me out there?"

"Yes."

"So you'll be there too, then. For the Imminence."

"Yes. Though being a Lacker and all, I'm not sure it will do me any good." I smiled and wiped her eyes with my hand.

"Maybe it will, Alice." She looked very serious. "Can Heather come too? And Uncle Roy?"

"Sure, we'll all go. It's probably not that far away—only a few hours from here."

"Really?"

"Sure. See, problem solved."

She looked relieved for a moment, but then she said, "But what about my parents? And the Littles?"

"Mary Fred, don't you think the Imminence is large enough to reach them wherever they are? After all, it's not as if they're Lackers."

"Oh, Alice, I don't know. I hope so."

"Of course it is." I made my tone as reassuring as I could, and said some more little comforting words. Then Puffin came back onto the porch with her hair in her funny ponytail and her flowered nightgown. She asked us what we were doing, and Mary Fred dried her eyes and said we were just talking, and that sometimes talking could be hard work but that we were doing a pretty good job of it. She didn't mention the Big Cat again that night, but I could tell she was still thinking about it, and I hoped that maybe I had managed to make her feel better, even though as far as I knew, there was no sub-stance at all to the comfort I had offered her. But then I thought, sometimes comfort is like that.

When the girls had gone to bed, I sat for a while on the porch swing, feeling the humidity against my skin, almost as if someone were touching me. Like Mary Fred, I needed com-forting, but since there was no one there but me, I had to make do with the night air. When I finally went inside, I walked through the house, turning out each light one by one, then lay in bed alone for a while, with darkness all around me.

THE BOOK OF HEATHER

When I took my first look at Mary Fred, I was sure there was no way we could ever be friends. In fact, I didn't even want to be seen with her in public. She was wearing a dress the color of mud, she hadn't shaved her legs, and her hair was in these weird braids—there was no way I would ever dream of going anywhere with her, not even to the Safeway.

Luckily, Mom didn't suggest any field trips, at least not for a while. By the time we had to actually leave the house together, I was okay with her. It wasn't that I didn't care what she looked like—I still did—but I got to the point where I could handle it. I had never been friends with a person like Mary Fred before, someone who was basically a dork, and it was hard for me at first. But after a while I almost liked that about her, and I kind of enjoyed going places together because people would look at her and wonder what her problem was. It made me feel like we were outlaws.

I was incredibly bored when we first met. Life was just dragging on. I hated school, though at least when you go to school there are people around you, all making noise, especially in the cafeteria, there's this roaring of people's voices. Their sounds make me feel better, like I'm not alone in the whole world. I guess that's why I watch TV, for the sound of it. Sometimes I used to cut school and take the Metro downtown and just walk around, up and down Connecticut Avenue. I would look in stores but mostly I pretended that I was going somewhere very important, like down Sixteenth Street to see the President, and that everyone was waiting for me there, a whole crowd of people sitting around in the White House going, "Where's Heather Cullison? Is she here yet?" And then finally my cab pulls up, or no, wait, my limo, and when I come into the room, everyone claps. I walk down the aisle to the front, where Bill Clinton and Al Gore are standing there, smiling at me. Bill probably wants me to meet him in a hallway somewhere, but I just smile back and stand at the podium facing the audience. They don't scare me at all, all those faces looking up at me and waiting for me to speak. "Greetings," I say, and everyone applauds again. I love the sound of applause, and sometimes when I hear it, like on a record, when my mom is listening to the soundtrack from *Woodstock* or something, I feel myself starting to almost cry, thinking about how it's all waiting for me somewhere, I just don't know where yet.

At first, Mary Fred and I did nothing but veg out in front of the TV. We just sat there and watched all the stuff I usually watched. She didn't have any particular preference, and that was a good thing since we never argued about the channel like I sometimes did with my uncle Roy. Although Roy had been keeping mostly to himself for a while now and didn't even try to grab the remote anymore. We sat there and for the first few days, we didn't say much to each other, though sometimes I'd have to explain the plots of particular TV shows. Mary Fred had a lot of weird questions, and I would answer them during commercials. Every so often we'd watch something on Nickelodeon, and she always wanted to discuss why the

Skipper's clothes never got old or dirty on *Gilligan's Island,* or why the people on *The Beverly Hillbillies* didn't just go back where they came from, since it was obvious that they didn't like it in California. Sometimes I had the feeling that she didn't realize that these weren't real people, but just actors on TV, especially when she'd get scared that Gilligan was going to get eaten by a lion or something, though I told her he'd be okay.

I can't explain it, but after a while, I started to be glad she was there. I liked that there was always someone with me, that when I sat in front of the TV, I wasn't the only one who could hear it. It was a beginning to my search for the crowd who waited for me—Mary Fred was just one person, but sometimes it felt as if she was clapping for me. I liked that she didn't say much—it was like we both just listened to the same things, as if there was now more sound in the room. A hubbub. That was one of my SAT words, and I liked to say it to myself. Hubbub. Hubbub.

I think the moment I knew she was really my friend was when I came back from France. It had felt so bad to leave Paris. One minute it was my birthday, and we were in the Tuileries watching the old men roll metal balls, and throwing francs to mimes, and the next minute we were back at Baltimore-Washington International at the same terminal we had left from, only it looked different now, tacky and ugly and full of boring Americans in T-shirts. Paris had been full of just the right kind of people, with interesting clothes on, like they had really thought about what they were going to wear and studied themselves in the mirror, like I do, to make sure they looked just perfect. And sometimes couples had stood on the corner and kissed in ways that you never see anywhere but in movies. Everywhere we went, people had smiled at us because we were a cute family, and my father spoke really good French so people didn't hate us for being Americans, and the twins were dressed in identical outfits every single day and were always carrying balloons or something that made them look like cartoon characters. Dad and Jemma held hands as we walked around, and though I like Jemma a lot, sometimes I found myself wanting her to just disappear, get poofed away like someone on *The X-Files,* so I could have my dad back. Though then I would think, well, the twins need their mom, and Dad really loves Jemma, and what good would it do anyway, things with him and Mom are over forever. Unlike most divorced kids, I knew that.

So by the time I came back from Paris, all this stuff was swirling around in my brain. I felt sad, and guilty, and angry, and guilty some more, and most of all I felt like just staying in Paris and being an artist or something, or a fashion model— though this would be impossible because of my big thighs— and just never going back to Maryland at all. But then I knew I would miss my mom too much to stay away for long, even though she really got on my nerves, and that made me sad too.

When my dad dropped me off in front of my house—not even coming in, because it would just upset Mom and he knew it—I went inside feeling weighed down by all these things that I felt I could only really say in French, only I didn't know French well enough, in fact barely at all, really, all I knew was that I should have been born speaking it because it suited me better than English.

When I see this poster that says "Bienvenue Chez Vous Mademoiselle Heather!!!!!!!" on it, I know right away that Mary Fred has made it, since my mom wouldn't think of doing something like that. She might mean to plan something nice, but it wouldn't occur to her exactly what to do. So for me the sign is like Mary Fred understands the whole thing somehow without my having to tell her.

* * *

Next thing that happens, I get sucked into this community service thing with her. By that time I was bored enough to think it was a good idea, plus the Board of Education required it, and I realized I'd have to cough it up some time, so why not now. I figured by next summer I'd be driving, and working at some glamorous job, so I wouldn't have time to stand around dishing out soup to all the crummy people hanging around our town. I used to see them standing outside the church on Maple Avenue, in the parking lot, waiting for the doors to open, and my exact thoughts were, EWWW.

But Mary Fred just kind of dragged me in there in that perky way she has and before I knew it, I was all emotionally attached to the people, who really weren't all that yucky when you got to know them, and Mary Fred and I were having a great old time dishing out whatever slop Mrs. Katz had concocted for them that day. At first, we tried to cook something that didn't look quite so disgusting, but Mrs. Katz seemed insulted when we actually made a main dish so we just stuck to desserts and salads.

Also, it was nice having someone to talk to. My mom was always at work or at the grocery store, and Roy just kept to himself most of the time except to make sarcastic remarks regularly, like that was his job, like we should pay him for it or something. So I really began to like the fact that whenever I thought of something funny, or odd, or even just stupid, instead of just thinking it to myself, I could open my mouth and say it to Mary Fred and she would always agree that it was funny or odd, though she never seemed to think anything anyone said was stupid, even when it was. For example, she thought my uncle Roy was hilarious and would always laugh at his jokes even though I told her not to because that only encouraged him.

So by the end of the summer, M.F. and I were palling around

like Siamese twins, and I had totally stopped noticing that what she was wearing was generally pretty horrible and embarrassing. She didn't like to discuss her weird religion all that much. I don't really know what it was, but I guess the deal was they had to wear brown all the time. I tried to get her to explore some other color options because with her light hair, brown was a really bad color for her and made her skin look sallow. I showed her some magazine articles about skin tone and I think they did make an impression on her, but she kept right on wearing brown, though I got her to wear some other stuff with it. I could see she really liked pink, so whenever we went shopping, I would find all these pink shirts and get her to try them on, even though I wasn't crazy about pink myself but at least it was an improvement.

All this was not a big problem when it was summer. I mean, in summer everyone looks like a slob because it's so hot out, people are just walking down the street melting anyway. Though personally I always make sure I look great before I leave the house because you never know who you might run into, even if you're just dashing into town to grab a video. On days when my hair frizzes, I won't go anywhere at all, though at the soup kitchen we had to put our hair back anyway so even when I'd spent an hour getting it just right, it ended up in a dumb ponytail. M.F. offered to put my hair in what she called French braids one day, maybe thinking I might like them because they were French, but I was able to get out of it without having to actually tell her how dorky they looked. I told her they would hurt my head, and she seemed to buy that.

Okay, so by the time August rolled around and it was almost time to go back to school, M.F. was not only my best friend, except for Emma, who had been away for the summer with her dad in Colorado, but she was even better than that, sort of like a cross between a friend and a sister. Not a real sister, since Emma had one of those and they really hated each other most of the time, but the kind of sister you see in old movies. But in spite of all that, by the middle of August I started to worry. I *hate* the middle of August anyway, when you start to be able to count the days till school starts, and just when you think you still have a week or two left, all of a sudden you're back at your locker and it's too soon, since it's still a hundred degrees out and you should be at the beach, and everyone is all sweaty and miserable. You should feel kind of excited because it's a new year, but I never do. I just want to get on with it until I can feel comfortable again and know where my classrooms are and not be wandering around like an idiot trying to find things.

I began to worry more and more every day, and when we got up in the morning, I would see M.F. in a whole different way, not as my pal who was fun to be with but as this liability. SAT word. Liability: n. something disadvantageous. It occurred to me that if I'm walking around being best friends with someone who is basically a dork, then that pretty much makes me a dork too. I would look at M.F. when she came downstairs all smiling and fresh, her hair in those freaky braids, and I would think oh HELP. I imagined myself back in the hallways, looking around for a sign of Dylan Magnuson, as I always did, usually spotting his hair first when it was spiky, or his T-shirts that said things like "Meat Is Murder" or "Have You Clubbed a Baby Seal Today?" (His mother worked for Greenpeace.) As I sat in front of the TV watching *Jenny Jones,* I went into my usual fantasy about Dylan. He would come up to me and say, "Heather, I'd really like you to come with me to the demonstration against the U.S. involvement in [insert foreign country] in front of the Capitol this Saturday—can you make it? We can go to Sonny's Kitchen afterwards and eat some kimchee." And I say, "Oh, okay," like I'm interested but not totally insane about him or anything, in other words I don't fall on the floor and scream, though I'd like to. Instead I am very "poised." That's a word my mom uses: "1. A state of balance or equilibrium. 2. A dignified, self-confident manner or bearing." Being poised made me feel like I was ready for anything—poised on the brink of, whatever.

Suddenly, in the middle of my wonderful Dylan fantasy, a horrible thing happens. Mary Fred walks up to me—right next to me, standing by my side like she really is my Siamese twin—and says, "When are we going?" She is wearing a pink sleeveless top that we made her buy at the mall, and a brown skirt the color of dog doo, and her hair is in pigtails that stick out on both sides. "No, no!" I say out loud.

"Yeah, she looked better before," Mary Fred says. She thinks I'm looking at the TV and commenting, as I usually would be. We're watching Jenny Jones make over a bunch of tacky old moms. The moms go into the back room wearing sweatpants and baggy T-shirts. They come back wearing black miniskirts and black lace tops with their bras showing, and when they reach the stage, they prance around like they think they're pretty hot stuff, though they're still fat, and old, and they have eighties hair, the kind that's long in back and short in front.

Suddenly I have an idea.

That was the beginning of what I secretly called The Mary Fred Project. "M.F.," I say, cagey, my eyes still on *Jenny Jones,* "we should do that to ourselves."

"What?" M.F. asks, very innocent.

"Makeovers. We should make ourselves over."

M.F. claps her hands. "Great idea! You make me over, and I'll make you over."

OhmyGod no, I think. But I say, "No, let's do this. Let's both of us make over both of us."

"Can you do a makeover on yourself?" she asks.

"Of course," I say.

So we go out to the Cosmetic Center and buy all kinds of crap on sale—eyeliner, mascara, gel with glitter in it, face powder. Then we go to Rave, the sluttiest store in the mall, and I force M.F. to buy a short black skirt. "Just like the moms on *Jenny*," M.F. says when she sees it. Yeah right, I say. We find a see-through top to go with it, kind of a lavender, which is close enough to pink for M.F., and we buy her a little metallic flower clip to pull her hair back with. I buy a bunch of the usual stuff I would buy, on sale. Mom has given us a handful of money and said, "Don't get too crazy in there." She's down the hall at Ward's looking at air conditioners. "We really ought to get one," she says every year. "It's just so *hot.*" Then she doesn't buy one because, she says, they're too expensive, and every year it is hot again, hot as hell, I mean *just* like hell, it just scorches you, and Mom is all surprised like it's never been hot before.

When we get home, M.F. and I go up to my room and put on all our new clothes. It's awfully hot for black tights, but we put them on anyway. I sit M.F. down at my dressing table and slather eye makeup on her, and powder, and I stick the little flower in her hair, leaving it kind of messy, and before she can protest I slap some gel in it to make sure it stays that way. We go downstairs screaming "Fashion show!" with me leading the way. When we get to the foot of the stairs, Mom and Roy are staring past me. I turn around and look at M.F. Instead of my uncool pal, I see this awesome model girl standing there. Even Roy is gaping at her, and he doesn't usually notice anything but himself. I knew that M.F. had potential, but her skinny body suddenly looks incredibly chic, and her eyes are big with

the black gunk all over them. She looks like she just jumped
out of MTV.

"How do I look?" she says, twirling around.

"Oh, my goodness, honey," Mom says. "You look—beautiful. It's almost scary."

I'm sizing up M.F. and thinking, well, her nose is a little too
long and her teeth stick out (though the purple lipstick helps
this a lot), her blond hair is a shade too close to dishwater and
kind of stringy, but she has great legs (I'm so jealous. My
thighs will never look like that, long and lean like a model's)
and best of all, she doesn't look like a dork. At all. Now if I can
only get her to dress this way all the time, I think.

"This is what we're wearing the first day of school," I tell
Mom and Roy. They both look a little shocked, even Roy, but
they don't say anything.

"Is it dress-up day or something?" M.F. asks.

I tell her yes.

The night before the first day of school finally comes. I'm
sad, because I love summer when it's over, it always seems so
magical. In retrospect: n. Contemplation of the past. I think
of all the fireflies and wonder where they go, and I think
about the ocean and how it's always warmest right about now,
which is such a waste. I think when I get old and live on my
own, I will always take my vacation at the beach this week,
the first week of school, and bob around in the water all by
myself, laughing out to sea. I don't contemplate the past
much, in general—I think about the future, and I see myself
in it, grown-up and business-like, carrying a briefcase and giving out my business card to everyone I meet. Heather
Cullison, Attorney. Heather Cullison, Consultant. Heather
Cullison, Head Buyer. Heather Cullison, Account Executive.

My mom said once that she could get me a job at the library. I DON'T THINK SO.

Of course, it's not like I'm doing great in school. But my friend Emma says it doesn't matter, that high school is totally bogus and just a waste of time, and that we'd all be better off staying home. I copy Emma's math homework a lot and feel like I'm getting away with something. I'm hoping we'll be in the same math class again this year. I find myself wondering if M.F. will be good at Algebra II.

I just feel so sad. School just seems like a big locker door about to shut on me. I can hear it clanking, locking me away for the whole year, ringing bells every so often to get me to move on to the next period. When is something exciting going to happen? I ask myself in the mirror as I practice putting on my makeup for tomorrow. My hair is up in a ponytail, ready for bed. I can only hope tomorrow will be a good hair day. Otherwise, I may have to pretend to be sick. I have stuck my finger down my throat on many mornings just because of some frizzing.

"Let's lay out our clothes for morning," I say to M.F. She thinks this is a great idea, since she's very organized and neat, so I go to her closet in what used to be the guest room and take out the see-through lavender shirt, the black skirt, and a pair of black sandals I made her buy at Payless. I promise to do her hair in the morning and she doesn't even protest.

The first week of school is tough. Not only are we lost in the halls most of the time, but I only have two classes with M.F., and one with Emma, and the rest of the time I'm stuck with a bunch of people I don't like. I have to sit behind Danny Fox in Chemistry and he smells so bad I almost puke every day before class is over. I've known Danny since I was little, and the truly embarrassing thing is that we used to play together because his mom and my mom used to be friends, before the Jemma business. (Danny's mom Libby sided with Jemma.) I always pretend I don't know him, in fact that I've never seen him before in my life, but he always says things to me like, "Hey Puffin, how's Stinky?" Stinky was my cat that got run over by a car. Danny knows that Stinky's accident was years ago, but he still says things like this just to prove that he knows me, and sometimes other people hear him. Emma always says things to him like, "Who's Stinky, Danny? Your imaginary friend?" Though Emma knew my cat too, in fact she used to put doll clothes on him.

One time we were in the food co-op and my mom and I ran smack into Libby and Danny in the bulk aisle. Usually when my mom sees Libby she has time to run the other way, but this time we were pushing a cartload of disgusting frozen vegetarian entrees along when we nearly crashed right into them. "Hello, Danny," Mom said carefully, like she was picking glass out of a flesh wound. "Libby. How nice to see you both." She smiled like someone was poking her with a hat pin.

"Hello, Alice," Libby said in a tired voice, like she was already sick of the sight of us. "Is this little Puffin?"

I wanted to smack her face and tell her that I was Big Fucking Heather, thank you, but I didn't say a word, just nodded. Normally Mom tells me afterwards that I should have been more polite and answered back instead of just standing there like a lump, but this time as we walked away, she only coughed like she was choking on something, and she never mentioned it again.

Every so often, I run into M.F. in the hall. The first day, she looks totally great, and I can tell that a lot of the boys are asking who she is. I tell a couple of people that she is my cousin

Mary from California and that she's living with me now. I figure if I tell enough people this, the Fred will disappear from her name, and that would be best for everyone concerned. The second day, M.F. wears a pink sleeveless top with the black skirt, and on the third day I make her borrow a top from me, a purple and black tank with spaghetti straps. "My brassiere is showing!" she says in horror when she sees it, but I loan her a black bra, even though her chest is a size bigger than mine and she's kind of bulgy in it. On the fourth day, though, she's back in a brown skirt and another pink top, and she's not wearing any eye makeup because I overslept and didn't have time to put it on her. But I do clip her hair messily in the flower clip so she still looks kind of cool and casual. Still, signs of dorkiness are starting to pop back up, and I'm worried that she can't keep coolness up indefinitely. Luckily it's a three-day weekend, and I drag her back to Rave to buy another top and a skirt, but I'm a little worried about when the seasons change.

"How was school?" Mom asks us every night when she comes home. I always say it was fine and don't elaborate much, but M.F. sits there and tells her every little thing that happened all day. She spends a lot of time talking about her classes, which are Regular and not Honors, even though she is clearly smarter than I am but didn't have time to be tested for placement last year. She talks to Mom about the three branches of government, and about isosceles triangles, which they are reviewing (she's only in Geometry, unfortunately), and about oxygen. Mom acts fascinated, though I'm pretty sure she already knows all that stuff.

On the weekend, we go back to the soup kitchen, though we have earned nearly enough community service hours. M.F. and I decide that we will still work there one day a week just because otherwise we would miss everyone, and the desserts might get bad again if we weren't around to help out. Nothing has changed at the soup kitchen while we were away. Mrs. Katz still can't cook and is a bitch. Mr. Williams still doesn't like tomatoes on his salad. Monica is still there with her three kids, and they're still living at the shelter, and her youngest kid still has a runny nose and no Kleenex.

Every day when we come home, I throw myself onto the couch and am about to turn on the TV to watch all the usual stuff but M.F. plunks herself down at the dining room table and spreads out all her books and asks me to come help her, so of course I do. I'm not even sure that she really needs help, but we sit there and work on all this boring crap until Mom comes home carrying bags of groceries to be put away. When Emma calls and tries to tell me all about her summer in Colorado and all the cool boys she made out with in the woods, I never have time to talk to her, and I think she's getting a little offended but I can't help it, I'm busy.

Finally, I feel like I know my way around, and I can find my classes without being late, and I know when I have time to go to my locker, and who to sit with in the cafeteria. (I don't have the same lunch as either Emma or M.F., so I sit with a bunch of girls I knew in middle school.) By the middle of September, it isn't so hot out all the time and I can start wearing shirts with longer sleeves and jeans instead of shorts or short skirts. M.F. is still doing okay with clothes—between borrowing from me and rotating the outfits we bought at the mall, she's in pretty good shape. Boys are still watching her walk down the hall, and of course she doesn't notice it. She has grown some since she came to live with us, and the brown skirt has gotten shorter and tighter, which helps. I notice that when I walk past the cafeteria while she has lunch and I'm on the way to

English, she's starting to sit at the popular table with all the jocks, preps, cheerleaders, and some arty people who seem to be hanging out there by mistake. Later I try to tell her that it isn't really considered cool to be popular, but she says they just asked her to sit with them and she said yes, and that they seemed really nice. Oh, sure, really nice, I say, thinking of what buttheads all the jocks are, not to mention the cheerleaders. At one point M.F. tells me that someone has asked her to try out for cheerleading, but I manage to convince her it would be bad for her studies.

Emma and I have U.S. History together. It's the kind of class where you can't talk but you can still pass notes, so we send a lot of tiny little pieces of paper back and forth with our smallest writing on them. Our teacher, Mr. Hale, has bifocals and we're betting that he couldn't read any of our notes if he happened to find one. Emma has sent me a lot of descriptions of the boys in Colorado and then information on her newest crush, a guy named Nick who is in her drama class. I think he's probably gay but I don't mention this to her. Emma says I've changed since Mary came to stay with me. She says I'm not as sarcastic. She says she's worried that I'll become some kind of Christian fanatic, but I assure her that there's no chance of that. M.F. never talks about her religion at all. Emma says that people like that are always trying to convert everyone, but I tell her I get the impression that they don't want anyone to join, in fact they just keep to themselves and mind their own business. I say this so Emma gets the idea that minding your own business might be a good thing.

In fact, I'm not sure I even like Emma anymore. She wears too much eye makeup, and her skin is so pale it looks like she's drunk embalming fluid for breakfast (this is what Roy said last time she stayed overnight at our house). She's always saying nasty things about everyone, and I used to enjoy this—we used to go to the mall and just sit there making fun of everyone who walked by. But lately I haven't felt like making fun of people, it just seems mean. M.F. always says that a person can't help the way he or she looks. Of course, that's not true, and I point out to her how people could have worn a different outfit or done their hair differently or at least washed it once in a while. But M.F. says it's what's inside that matters. I tried telling that to Emma and she threatened to puke all over me if I ever said it again.

I've tried hanging out with both Emma and M.F. a few times, but it's really not any fun. I can tell that M.F. doesn't really understand much of what Emma says. When Emma tried to talk to her about existentialism, M.F. said she had never heard of essisenstualism but that it sounded kind of grim to her. Emma rolled her eyes when M.F.'s back was turned, and I didn't appreciate that. Later, M.F. asked me to explain essisenstualism to her, and I at least taught her how to pronounce it but apart from that, I didn't do a very good job of explaining it because the truth was, although Emma and I had called ourselves existentialists all last year, I didn't really understand it myself.

So pretty soon it was fall, and the football games started at school. M.F. wanted to go to them because she liked football and a bunch of her new friends were on the team, though it was obvious she didn't really understand the game and kept asking Roy to explain it to her. He didn't know anything about it either, but he kept trying. They'd sit in the living room with the TV on talking about downs and flags, and I could tell that he was making up half of what he said. I told M.F. that it wasn't cool to go to football games, or to Homecoming, and that we weren't going, though the truth was that if someone had asked me to the dance, I might have considered it, but no one did. The kind of guys I liked wouldn't be caught dead at a dance unless they were standing around outside trying to buy some weed. A couple of guys asked M.F. to the dance, but they were jocks, of course, and I explained to her once again that she couldn't go out with jocks because they weren't cool. M.F. said they seemed nice, but I said niceness didn't matter, it was coolness that did.

I kept a pretty close watch on Dylan Magnuson. As far as I could tell, he didn't have a girlfriend, and I didn't think he was gay. He seemed to keep to himself, though sometimes I saw him in town on weekend nights, standing around outside the video store, where people sometimes hung out. Dylan was a senior, and though I hoped that he would be in one of my classes anyway, he wasn't. I had wanted to take Psychology with Dylan because you got to marry someone and carry a sack of flour around with him for six weeks, pretending it was your kid, and I was hoping maybe I could hook up with him that way. But they wouldn't let me register for it because I was only a junior, and seniors got first preference. It turned out that this year, they stopped doing the flour sack thing anyway, maybe because a lot of parents complained.

So I'm looking at the back of Danny Fox's head and trying not to inhale through my nose. He always smells like some breakfast cereal, I think it's Cheerios, and shampoo, and some sweaty boy smell that I hate. When the teacher assigns us lab partners, I cross my fingers and close my eyes and pray that I don't end up with him, but when I open my eyes, there he is sitting next to me in front of a Bunsen burner. He's wearing a Dragon Ball T-shirt, which is one of those dumb Japanese comics that he likes, with a picture of some stupid-looking guy with too-big eyes, and his jeans have obviously not been washed since third grade. Danny is famous with those of us who were in third grade with him because he peed in his pants one day and was afraid to tell the teacher, so he just sat there, and pee started trickling out the ankles of his jeans and into two puddles on the floor. For years people called him Pee-Man and sang the song from *He-Man* to him, and every so often I still hear someone say it.

Maybe it's just because I know about the pee that Danny seems so icky to me and seems to smell so bad. Of course, by mid-fall it isn't hot out anymore and people aren't reeking so much, but he always seems to have this cloud around him like Pig Pen. It might just be a cloud of ickiness. Anyway, he's pretty good at chemistry, so it's not that bad being his lab partner. The bad part is he keeps phoning me to talk about school stuff, and it's *really* embarrassing that I have to talk to him. Sometimes Mary Fred gets on and chats with him and then hands me the phone with this "He isn't so bad" look on her face. I always roll my eyes, but I take the phone and listen while he blabs away about our boring homework and the group project we have to do. The only good part of chemistry is that we get to make helium balloons, but that's not till spring.

By October, Mary Fred seems pretty settled into school, in spite of her bad taste in lunch partners, and things are fine. It's not that I actually like school or anything, but I still like the feel of people. When we have an assembly and I sit there not really listening to lectures on drugs, or African storytellers, I feel the rustle and hum of everyone around me, and when we all clap, of course I imagine myself in fifteen years, coming back to tell the new kids of Mt. Pleasant, kids that are just being born right now, how they can grow up to be as successful as I am.

Toward the end of the month, M.F. starts freaking out about Halloween. Every year I say I'm not going to trick-or-treat any-

more, but then Emma and I end up putting on the witches'
hats that we keep meaning to give to Good Will, and eye masks
so no one will recognize us. When it gets dark, we walk around
the neighborhood. Everyone is giving away all the candy they
have left so they won't eat it and get fat. There are a lot of
tough, nasty boys on the street at that time of night but we
know how to walk fast so they won't bother us, and if we get
scared we just ring someone's bell. A few years ago a tough-
looking guy stole Emma's bag of candy but apart from that,
we'd always liked the holiday and we looked forward to it.

But M.F. seems to think it's some kind of satanic festival
and it seems to really bother her. There's a big Halloween
dance at school, and she thinks that's horrible. And another
thing, she not only doesn't want to put on a witch's hat and go
out with Emma and me, but she doesn't even want me to go.

"Don't suffer a witch to live," M.F. says whenever the subject comes up.

"It's just a costume," I say each time. "I'm not really going
to be a witch. And anyway," I press on, finally, though I know
I should keep my mouth shut, "Wicca is a perfectly decent religion. I know lots of people who are witches," though actually
I don't, just my mom's friend Kathy, who works at the antique
shop in town. "They're perfectly nice people."

"Heather," M.F. says in an exasperated voice like she is talking to an idiot. "They worship the *devil,* for pity's sake."

"No, I don't think they worship the devil. I think that's just
a myth."

"Heather, I think everyone knows that witches worship the
devil."

"No, M.F., I think it's the Great Goddess. And Halloween is
like their big holiday or something." I suddenly realize that
M.F. and I are having an argument. It's our first one, and I

don't like it. I've argued with Emma a million times and made up. Sometimes we've gone weeks without speaking to each other, usually over something really stupid, like the time I was at her house and accidentally spilled glitter all over her rug, and she said I was a moron. Emma and I know how to have an argument, after so many years of practice, but I'm finding it scary to argue with M.F. What if she doesn't talk to me for a week? What if we stop being friends at all? It would be so awkward at the breakfast table. In fact, I suddenly realize that not hanging out with M.F. would totally suck. I would have to go back to doing everything alone, cutting school and wandering around D.C. by myself again, and I just don't think I can handle that after getting used to having someone there to talk to all the time.

"Heather," M.F. is practically shrieking now, "I know this is a bad thing, okay? I just know it. It's evil. It's part of the devil's big plan."

"Okay, okay, M.F.," I find myself saying. "If you don't want me to, I won't dress up. I won't go to the dance or anything. We'll just stay home—" I try not to say anything sarcastic but the words "we'll bob for apples" pop out of my mouth. Luckily, M.F. thinks this is a great idea.

On Halloween night, we try to sit around in the living room, doing our homework or watching TV as usual, but from about four o'clock on, a thousand little kids in costumes come to our door. Mom has bought a million bags of miniature Hershey bars, though she says she feels bad giving kids candy and would really rather give them fruit, which is better for them, but you can't give out fruit anymore since people always think there are razor blades in it, and anyway, the fruit would be a *lot* more expensive than candy, and we can't really afford it. Mom is at the computer in her little corner, doing stuff for work, and M.F. and I are trying to watch a made-for-TV movie about ice skaters, but the doorbell keeps ringing and we have to keep jumping up, which kind of ruins the movie for us.

I open the door the first few times, but after a while I get M.F. to do some opening, and I stand behind her with the bowl of candy. "Twick or tweat," say a bunch of tiny little boys and girls with goofy plastic masks on the tops of their heads (I remember that it's too hard to breathe through the nose holes of those things), or funny hats and spots of red on their cheeks. "Oh!" I hear M.F. say the first time, and she turns to me and says, "Give them some candy, Heather." I plunk a little candy bar into each bag, and some of the kids thank me, and others run back to their parents and the parents tell them to say thank you, and then some do and some don't. When the doorbell rings again, M.F. jumps up and runs to open it. "Here's a treat for you," she says, and for a moment I'm afraid she's going to give them a big lecture on Satan, but she just grabs the candy bowl and starts flinging candy into everyone's bag. When she turns around, I see she's smiling like she's having a great time.

Our fight is over. I'm relieved.

Just before Thanksgiving, M.F. makes me go bowling. My idea of physical activity is to walk from the couch to the fridge, but M.F. says she needs to move around some and now that it's getting cold out, we're not walking to the soup kitchen or to the video store. I guess she's used to milking cows or whatever it was she did on that farm. M.F. works on me about the bowling for a few weeks until finally I say, "What*ever.*" It turns out that she has met this guy named Jack in her U.S. History class and that he wants us to go bowling with him and his friend Todd. I'm totally horrified when I hear this because it's bad enough that we have to go bowling, but now it seems we're going on some double date with a couple of dorks, or maybe jocks, which is even worse.

But M.F. just hammers away at me about how nice Jack and Todd are and how much more fun it is to bowl with four people than two, and how it's not really a date, since she's not even sixteen yet and much too young to date, it's just for fun. I don't think it sounds like fun at all but finally there we are, on our way to bowl. Mom won't let us ride in cars driven by teens, so she insists on taking us to the bowling alley to meet Jack and Todd, which makes me feel like an even bigger geek. We make her drop us off at the corner so no one sees us. My eyes are darting around to make sure Dylan Magnuson is nowhere in sight, but of course he's not the type of person to bowl anyway.

I'm a little surprised when I meet Jack and Todd because it turns out that they're African-American, and there is no reason why they shouldn't be, but it just surprises me. It also turns out that they are pretty terrific bowlers. M.F. isn't too bad at it, being kind of athletic, but I have a problem with the ball going in the opposite direction of where I want it to go. Jack and Todd keep trying to show me how to hold the ball, and where to put my feet, and M.F. keeps saying, "You're doing just fine, Heather, just fine." The first game we play is girls against boys, and they totally liquidate us, but the second game it's Jack and M.F. against Todd and me, and that works out a little better, though we still lose. Todd has a pierced eyebrow and is actually kind of cute, but he doesn't seem interested in me that way and anyway, when you get right down to it, I only have eyes for Dylan Magnuson.

"Why don't you try talking to him?" M.F. is always saying to me when I start whining about Dylan Magnuson, about how I saw him in the hall and he brushed against me when he passed, though it was mostly because some jocks behind him had shoved him in my direction. "How romantic," Emma says when I tell her things like this, but M.F. is always encouraging, and says, "Just go say hi to him. Tell him you need some help with your math and that you heard he's really good at it. Tell him you noticed he has a Nine Inch Nails patch on his book-bag and that you really like Nine Inch Nails." She goes on and on with these helpful suggestions and I just keep saying, Okay, okay, I'll try that, okay, Mary Fred, I will, but then of course I don't do anything at all, I just stand at my locker and wait for him to walk past so I can see if he's with a girl, or if he's gotten any piercings. In fact, he's never with anyone. I have a theory that he has a pierced tongue, and I keep trying to see him talk so I can check, but he never says anything.

So all in all, life is fine. School isn't too bad, and after a few months, I notice I haven't skipped class to go downtown, not even once. I can't cut even if I want to because I have to be back in time to walk home with M.F., and she wouldn't approve of it anyway. I told her once that I used to ditch school and all she could say was "Why?" She totally didn't get it. Anyway, I'm not hating it too much. M.F. and I stay busy working at the soup kitchen once a week and going bowling every other Friday or so. Bowling is pretty okay, as long as no one sees me going in there.

The one thing about school I really don't like is when I walk past the cafeteria at lunch and see M.F. sitting there at the pop-ular table. One day I stand in the doorway, waving and trying to get her attention before the bell rings and I'm late to English, but she's laughing with some big football-playing creep, throwing back her head and giving him one of the biggest M.F. laughs I've ever seen, like he's David Letterman and she's a guest on his show. I feel myself getting annoyed and wanting to yell her name across the room, even though that would be totally uncool, and as I stand there I get madder and madder until finally the bell rings and I'm late, and Mrs. Flitcraft makes me go to the assistant principal to get a note. By the time I get back to class, I've missed the discussion of what's going to be on the quiz, and as I sit there I feel myself getting more and more pissed off at M.F. When I get back a D a few days later, it feels like it's all her fault.

"I always see you in the cafeteria talking to jocks," I say to her on the bus on the way home the day after the quiz. The bus had been late, as usual, and we had to stand around waiting for it for a while, and a carload of jocks and cheerleaders drove right past us, honking and waving to M.F.

"Jocks?" M.F. knows perfectly well what jocks are, since I have explained the whole thing to her about a million times, who all the various groups are and which ones she should avoid.

"You know who I mean. Those guys from the football team."

"Justin and Carl?"

"I don't know their names, M.F." I explain to her that I'm sure they're very nice, but like I told her before, they aren't cool.

M.F. says she doesn't really care if people are cool or not. I roll my eyes and explain that if she talks to the wrong people, it will reflect badly on me. Then I realize that this sounds horrible and selfish, but by this time we're being dropped off on our corner and I manage to change the subject.

When I think about it later, I realize that the truth is, I'm jealous. And it's the worst kind of jealousy, the two-way kind. I'm jealous of all those stupid football people for taking M.F. away from me, and then the weird part is that I'm also jealous of her. Like there's part of me that wishes I was blond and perky, with a great figure, and that jocks hung all over me drooling whenever I laughed at their jokes. Though I have basically been more or less cool ever since my nerd period in seventh grade, I am now horrified to discover that I have this secret desire to be popular. I shudder at the thought and re-solve to try to get over it.

But the idea kind of haunts me. Maybe it's because when I see them all sitting there in the cafeteria together, talking about dumb stuff, like whether the Redskins will make it to the Super Bowl (answer: of course not), they just look so nor-mal, like they all go home to mothers in aprons who offer them brownies and milk, and dads who come home at five and play catch with them out front, and even though I happen to know that their parents are all divorced, just like mine, and that no one is normal anymore, still, I find myself wishing for a horri-ble moment that I was a cheerleader and that my mom had perfect fake blond hair, and that she stayed home all day and helped me with my algebra, and then we brought Dad his slip-pers and pipe and he read the paper while we sang songs from the sixties at the piano. But we don't even have a piano, and the thought of Mom with perfect hair, even reasonably decent hair, makes me laugh, even though at the same time, I'm sad.

The next day, I tell M.F. she can talk to whoever she wants.

By the time Thanksgiving break rolls around, I do a per-sonal inventory, like Mom says to do. M.F. is still hanging around with the wrong people, but even if it bothers me, I just keep it to myself. Mom still gets on my nerves, but I notice that I have stopped screaming at her quite so much, which is good since I never wanted to scream, it's just that she can be so an-noying sometimes. M.F. always looks so shocked when I raise my voice to an adult that it's inspired me to cut way back on it. Roy is still, well, Roy, but he pretty much stays out of my way. I still don't see too much of my dad, since he works all the time and does soccer with the twins on weekends, but I'm more or less used to that. So overall, I have to say that things are fine,

like if life is a big volleyball game, say, against the team of evil
and doom, my team is still a few points ahead.

On Thanksgiving Day, Mom, M.F., and I cook a huge turkey
with stuffing, broccoli, corn, and potatoes. M.F. bakes two
kinds of pie, pumpkin and pecan. We all sit down at the table,
and Roy isn't even late, and it looks like he's wearing a clean
shirt. Mom makes us all tell what we're thankful for. Roy says
he's thankful that we made two kinds of pie, since he likes
both of them. I say I'm thankful that we have a lot of food,
since I'm really hungry. And some people don't have any food
at all, Mom says, to try to give my statement some relevance.
Yeah, I say. We all turn to M.F. She says, "I'm thankful to be
here with you," but she looks sad, and she is probably thinking
about her real family, wherever they are now, in jail and in a
bunch of other foster homes. Mom puts her hand on M.F.'s
hand as if she knows that M.F. is thinking that, and she says,
"I'm so thankful that we're all here together, and I think the
thing we're the most thankful for this year, Mary Fred, is that
we have you in our lives." I wait for Roy to say something sarcastic, but he doesn't. The fact is, what Mom said is basically
true, though I would never say it out loud.

As soon as Thanksgiving is over, I start to get this knot in
my stomach. I used to like Christmas when I was a little kid,
but since my parents got divorced, I've dreaded the holidays.
Every year I go to my dad's for Christmas Eve, and then late at
night he brings me home so I can wake up where my presents
are, with Mom. It's always at least midnight when I get back,
because Dad and Jemma have a big party with lots of her relatives there and it lasts a long time. When I was younger, while
Dad drove me home I would try to stay awake so I could look
at the sky and see if Santa was flying by, but the only thing I

ever saw that was at all interesting was a bunch of police cars surrounding some people in a van.

In the morning, I always wake up excited because it's Christmas and I like getting presents, but at the same time, I feel sad when I realize I'm not at my dad's anymore, and that while I open my presents with Mom, he's down in Chevy Chase opening presents with the twins, who always get a zillion things and then go on to ruin them all. If you give them Barbies for Christmas, by New Year's Day, the dolls will be stark naked and have weird punk hairdos that have been dunked in the toilet.

It has always seemed to me at Christmas that there were just not enough people in our house. There was Mom and me, and sometimes Roy. Even when all three of us were in the living room, and it's not a big room at all, it seemed like there weren't enough of us, like no matter how hard we tried, we just couldn't fill up enough space.

Before Christmas, both Mom and Mary Fred each have a birthday. Mom's comes first. Usually I just make her a card, but M.F. insists that we go out and buy her a nice present. We go to one of the cutesy little stores in town and get her a necklace with a fairy on it. I don't think M.F. realizes it's a fairy— she thinks it's an angel, and I don't bother to correct her since she'd probably just think fairies were satanic anyway. We each buy Mom a nice card, and when her birthday comes, we make dinner and serve it as if we were waitresses. I can tell that Mom is really touched, and I kind of wish I'd thought of doing all this for her before, but it never occurred to me.

M.F.'s birthday is an even bigger deal. Mom wants to have a party for her, but I talk her out of it. Mom has asked who M.F.'s friends at school are, but I've told her that she doesn't have any, since the last thing I want is a bunch of jocks and cheerleaders at my house. Mom has met Jack and Todd and thinks they're nice. She says that since bowling seems to have become very important to M.F., maybe we should all go to Copacabana Lanes for her birthday. It's true that M.F. has gotten serious about her bowling and is doing better every time. As for me, every now and then I actually hit a pin or two but mostly it's gutter balls all the way. I picture Jack and Todd and M.F. and me bowling with Mom and Roy, and tell her that no, there is *no* way M.F. would want to bowl on her birthday. Mom says that we'd better just do something at home for her. She suggests inviting Diane but almost instantly shakes her head no and says, "We'll just have family."

The day of M.F.'s birthday, we go out and buy party hats and noisemakers and a huge cake with flowers all over it, and we cook her favorite fish (red snapper) and we don't let her help with anything.

At dinner, I can see that M.F. is having a terrific time. Roy is making lots of jokes, and we're listening to the new Backstreet Boys CD I bought for her. I *hate* the Backstreet Boys, so it's a big sacrifice on my part. M.F. loves the fish and keeps oohing and ahing over our cooking, which is really nothing special. We're all wearing party hats, and she keeps blowing into her noisemaker. There are crepe-paper streamers hanging above her head like a pink and white frame. "I'll be right back," Mom says, and I know she's gone into the kitchen to put the candles in the cake. I stand up and am about to dash in to help her when the phone rings. I pick it up and hear a man's voice asking for Mary Fred Anderson. "It's for you," I say to M.F., handing her the phone without really even wondering who it is, since I am only thinking about cake. She says hello into the phone and then she gets this weird look on her face. Her eyes dart to the stereo, and I turn the sound down so she can hear better, though what I really want is to hear for myself. Her eyes are misting over and she sounds like she has suddenly developed a Southern accent. "Oh, thank you," she says, then listens for what seems like an eternity. "Bless you and keep you in the One," she says finally. "You too, Papa." She hangs up the phone and sits there without saying anything.

I stare at her. "That was your dad calling?" It has been some time since I'd given any thought to M.F.'s real parents. I had grown so used to thinking of her as ours. "He was wishing you a happy birthday?" She nods. She looks too upset to talk, so I say, "That was really nice of him, wasn't it? You must be relieved to hear from him." She nods again, then stands up and goes to turn off the stereo. The Backstreet Boys stop in the middle of a sentence. She sits back down at the table and is just opening her mouth to say something when Mom bursts through the kitchen door carrying the cake lit with sixteen candles plus one to grow on. As we sing to her, I can see that M.F. is trying not to cry, but by the time we finish the song, she looks pretty normal again, and she blows the candles out in one breath without even trying. "Blowing the candles out is just like bowling," she says. "You have to aim at the middle." Her voice still sounds weird.

When M.F. went upstairs to wash up before bed, I told Mom about how M.F.'s father had called, and how she had turned off the music afterward as if she had suddenly remembered her old self. "Oh, the poor baby," Mom says. "What can we do? She must be really upset." We start talking about how we can cheer M.F. up, as if her father had just ruined her day. Later it occurs to me that of course M.F. was glad to hear from him and that it's not that he's some terrible usurper. SAT word, to usurp: to seize or hold by force or without legal right. As I lie in bed, I realize that of course, *we* are the usurpers. I suddenly see us as trolls in a fairy tale, evil trolls who are holding the princess captive and never want to let her go.

By the week before Christmas, the knot in my stomach always expands to the size of the *Titanic.* I am walking around nearly doubled over with the ickiness of it all, how I hate my parents for getting divorced, and I hate my life, and most of all, I hate Christmas, I just hate it. I'm back to screeching at my mom—I can't help it, everything she says irritates me. As usual, though, I look to M.F. to cheer me up, to make me see the sunny side of divorce or something, which she is usually good for. But M.F. does not seem to be doing so well herself. Ever since her father's phone call, she has been different—not distant, exactly, but a little distracted, and she seems edgy, like something is worrying her. It's not just the usual sadness you always see when she's thinking about her brothers and sisters, but more of a nervousness. She picks at things when she sits around, pulls loose threads from her sleeves and twists her hair around her fingers. Since her father's phone call, she is back to wearing a lot more brown, and she has even put her hair in french braids a few times, though I try to talk her out of it by saying that her head will be cold, since it has gotten to be winter. Though we bought her some cute boots at Parade of Shoes, she is back to wearing the sensible shoes she brought with her, though that's okay because they look a little bit like Doc Martens.

The week before Christmas, M.F. insists that we go to the store and buy decorations. Mom takes us to Kmart and lets us go wild filling the cart with cardboard angels, plastic holly wreaths, and icicle lights. We buy electric candles to put in each window, a plastic snowman to hang on the front door, and some branches from pine trees. I pick up a Santa doll, but

M.F. makes me put it back—she says Santa has nothing to do with Christmas, really, and that if I read the historical information I would know that. She also says no to a Baby Jesus that I figured she would like. She says that models and pictures are raven images, or something like that.

We stop and buy a tree on the way home. Usually we wait till the day before Christmas because they go on sale then, but Mom thought that M.F. would want to spend the whole week decorating the tree. When we get the tree home, M.F. says that actually, the whole tree business is some kind of pagan thing. I'm not sure what "pagan" means but from the way she says it I'm pretty sure she thinks it's satanic. Mom goes up in the attic and gets out the big box of ornaments, and we start putting them on the tree. I've had a pretty good time so far buying stuff at Kmart but when I open the box of ornaments, the knot in my stomach suddenly grows larger, like I have accidentally swallowed a barrel of broken glass. Each ornament reminds me of when I was a little kid. I remember the elf, the tiny little house with angels on it, the nutcracker soldier, the signs of the zodiac. (Cancer for me, Sagittarius for Mom. Dad is a Leo, and his sign hangs on his and Jemma's tree.) Even the lights make me feel sick because I remember Dad draping them all around the tree, trying to get them just right, and Mom sitting there laughing at what a perfectionist he was.

By the time I finish looking through the box of ornaments, I'm ready to just throw up all over the tree. But I don't say anything about it. M.F. goes through the box holding up each ornament and squealing about how precious and cute it is. We decide to wait until two days before Christmas to actually decorate the tree, so we can make a big deal of it. School finishes that Wednesday, and the next day we get up, put on the one Christmas CD I can find, and get to work. As I pin the ornaments on the tree, trying not to really look at them so I won't keep getting dragged into the past in my mind, all these horrible folksingers bleat Christmas songs in the background. When we get to the star that we always put at the top of the tree, M.F. hands it to me and says, "Here, Heather, you're taller than me." Actually, I'm two inches shorter than her, but I think she realizes that putting the star up is kind of an honor. I reach up the side of the tree with it, but I can't get the star all the way to the top, so I get a chair from the dining room and stand on it. As I teeter at the top of the tree, I see my parents laughing, and me small, and Mom sticking the star up there, Dad standing behind her to make sure she doesn't fall. Mom's face looks younger and her hair isn't graying, and Dad doesn't have his bald spot, and I am just their little Puffin.

"Heather, are you okay?" M.F. comes up behind me like she is going to catch me if I fall.

"I'm a little dizzy," I say, getting down off the chair and handing her the star. "You'd better do it. I think I'm afraid of heights."

"Heights?" M.F. lets out one of her peals of laughter. Then she sees my face and says more seriously, "Come on, Heather, it's okay. You'll get through Christmas somehow."

Then I realize that she is having just as much trouble as I am. "Did your family have a Christmas tree?" I ask her as she stands at the top of the tree, rearranging the tinsel so it fits around the star better.

"No, we always decorate a pile of straw," she says. "A *huge* pile of straw. All the kids in the Compound get together and make ornaments for it every year. Mostly papier-mâché, but sometimes we make things out of clay, or construction paper. The little ones make a lot of doilies. Then we get together and hang them all up. I guess that's what they're going to do tonight, at the Compound. That's when it would be, tonight. It'll still be decorated when we get there. We never take it down till the middle of February. It gets kind of dirty but that's part of the meaning of the straw."

"When we get there? What do you mean?"

"We're going there, Heather. Didn't you know that?"

"We are? When?"

M.F. gets that nervous look that I've been noticing and says, "January seventh. Didn't Alice tell you? She says she's going to take us all there."

"Really? I didn't know that." I think for a minute. "But isn't that a school day?"

"Yep. It's supposed to be."

"And Mom said we could take the day off? Or are we going after school?"

"No, we have to be there by noon, so we'll have to miss school." M.F. stands there twisting a big clump of tinsel in her hands. Her face looks tense, like someone is pinching her.

"And we're going to the Compound? Where is it?"

"It's out in Virginia. Frederick County. It's pretty there, you'll love it."

"Are there horses? Can we go riding?"

"I think the horses will be shut away that day," M.F. says. "It's going to be kind of—different."

"Is your, um, real family going to be there?" The minute this is out of my mouth I'm sorry, but M.F. just shakes her head and says she doesn't think so, though you never knew for sure just what was going to happen. She explains how all the Littles have gone to nice homes with wonderful families like us, and they won't be able to be there but that will be okay, though. She looks like she's not so sure just how it will be okay, but I nod and say I just know the Littles are doing great wherever they are.

M.F. looks sad again, which I hate, and says, "Well, I'm glad you and Alice and Uncle Roy will be there."

"Me too," I say, though so far I'm not feeling glad at all. Looking at M.F., all I feel is worried.

Every year Mom drives me to Dad's and lets me out of the car. She waits just long enough to make sure I get in the door, and then she speeds away. I don't even know what she does when she gets home. Sits there all alone, I guess. Every year I feel awful as I climb up the steps to Dad's house. Through these big panes of glass on the sides of his front door, I can see lots of people standing around holding drinks and eating these little fancy snack things. Everyone is laughing and talking so loud that no one ever hears the bell when I ring so I have to walk right in. I turn around and wave to Mom before I go in, but she is always gone before my hand is even all the way up in the air.

This year will be different, though. I have forced M.F. to come with me, even though she has said she doesn't want Mom to have to stay home alone. "But what about *me*, M.F.?" I keep saying. "I really need you to be there."

"Why don't we just clone her?" Roy says when he overhears us. "We need about six of her." Then he says he'll stay home with Mom and they will sing "Frosty the Snow Man" over and over all night. He says it's his favorite song, and all day long every time we see him, he goes, "Hippety-hop-hop, hippety-hop-hop, hey, look at Frosty go." Like that's going to convince me.

Anyway, somehow I drag M.F. along. She's wearing a dark green velvet dress that we got at Kmart and she looks really pretty, like someone in an old movie. I find myself feeling a little jealous of her prettiness for a moment, but I give myself a pinch and tell myself to get over it. I'm wearing a long black velvet skirt with a big slit up the side and a skintight maroon top with a low neckline. I've borrowed M.F.'s Doc Marten–looking boots, though they are a size too big for me, and as we go up the stairs, I make a clomping sound. It feels to me like my thighs are so big that when I walk, I make a booming noise like a giant. "Maybe there will be some cute guys here," I say to M.F., though I know that the only cute guys here will be five years old.

I manage to find Dad and introduce him to M.F. He says hi to her and gives me a big hug, too big a hug, like he is making up for all the days he hasn't hugged me. Then he says, "Puffy, I'd like you to meet one of my associates," and he drags me over to some old guy and says that I'm his daughter, leaving M.F. standing back at the food table alone. If there's anything I hate more than being called Puffin it's being called Puffy, but Dad doesn't seem to know this. Maybe I've never mentioned it to him.

When I get back to M.F., she is standing at the food table eating a big hunk of poached salmon with some kind of cold white sauce on it and talking to some old woman who I guess is a cousin of Jemma's. "Here she is now," M.F. says, introducing us and telling me that the woman, whose name is Helga, is a painter and that she currently has a show at some gallery in town. We talk about this for a while, and I am so bored I think I'm going to just fall right over into a wheel of brie. "Wasn't she nice?" M.F. says when Helga totters away. I'm just stuffing my mouth full of a piece of pizza with green slime all over it when Jemma rushes up, gives me a kiss on each cheek, and says, "This must be your friend Mary Sue."

"Mary Fred, ma'am," M.F. says, shaking Jemma's hand. "Nice to meet you."

"Have you met the girls?" Jemma says, like the twins are the only thing of interest around here. "I think they're upstairs with some friends. I'll call them down."

"That's okay," I say. "We'll go up and find them." I actually like the twins, well, at least Kate—Samantha can be a major brat. But it always bothers me when I walk into their playroom and see how big it is, and how it's totally filled up with all kinds of girly crap that they like, shelves full of dolls and stuffed animals and a huge dollhouse that they're not really supposed to touch. Everything is pink and flowery, and their bedrooms are exactly alike except that Kate's is pink and Samantha's is purple. I have a room of my own on the third floor, though I'm almost never there, and it's pretty and flowery too. I hate it.

When we find the twins, they are in the bathroom with about ten other little girls, making a big mountain of foam in the sink with some shaving cream they must have stolen from Dad's bathroom. Some of the kids are rubbing foam on their chins. They think they look like Santa Claus but they just look like a bunch of bratty little kids with shaving cream all over them. Samantha has just finished writing "Fuck" on the mirror. When M.F. sees it, she takes a towel and wipes it off—it's a word she knows well from school, where everyone says it a lot. "Hey, guys," I say to Sam, "what's up?"

Kate sees me and throws her arms around my waist. Sam just keeps on doing whatever evil thing she is up to at the mirror, but she grins at me, like she's sure I approve. "Hey, monster," I say to Kate, tugging on one of her pigtails. "What's going on in here?"

"We were making a potion," Kate says.

"With shaving cream?"

"Yeah." Kate and Sam are wearing matching velvet dresses except that Kate's is red and Sam's is green. They have lace around their collars and white bows in the back, and they've got matching hair ribbons around their pigtails except that Sam is missing one of hers.

"Cool," I say. "Hey, this is my friend Mary Fred. Actually,

she's my foster sister. So that kind of makes her your sister too."

Sam looks around at M.F. like someone studying a bug and then turns back to her pile of shaving cream. Kate says hi to her and then says, "How can she be your sister? Your mom isn't married anymore."

"It's like she's adopted," I say.

"I thought people just adopted babies," Kate says, looking worried, like she's afraid Dad and Jemma are going to buy her a whole new set of siblings.

"I'm adopted," says this Asian girl who is helping Sam with the shaving cream. She squirts the last of the can into her hand and smears it on the mirror.

"It means you're really special, doesn't it?" M.F. says to her.

"Sure," the girl says, looking at herself in the mirror through a layer of foam.

"We better go downstairs now," I say, thinking that I really ought to stop them from making a total mess of the bathroom but that I don't feel like it. It's not like I'm an adult or anything, and it's really not my problem.

When we get downstairs, the party has gotten even more crowded, and someone is playing Christmas songs on the grand piano. They sound all jazzy, like the soundtrack to a movie. I feel like a lounge lizard, whatever that is exactly. There is a huge Christmas tree in the living room, pretty near the fireplace, and the fire is lit. I can't help imagining the tree and then the whole house going up in one big conflagration (SAT word: a large and destructive fire). People are crowded into every room, even the kitchen, laughing and talking in what begins to sound to me like a horrible roar. Instead of liking this crowd, I start to think of them as lava pouring from a volcano in the living room. I imagine them all turning to me and instead of applauding, they rush at me and try to eat me, like in *Night of the Living Dead*. This is not good, I think to myself, and I say to M.F., "Come on," though I don't know where I want her to go.

We pass through the kitchen and out the back door. It's freezing outside and we have left our coats upstairs on the bed, but I sit down on the top step of the stairs that lead into what Jemma calls the garden, though it is just an ordinary backyard. M.F. sits down next to me. "You hate this, don't you?" she says.

"It's not so bad," I say. "It's just that—"

"I know," she says.

"The twins are cute," I say.

"Yessirree," M.F. says. "Those are some cute twins."

"I like the twins," I say. "And I like Jemma."

"Things can't stay the same," M.F. says, looking away. "I figured that out. You might want them to stay the same, but they can't."

"I don't know if I'd want them to stay the same. I wouldn't want to be in eleventh grade for the rest of my life."

"Lately, Heather, I've been wanting everything to just stop. Don't you feel like we're about to fall off the edge of time?"

"Roy says it's not really the Millennium. He says the real Millennium is next year and that people are just a bunch of idiots."

"But the numbers are changing, Heather. It's a sign. Everything will change."

"Are you talking about that big whatever-it-is thingy?"

"Oh, Heather, I just don't want it to happen. I want us to just stay the way we are."

"Maybe not right here, though," I say, trying to peel my skirt off the step, which is frozen and is sticking to me. But I know what she means. "Sometimes I just want to get all my toys out of the attic and play with them," I say. "As if that would bring everything back. Have you ever wanted to do that?"

"We didn't really have toys. We used to make things out of wood, but they always broke or we threw them into the bonfire."

"I had all these Care Bears. I loved them. I used to line them up in rows, and then I'd have them get married and stuff like that. And then they'd have babies—Baby Hugs and Baby Tugs."

"Really?" M.F. looks interested, like she wants to go play with them now. Then she looks serious, like she's just realized that Care Bears are evil and is about to give me a lecture on them. "This is supposed to be a holy day, you know, Heather. It's not just supposed to be a bunch of cocktails."

"Well, whatever. It never seems very holy to me. In fact, nothing much seems holy at all. It must be nice to have a real religion. We're just sort of nothings."

"It is nice, Heather, but it's also—it asks a lot of you. I never knew any other way to be. But sometimes I think well, maybe it asks for things that . . ." Her voice kind of trails off.

"I couldn't even get up in the morning to go to church if my life depended on it," I say gloomily. Now I'm sitting here wishing I had a religion like M.F., and that I knew exactly what the meaning of life was and what I was supposed to do.

"I just wish the Big Cat wasn't coming. So soon," she says. She looks out at the line of trees at the edge of the backyard. Then she stands up and starts walking back into the house.

I follow her and when we get to the back door, I say, "Well, maybe it won't happen."

"I wish I could believe that," she says. "But I just know it will."

"I guess we'll find out soon enough, won't we?" I say. We go back into the living room and stand next to the food table.

Jemma has put out six big cakes, and we dig into them like we haven't eaten in decades.

When we get home, Mom and Roy are sitting in the living room together watching an old movie. The people in the movie are singing "White Christmas," a song I happen to hate. I think it reminds me of all the things Christmas is supposed to be like. It never snows here on Christmas, not ever. It will snow the week before, the week after, or in March, but on Christmas, forget it.

When Roy sees us, he starts singing "Frosty the Snow Man." Mom chimes in, like they have been singing it all evening, and they chant "Hippety-hop-hop, hippety-hop-hop!" as if they have been practicing. "Did you girls have a nice time?" she asks us when they have finished.

"Yes, Alice," M.F. says, like she doesn't want to give too much away.

"They have a nice house, don't they?" Mom sighs. Sometimes she says she doesn't know what they need with all that space, but mostly she tries to control herself and only say positive things about my dad and Jemma. "And the twins are so cute."

"Yes, ma'am, they sure are."

"Did you get enough to eat?"

"We sure did, didn't we, Heather? We stuffed ourselves till we were fixing to burst."

"Did you see Santa Claus on your way home?" Roy asks.

"Nope," I say.

"He's probably in a traffic jam somewhere over Alaska. Don't worry, he'll get here."

"Oh, good." I can see that Mom has put a bunch of presents under the tree. Even when I was little, I could never understand what it is exactly that Santa is supposed to be bringing.

The presents are always already there, and I have always known that Mom bought them because I saw all the bags.

"What's the deal with Santa?" Roy says like he is reading my mind. "I mean, you've got this fat old white guy and he's supposed to make all that stuff in his workshop, but then, it all looks like it comes from Target." Roy says something like this pretty much every Christmas.

"You're exactly right," M.F. says, looking excited that someone finally agrees with her about something religious. "He's got nothing to do with Christmas, Uncle Roy. Reverend Thigpen says that Santa Claus is a pagan god. He says we should be careful not to worship at his altar."

"I guess we should get rid of all your presents, then," Roy says, laughing at M.F. like he usually does. "I guess you don't want any of those pagan gimcracks."

"Presents? For me?" M.F. looks surprised, even though she had to know perfectly well that we'd all gotten her stuff, and I know she got presents for us too. "It wouldn't be polite, Uncle Roy, if I refused your hospitality by giving back all those presents. It just wouldn't be right."

This is the first hint of sarcasm I've ever seen from M.F., and I like it just fine.

When I wake up on Christmas morning, for a split second I feel excited when I remember what day it is. Then I remember that I'm not five anymore, and that it's more or less an ordinary day. But then I remember that I bought M.F. a really cool pink necklace and I can't wait to see if she likes it. I lie in bed for a while just feeling cozy and trying to pretend that I'm in a snowbound cabin in somewhere like Maine, or Canada, and that the only food in the house is the goose I shot out back during the snowstorm and a bunch of Little Debbie snack cakes. I snuggle up in my blankets and am about to roll over into a snowy dream when I hear my door open, and someone plunks down at the foot of my bed.

"Heather," M.F. says in a keyed-up voice. "It's Christmas morning. Get up! We have to go make breakfast before everybody wakes up." I look up at her through my slitty eyes and she laughs at me. "You look all rubbery," she says. "Come on!"

There's something in her voice that makes me feel as excited as I was just wishing I was, like we have some big plan to go bring joy and waffles to those less fortunate than us (that is, Mom and Roy), and we are conspirators (SAT word: n. Those who cooperate in accomplishing some unlawful purpose, only our purpose isn't unlawful). I find myself practically leaping out of bed, like I am ready for my secret mission.

On the way down the stairs, I try to say "Waffles or pancakes?" to M.F. but it just comes out as a mumble. But she understands me and says, "I thought we'd try omelettes with red and green peppers."

"Great idea," I mumble. We burst into the kitchen like storm troopers and before long we are chopping, beating, and frying everything in sight. While M.F. tends to the eggs, I set the table with the good china and the special holiday mugs we have had since I was little, though they're all chipped and faded. When we're all finished, I go up to Mom's room and wake her. She's already lying awake in her bed, looking kind of sad, like she's been thinking of all the things I've been thinking of. She seems glad to see me and gets up right away, puts on her bathrobe and slippers, and goes to get Roy. Roy is hard to wake up, but we've made a lot of very strong coffee to pour down his throat once we lure him to the dining room.

Roy is never hungry in the morning, and just wants coffee, but none of us ever has the heart to tell M.F. this. Somehow he manages to drag himself down for breakfast, and we all sit around the table. Roy and I are too sluggish to say much, but Mom and M.F. are chattering away about what we're going to do all day, how we're going to open our presents, then take a walk around town, then watch some TV. (Mom is sure that M.F. will like *It's a Wonderful Life,* which is on six times today.) At three we'll put the turkey in the oven and then we'll have a big dinner and relax.

"Don't you just *love* Christmas Day?" M.F. says. Even Roy says yes.

It turns out that everyone likes their presents. Mom loves the art book M.F. and I got her of paintings by women. Roy loves his Jerry Garcia tie, or at least he says he does. I'm crazy about everything. Mom bought me a bunch of sweaters and a black fake leather skirt, some earrings, a necklace, a gift certificate to Best Buy so I can get some CDs, and a book on dreams. She bought similar things for M.F. but all the sweaters are shades of pink, and instead of Best Buy, it's Barnes and Noble, and instead of a book, she got her a Mozart CD. M.F. looks totally thrilled with everything, especially the necklace I bought her. The funny thing is that the whole time I've known Roy, which is all my life, I can't remember him ever giving me a present, but this year he gives Mom some dried flowers and M.F. and me each a box of Belgian chocolates. This is especially amazing because since Roy doesn't have a job, he doesn't have any money, and I can't imagine how he paid for these things. He probably got the money from Mom, but it still counts.

Our hike around town isn't too much fun because, although of course there isn't a drop of snow anywhere, it's freezing cold out and the wind is whipping against our faces so I know I'm all purple and snotty. M.F. gallops along like she's just getting warmed up, and I have to dash to keep up with her. Roy has stayed home by the fireplace, and I think that was smart of him, but Mom is hanging in there with us, though she looks like she's shivering. As we walk up and down Laurel Avenue, I look for Dylan Magnuson, but all the stores are closed and I know I won't see him. I'm basically hoping that I won't because I know I look horrible. Someone drives by and honks at us, and when we turn to look we see that it is Danny Fox and his mom. Mom waves at them as they pass by and says in a thoughtful voice, "We should invite them over for hot chocolate, shouldn't we?" As I say "NO" very loudly, I notice that M.F. is saying yes with total enthusiasm (lively, absorbing interest or involvement). Oh GOD no, I think, does she have a crush on Danny Fox? I resolve to talk her out of it when I get a chance.

Luckily Mom gives up on the hot chocolate idea, since she must have remembered that she and Libby Fox aren't friends anymore, and we go have a huge dinner and then a nice quiet evening in front of the TV. Emma calls me in the middle of *It's a Wonderful Life* to tell me that there is a big Y2K party at Sara's house on New Year's Eve, and by the time I get back, Mom and M.F. are crying hysterically and Jimmy Stewart is hugging Donna Reed for the seventy-zillionth time. Roy is sitting in a chair by the fire watching, but he doesn't seem to have the heart to make fun of them. He's slipping.

Sara is one of those people that you're basically friends with, but you don't really like her. I tried explaining this to M.F. when I told her that we *have* to go to this party, but she totally didn't understand it. "But if you don't like someone, then you're not friends with them, Heather. I mean, it doesn't make sense any other way."

"It does make sense, M.F. See, Sara's friends with Emma, and their parents are friends, and they go on vacations together and stuff, and Emma's father defended Sara's father when he got put in jail for refusing to divulge his sources back in the eighties or something like that, so I have to be friends with Sara because I'm friends with Emma."

"What don't you like about Sara?" M.F. asks, still not looking convinced.

This is a tough question. I don't like anything about Sara. For one thing, she's very polite and self-confident, and she talks to adults like she's their oldest friend. Her clothes always look all beat up but I happen to know they all come from Nordstrom. "She's snotty," I say finally, though that isn't really it. I guess the main thing I don't like about Sara is that she's always judging everyone. She makes these remarks about people that leave you totally sure she's going to say the same thing about you the minute you're gone. Another big thing I don't like about her is that she's crazy. She's always doing things like shoplifting, and buying drugs from weird men in the grocery store, and taking off her clothes with strange boys but not having sex with them because she might get a disease. "And she makes me feel like a geek," I add, though that isn't it either.

"Then why do we have to go to her party?"

"Because it's the big event, M.F. We have to be there or—or we might miss something."

"What if we miss something bad?"

"You sound like Mom." Mom doesn't want us to go out on New Year's Eve because she's scared of the Y2K disaster that is going to shut down the world and give us a week of nuclear winter. She knows people from the neighborhood who have actually moved to Hawaii and set up self-sustaining communities just in case. Mom's solution to the problem was to buy a cord of wood from some guy in a flannel shirt and stock up on cans of tuna fish and gallons of spring water. Roy begged her to buy him some Spam but she refused because she says it's full of bad chemicals. The day before Christmas, she got the camping lantern out of the attic and a bunch of sleeping bags, and we are now ready to camp in the living room by the fire eating tuna fish for as long as six months if we have to. "It'll be fun, M.F., you'll see."

Of course, the party is not fun. The party as a matter of fact is like a celebration in hell. From the moment we walk in, I know it's going to be horrible. A bunch of guys are sitting on the couch in Sara's living room, and I take one look at them and see they're all drunk and high. There's nowhere to sit, so M.F. and I sit on the floor next to the fireplace, where a crummy little log is burning. The girls are sitting on the couch opposite the boys, and no one is saying anything. The stereo is playing some cheesy band like the Goo Goo Dolls. It's all so uncool that I'm shocked.

Sara's parents' house is one of those old bungalows like our house so they don't have a rec room or anywhere to escape to, and though I can see that her parents are trying to pretend they are staying out of our way, they are also watching us like hawks all night from the kitchen, and they keep coming into the room as if they'd forgotten something, then snapping their fingers as if they'd suddenly remembered where it was. Every fifteen minutes or so, they walk in carrying hand-woven baskets full of organic potato chips and clay bowls of onion dip made with real onions and yogurt. They leave food on the coffee table and act like they're not looking at us to see if we're doing anything bad. Whenever Sara's parents are out of the room, the moronic boys on the couch take a bottle of vodka out of their backpacks and swig a bunch of it down straight, while the idiotic girls pour it into their Cokes. They all laugh like they are doing something really clever. I find this incredibly boring, and M.F. doesn't seem to get why they're all drinking water out of a little bottle. I tell her they're thirsty.

After a while, the boys challenge us to a game of Truth or Dare, and they flip a coin to see who has to go first. No one wants to do Dare, since Sara's parents are in the next room, so we spend an hour listening to people confessing their love for guys in their Math class or describing the sexual experiments they've performed out behind the gym. (Luckily, M.F. seems to have no idea what they're talking about.) When it's my turn, I tell everyone that I have a secret passion for Kermit the Frog, in fact he makes me really crazy with lust. Everyone looks disappointed and accuses me of just making that up so I don't have to tell the truth, but I swear on my honor as a Presbyterian that it's true, and that anything green makes me crazy. Some of the guys are messed up enough to believe me, and one of them is wearing a green Polo shirt and gives me what he thinks is a sexy look. I wink back at him, even though he's drunk and stupid-looking. M.F. gives me a confused look. For a moment, I feel morally superior to poor naïve M.F., and then I feel guilty. Heather, you're a bitch, I say to myself.

The night wears boringly on, with the guys getting more and more obnoxious, and the girls looking increasingly drunk and slutty. Finally, after a few hours of this, the guys end up playing catch with a rock that was sitting on the coffee table. The rock has the word "Listen" engraved on it, and they start hurling it back and forth, shouting "Think fast!" to the girls on the couch, who squeal and duck their heads. Eventually, just as the game was getting to be a tiny bit fun, someone tosses the rock so hard that it crashes right through the front window. This seems to be the last straw for Sara's parents, and they call a bunch of kids' parents and then drive the rest of us home in their minivan. All I can think of when we get dropped off is, thank God Dylan Magnuson wasn't there.

When we get home, Mom is still next door at Paula's. Paula is having a big Millennium party and we can hear loud music blaring from her house. That song "1999," which I am getting totally sick of, plays over and over and I can hear loud laughing and thumping noises like they are all dancing or something. Ick.

When Mom finally comes home at 12:30, M.F. and I are sitting in the living room watching TV. We gave each other a little hug at midnight and toasted with glasses of grape juice, and by the time Mom gets home we are definitely having more fun than if we were still at Sara's stupid party. I halfway expected the TV to go off at midnight and for everything to shut down for a nuclear winter, but by the time Mom walks in it's still business as usual. "Oh, good, you girls are home. How was it?"

"Oh, we had a great time," M.F. says, and when I look at her I see she isn't kidding.

"That's good. Well, I'm glad you're home."

"Me too," I say, and I notice that I'm actually telling the truth. I would much rather be home with Mom and M.F. than at Sara's horrible party.

Mom walks over and gives each of us a kiss on the cheek, and when she gets to me I notice that she smells horrible.

"Oh, my God, Mom, what *is* that? You smell so *gross.*"

"Oh, that's Paula's new aromatherapy spray. There were a lot of psychic healers at the party and they were all working on me. I guess they thought I needed some healing."

"Are you sick?" Mom never gets sick, and the mere idea freaks me out.

"Oh, no, honey. They thought I needed some help with my love life."

"Mom, you don't have a love life."

"That's why they thought I needed help."

"What did they do?" I am suddenly interested, like maybe there is something I can do to make Dylan Magnuson fall madly in love with me.

"Oh, they sprayed me with this stuff, and they all stood around me and meditated on my aura. There were six of them, and they all took different parts of my body and worked on them."

"Ew, gross, they didn't like feel you up or anything, did they?"

"Puffin, please. Of course not. They just worked on my energy."

"Sounds like voodoo to me," M.F. says, which is almost a Roy comment.

"Well, I figured it couldn't hurt. What have I got to lose?"

"Smelling okay," I say. But Mom is right. Maybe I'll go over to Paula's before school starts back up on Monday and see what she can do for me.

Paula stands over me with a huge lavender spray bottle and says, "Honey, this is going to wake up all your estrogen. Men will follow you wherever you go."

"Is that a good idea, Paula?" M.F. asks her seriously. "I mean, it's bad enough as it is, what with men whistling at us on the street and stuff like that."

"It's really only one man I'm interested in," I tell her. "Or boy. Can you make it just work on one person?"

"Not unless you go spray some of this right on him." She laughs and tosses her hair back. She's wearing a long blond wig that looks like it comes from an old movie, parted on the side and kind of wrinkled, like Ginger Rogers's hair.

"I don't think so, Paula. He might think that was kind of weird."

"All right then, Puffin. Spread your legs."

"Excuse me?"

"Spread 'em. I need to spray you where it counts."

"Oh, ICK, Paula. Are you kidding?"

"Darling," she says, putting one hand on her hip and holding the bottle in the air with the other. "Do you want this or don't you? Auntie Paula has lots of things to do today."

I sit and think about Dylan Magnuson walking around school like a zombie, mad with love for me. "Okay, Paula, go for it." I make my knees move apart, though they don't want to, and Paula sends a cold jet of this stinky, disgusting smelly stuff right up my skirt all over my pantyhose. When she has finished, I say, "Oh, God, that was *so* gross."

Paula makes us each give her a kiss on the cheek and then shoos us out the door.

"You smell like a pink poodle," M.F. says as we take a short-cut home through the bushes. I turn around to glare at her and see that she is laughing, like she thinks the whole thing is just too silly for words. I get a little annoyed and think, well, maybe it is, and maybe it isn't.

The next day, school starts again, and I just walk around the halls and wait. It took me hours to get that smell off last night, and Mom was pretty freaked out when she found out where Paula had sprayed me. We run into our bowling buddies Jack and Todd in the hall right away, and Todd puts his arm around me, which he has never done before. "It's working!" M.F. hisses to me when they're gone. If it was anyone else I'd think they were kidding, but knowing M.F. she means it.

In Chemistry, Danny Fox keeps looking at me weirdly, like he has never seen me before. Oh, *great,* I think.

It takes me all day, but finally I walk past Dylan Magnuson in the hall. I have walked past him a million times and he has never noticed me, but today for the very first time, he raises one eyebrow and his left eye meets mine as he passes by, moving very fast without stopping, his messy, uncombed-looking hair flopping as he walks away.

For the next few days, I'm feeling pretty good, as if something exciting is going to happen, like Dylan Magnuson will finally not be able to stand another minute of living without me and will fall at my feet outside of Algebra II and ask me to be his. I try to think of how he will say it—"Will you go out with me?" he begs, looking up at me past his dark eyebrows, his voice all low and sexy like someone in a rock song, maybe that guy from Pearl Jam.

"Of course I will, Dylan," I say sometimes, and at other times, I hesitate and make him squirm just a little. But we end up kissing in the hallway and everyone around us kind of oohs like they're watching fireworks.

After a few days of wandering around in my happy little bubble of aromatherapy fantasy, I notice that M.F. is not looking too good. She acts normal most of the time but I sometimes catch her rubbing her hands together like she's trying to start a fire, and she gets this terrible look on her face when she thinks no one can see her like she's thinking about something scary.

It doesn't take me too long to realize that this isn't just the normal sad look she gets sometimes—no, I figure out that she's worrying about the Big Whatever It Is, and at first I'm relieved that that's all it is, because since the Y2K turned out to be no big deal, I'm not at all concerned about possible disasters. I mean, why worry. But soon it starts to upset me that poor old M.F. is such a wreck, and it just seems to get worse and worse, and though part of me wants to yell "Get over it!," another part of me just wants to cry whenever I look at her. By January 6, she is unable to eat, and she looks like she's going to burst into tears any time. That morning, when Mom writes us both a note to give our homeroom teacher saying that we won't be in school the next day, I remember that we're supposed to drive out to the middle of nowhere and blow up with M.F. Or something.

That night, dinner is totally depressing. M.F. isn't saying anything, is just picking at her food. Mom is scurrying around like a deranged hamster trying to make everything better, but what can you do about the end of the world? I'm grumpy because Dylan Magnuson has so far still not fallen at my feet, and what if the world *does* explode tomorrow, will I die a virgin, never having known the whatever of love? It's too late in the day to go throw myself at some guy just in case, but I wish I'd thought of it sooner.

As if things aren't gloomy enough, Roy is being difficult too. "Geeze, Al, I really don't have time to go schlepping out to fucking Virginia tomorrow," I can hear him saying from the living room while they think M.F. and I can't hear because we're in the kitchen doing the dishes. "I mean, I'd like to do it for the little chick, but I can't."

"Roy, damn it, I don't ask much of you, but Mary Fred needs us all to be there and I damn well want you to be there." I have never heard my mom talk to Roy this way, though there have been a million times when she should have, and I'm kind of impressed.

"But Al, I have to—"

"Roy, you live here rent free, you go out every day and as far as I can tell you do absolutely nothing, *nothing*, and I am telling you right now, this is one thing you just have to do." Mom's voice is like steel, and even I feel scared.

Sure enough, at six in the morning, when I come downstairs, there is Roy, drinking a big mug of coffee.

It takes Mom a while to start the car. She has to pump the gas, pull out the choke, then wait, then try to start it, then wait again. Roy suggests at that point that she should get out and do a little dance, too, but Mom just glares at him. I hate Mom's car. I will never learn to drive because I wouldn't be caught dead driving it. It's an old rusty orange Volvo with a million bumper stickers on the back, stickers for Amnesty International, some failed political candidates, and one that everyone in our neighborhood has that says "Friends Don't Let Friends Vote Republican." I'm saving up to buy my own car, and I figure that with my allowance, I will be able to get one in about fifty years.

Actually, Dad offered to buy me a car, but Mom wouldn't let him. They had a big argument about it a year ago, and it was one of the few times I'd seen them talk to each other since the divorce. They both spoke in exaggeratedly pleasant voices the whole time, but I could see that they were really mad. "She'll be sixteen soon," Dad said, "and she needs a car." "I don't want her driving," Mom said. "It's dangerous. We have good public transportation." "You just want her to be a little kid forever," Dad said, smiling with his teeth clenched. "Maybe I do," Mom said, "is that so bad? Kids grow up too fast nowadays." When it was all over, I knew that I would never have a car, and the truth was, I didn't mind that much. It seemed like too big a responsibility for me anyway, especially the driving part. I have enough trouble just walking without bumping into anything.

Finally Mom gets the car started and we take off down the road. It's only seven in the morning and everyone is still asleep, and there are no other cars on Laurel Avenue when we drive down it, just a school bus. I check out the windows just to make sure Dylan Magnuson isn't on the bus, though I know he's too cool to take the bus to school. I see him in the parking lot at school most days getting into a banged-up Toyota when M.F. and I are waiting for the bus, which is always late, and sometimes I actually walk over to the parking lot to watch him, pretending I am heading toward my own car, but I just can't remember where I parked it. I stand outside someone's brand-new Jeep and dig in my purse like I can't find my keys while he speeds by, and I can hear the stereo on really loud inside his car but I can never figure out what he's playing, though one day I'm pretty sure it was Rage Against the Machine. When I get back to the bus stop, M.F. is always freaking out because she made the bus driver wait for me and she doesn't want to make him late, since he has to get to his other job. I tell M.F. she has no sense of romance.

Right now, I look over at M.F. and see that her face is tight and pinched, like something hurts her. I can't actually see through the windows—they're all frosted up because it's cold out and still dark. We drive past all the locked-up stores in town, then onto a bigger street, and finally we're on the Beltway, cruising. I settle back in my seat to take a nap, but I keep waking up and looking at M.F. She is staring out the window like she's expecting to see something horrible coming down from the sky, the devil (if she even really believes in the devil, I don't know for sure), or poison arrows, or aliens. I have no idea what the deal is with this Big Thingybob, and I don't want to know.

We drive all the way to the other side of the Beltway and then head west. I am in and out of a doze, and traffic picks up after a while, though the cars all seem to be headed the other way. I see a sign for Manassas just as my eyes close heavily and I start to dream. I am in the hallway at school and at the far end, I see Dylan Magnuson walking with Danny Fox. They are talking in a whisper, and when they see me, they're suddenly quiet and I just know they were talking about me. I'm standing there by my locker and suddenly I realize that I smell really bad, like that lavender spray stuff only worse, like a whole florist shop has rotted somewhere inside me and I am just reeking of dead orchids or petunias or something. I see Dylan Magnuson start to move toward me and I back away because I don't want him to smell me, but he is coming closer, closer, he is looking right at me with the same eye he looked at me with in the hall, plus the other eye, and he is about to say something. No, no, don't inhale, I think, but he comes up right next to me and says, "Beware, Heather, beware, because the Big Whatever It Is is coming and coming soon." I see Danny Fox in the background, and he is waving at me and grinning like he knows just what Dylan is saying and he couldn't agree more. I am about to say something back to him, to thank him for his concern or whatever, but when I start to talk I realize I am babbling in real life, in the backseat of the car, all smooshed up next to Mary Fred, who is wide awake and staring out the window looking pale and freaky.

I look out the window past her and see that we are on a small country road with big bushes on either side of it. There's only room enough for one car, but we are barreling along and I'm hoping that no one is coming the other way. There are hills to our right that rise up blue and cold with a pink sky behind them, and they look really creepy. For the first time, I start to feel just a little bit afraid. What if M.F. is right about this Big Whatsit? What if we're about to spend our last hour on earth in Mom's clanking mess of a car? I hear scary noises but then I realize that it is just the sound of Roy in the front seat, snoring.

"Are we getting close, Mary Fred?" Mom calls back.

"Just keep going on this road, ma'am," M.F. says in a small voice. "It isn't far now."

As we keep driving along, the road becomes more narrow and bumpy. Finally we come to a stop, and our brakes squeal, as always. I look out the front window and see that there is a metal gate in front of us with a big No Trespassing sign on it, and next to that, an empty guard shack like on a military base or something. "Here we are," M.F. says. She jumps out of the car, walks over to the gate, punches a code into a metal panel with numbers on it, and pulls it open. A chunk of frosty air has blasted into the car, and when she gets back in, cold radiates from her. "Drive on in."

I am pressed to my window, looking out, as we pass some fields full of barns and then a bunch of cabins. "Drive up to the main building," M.F. says. Mom keeps going and pulls up next to what looks like a really big log cabin. "The chapel is just behind it. You can park over here." Mom pulls up next to the building, beside a pickup truck. It's the only vehicle we've seen so far, and it suddenly occurs to me that it doesn't look like anyone else is here.

"Wake up," Mom says, giving Roy a big poke in the ribs. He jumps up in a way that normally would make me snarf, but I am suddenly feeling too frightened to think anything is funny. We all follow M.F. out of the car as she walks like a sleep-walker behind the big log cabin building and into what looks like a small church behind it. We walk in the double doors behind her. It's a wide room full of wooden pews with a big cross at the front. No one is there. The room looks still and dirty and smells like mildew, like no one has been in it for a long time.

We stay there for a while, a long while, listening to how quiet it is, as M.F. sits in a pew and sobs. Then we get back in the car and drive away.

M.F. cries in my arms for most of the way home.

For the next two days, M.F. does not come out of her room. Every so often I go in there and see her lying in her bed in the dark, pretending to be asleep. Sometimes I say something to her and she answers in a snuffly voice, like she's been crying some more, and then sometimes I say "M.F, are you awake?" and there is no answer, but I'm sure she's not sleeping. Luckily it's the weekend so we don't have to figure out what to tell the school, but it's horrible. Mom and Roy and I sit alone in the living room and every so often one of us looks up at the stairs, like we're expecting her to come down them like Barbra Streisand in *Hello, Dolly!*, but it's just the three of us all weekend long. Everything seems so dark and silent. Mom goes to Mary Fred's room every few hours with a tray of food, but when she brings the trays back down, the food is always untouched. Even Roy has a turn at going up and trying to bring M.F. back to normal. He goes out and buys her a Princess Leia Pez dispenser and brings it to her, but when he comes back down he says she was asleep so he just laid it on the pillow next to her head.

Monday morning I get up and the house is quiet, but just as I am about to start panicking about what to do about M.F., she sails out of her room and into the bathroom, emerges with her hair in a ponytail, returns to her room, comes out all dressed in a brown sweater and a heavy brown skirt and her fake Doc Martens. She doesn't smile or anything when she sees me, but she heads down the stairs, and when she pours herself a bowl of cereal, she pours one for me too. When I get downstairs, I am relieved when I see it. I guess I was afraid that she was never going to talk to me again, as if it was somehow my fault that the world didn't blow up on January 7 like it was supposed to.

We ride the school bus without saying much but by the time we get to school, she seems a lot more normal, and we walk down the hall together like we always do, stopping first at my locker, then at hers, and I watch for Dylan Magnuson because first thing in the morning is one of the three times a day that I am most likely to see him in the hall, and though I don't see him, M.F. waits for me and I almost feel like things are okay. By the end of the day when we go home together, she seems more or less recovered. She's talking, even smiling a little bit, and she doesn't look like she's been crying in the bathroom, which is the official place to cry. We walk from the bus stop to our house in the cold, and when I say something, she answers, like I say "I wonder who's on *Jenny Jones* today?" and she says "I hope it's not more 'From Geek to Chic,' I'm really getting tired of that." I feel all warm inside whenever she talks, like there is hope.

When Mom comes home, we all retreat to the kitchen and start dinner, and we do our usual jobs—M.F. gathers all the food from the fridge and cuts it up, I finish washing the dishes from breakfast and put them away, Mom stands at the stove flipping and turning things, and the kitchen gets warm and steamy from our cooking. Sometimes I get a warm and steamy feeling in my stomach from this, the three of us together, and I think, this is where I live, this is my life, and it feels squishy and cozy. I wonder if M.F. ever feels this? Not today, I think, looking at her. She's still pale and gloomy, like someone from a horror movie.

Dinner is quiet except for the pathetic sound of Roy trying to make jokes to cheer everyone up, and afterwards we go into the kitchen and wash everything without saying much. But finally I just can't take it anymore, and while M.F. and I are at the sink washing and drying, I say, "Listen, M.F., you can't feel so bad. You just can't. It's a good thing the world didn't blow up. I mean, you should be happy about that. Just think of all the good things in life we can still have now, and Mom and Roy and me aren't burning in hell or whatever. Everything is normal again, M.F. Everything is just ordinary."

"Oh, Puffin," she says, turning to me, her hands full of wet dishes. She's never called me Puffin before, but I let it pass. "I *am* glad that the world didn't end. That's part of what bothers me so much—how glad I am. I'm just so—" She stops and thinks for a moment. "Attached. And I was so glad you didn't have to go to the Judgment as a Lacker, and I didn't have to go up to the garden without you. I was just *so* glad of that, and then I realized that it was all different now, and I'm different, and I didn't want to be different but I am, and it scares me, it just scares me." Tears are starting to roll down her cheeks but she doesn't sound like she's crying at all, she's just talking in her normal M.F. voice, which is very sensible and plain. "And the other thing is—" Her voice makes a little choking sound. "I was so afraid when I saw that they weren't there. Then later, I realized, oh, maybe they all went to the Outpost. Maybe everything was changed, and they were there because—well, I didn't know. All I do know is that here we are, Heather, and it's already January tenth, and the prophecy was wrong. It was just wrong. And I'm so *glad* about it. And that's maybe the worst part. And also the best part. I'm really glad."

She didn't look glad, standing there crying, but I basically understood, at least I think I did. Anyway, I gave her a little hug, and we went back to our dishes.

*　*　*

After our talk, M.F. seemed fine. She got up the next morning laughing and joking like she always did, and on the way to
the bus stop, she petted the neighbors' cats and commented on
the Christmas decorations that were still up, which she liked.
She said she had a quiz in math but that she wasn't ready for
it, and I was about to say we should have worked on math all
weekend, but then I caught myself because I didn't want her to
think I was blaming her or anything. I had missed a chemistry
test while we were on our little trip to Virginia and I was supposed to make it up somehow, but I didn't feel like talking
about that either. We got on the bus, said hi to the driver, Mr.
Turner, and sat in our usual seats. This was our routine every
day, all week, as homework came and went and we traveled
back and forth, back and forth.

"T.G.I.F.," M.F. said on Friday morning. This was what she
always said, and I don't know where she learned it. We had
some microwave oatmeal for breakfast, since it was especially
cold out today and she said the oats would stick to our ribs.
M.F. and I had not mentioned the Big Non-Event at all since
our talk over the dishes, and I was glad about that. I hated
talking to people about serious stuff, and all I wanted was for
it to go away, and, I realized, what I really wanted was for M.F.
to stay with us forever and forget about her parents and the
Littles and the Fred people and the brothers who had died, and
to think of us as her family and live with us until we all got old
and I married Dylan Magnuson, and M.F. married someone,
hopefully not some dumb football player or worse, Danny Fox,
and we had kids and lived next door to each other, and our
kids would play together and think of themselves as cousins.

I was seeing all this in my mind through the whole school
day—in the morning as I headed toward my locker, with my
eyes glued on the end of the hallway, hoping for a Dylan

Magnuson sighting. He wasn't there, so I skulked around the building between all three lunch periods, looking for him, but all I saw was M.F. in the cafeteria at the table full of stupid jocks and preps, laughing away like nothing bad had ever happened to her before in her life. That made me feel kind of sick, but I ignored it and went down the hall, hoping that Dylan Magnuson was on his way to his math class which I happened to know met right there on the first floor in 1101. Instead I saw stupid Danny Fox coming down the hall, a Grateful Dead T-shirt under his coat, his icky long hair hanging in his face with little damp ends like he'd been sucking on it. Dylan Magnuson was nowhere to be found, so I finally went to my chemistry class, and Ms. Peachum made me go get a note because I was late.

When classes were over, I went to my locker to wait for M.F. Instead, I saw Danny Fox coming down the hall, swaying back and forth a little bit as he walked, as if he didn't look dumb enough just being Danny Fox but had to introduce a stupid walk into the picture too. I was hoping that if I ignored him he would go away, but he stopped to ask me a question about chemistry. I told him I didn't know the answer, which of course was true, so he went down the hall to his locker, luckily before someone saw me talking to him. I put my history book in my locker, since I wouldn't be needing it till next Tuesday and it weighed about a thousand pounds, and I looked in the mirror that I had hanging there next to some pictures of bands I didn't really like anymore (Korn, Metallica, the Beastie Boys) and was just about to fluff my hair up a little when past my locker door, down at the end of the hall, I saw Dylan Magnuson. I always saw his hair first, which was black and kind of naturally spiky, since he was pretty tall and his hair would poke above everyone's heads as he came down the hall.

A few feet behind him, M.F. was walking with some jocks. She saw me and started making faces at me and mouthing the words "Dylan" and "Magnuson" in a pretty uncool manner. I rolled my eyes at her to get her to stop, but she just went right on gesturing and winking. Dylan Magnuson walked right past me without looking at me, as usual, and started heading out the front door. I watched him walk away, and then I turned back to look at M.F. She was talking to this beefy red-faced guy in a Tommy Hilfiger jacket, and the guy was standing a little too close to her, his piggy eyes kind of looking her up and down. I went over to try to rescue her, but just as I reached them, she threw back her head and laughed at something he had said, and I thought, hey, M.F. doesn't want to be rescued, despite the fact that this guy is a creep and has a face like boiled ham. I turned back around to see if Dylan Magnuson was still in sight, but he wasn't. I went up to M.F., who was still laughing, and said, "I'll meet you at the bus stop."

"Okay, Heather," she said, not really looking at me, which kind of hurt my feelings.

I went back outside and was about to join the big crowd of people waiting for our bus, which was late, as usual, when I noticed that Dylan Magnuson was in the parking lot, opening the door to his Toyota. Very casually, I started to stroll in his direction, digging into my purse like the keys to my Lexus were in there. He climbed into his car and started it up, and I could hear loud music suddenly begin to boom from his speakers. I stood there, pretending not to watch him. I had once loitered in a phone booth on Laurel Avenue for several hours just in case he happened to walk by, and I was pretty good at appearing nonchalant (SAT word). I saw M.F. come out of the school, still laughing and talking to the stupid jock guy, and she went over and stood at the bus stop in the crowd of people waiting, right next to Danny Fox. The jock came and stood next to her, even though I knew he didn't take our bus, and he started putting his arm around her. I watched as she didn't even make him take it off, and it annoyed me. I thought, what the hell does this creep think he's doing? and I was just starting toward her to put a stop to this guy and his tacky moves when I heard a car come toward me. I turned to look and sure enough, it was Dylan Magnuson, and as I looked at him, he seemed to see me, he actually looked at me, kind of, and I thought, hey, that spray stuff is working! and for a moment I hoped he'd stop and offer me a ride or something, but he just kept on going. He floored his accelerator and the car made a little screeching noise, like it didn't really want to go anywhere but was being forced to, and then suddenly it just shot right past me, going much too fast into the circular driveway in front of the school. Then, as if in slow motion, instead of turning to the left and following the path of the driveway, the car plunged forward. Right before it drove into the crowd, in the moment before I saw several people just go flying right through the air, I heard my own voice screaming and screaming, "No! No!" and I didn't stop screaming for a long time.

THE BOOK OF ROY

When I first met Mary Fred, I thought, "That is one strange little chick." She didn't look like she was from this century. She dressed in these funky brown clothes all the time and wore her hair in those little ponytails girls wore back in pioneer days, or in weird braids that seemed to come from inside her head. She looked like she should have been riding on the front of a covered wagon somewhere just past Kansas, or in a spaceship, or both.

I thought Alice was totally insane to bring some new person into our wretched little lives, but I didn't tell her that that's what I love about her. When we were kids, she was always bringing home cats with missing legs, or dying birds that we would have to bury in the backyard, or when she got older, boys with crossed eyes, or withered arms, or idiots like that ex-husband of hers who was obviously just looking for someone to revere him while he grew up to be someone who did not appreciate reverence. I would never say any of this to Alice—all I would say to her is Al, you're nuts. Which she is. But she is also a good person, and a good sister, and secretly I admire that, though I slime everything over with sarcasm, everything.

So the whole deal with the Little Chick seemed to be more

of the same, business as usual for Alice. That's how I came to think of her, as the Little Chick, though I never called her that to her face. Sometimes I called her M.F., like Heather did, because it cracked me up that she didn't know that it stood for Motherfucker, a word she'd probably never heard in her life and wouldn't understand if she did hear it. Hell, I don't think I understand it either. I mean, what is that word about? Please. I heard it a lot when I was six years old and the tough guys in the third grade used to chase me home every day and try to knock my books on the ground. Most of the time I waited for Alice to walk with me because she was bigger than they were, and when she saw them, she would give them her most reproachful look, the kind of look that shoots hideous remorse into the heart of every man. I always hated it when she used it on me, like her eyes were saying, Oh, *Roy*, I had such *high hopes* for you, even when her mouth was telling me it was okay, whatever it was I did this time.

Well, the Little Chick was an imposition in my life, I have to say. I was used to going out and doing my thing all day, whatever my thing happened to be at that time, and coming home and finding my niece Puffin on the couch, staring at the tube, incapable of speech, which suited me fine. Sometimes I would sit with her for a while and just collect myself. That's how I thought of it, like little pieces of me were shredded all over the place, and I had to sweep them all into a big pile before Alice got home, because I didn't want her to see through me.

It amazes me even now that I could go that long without her knowing about the heroin. I just thought it was so obvious—the signs were so clear. I never had any money, I was in and out of these hazy moods, I went out and never said where I was going, I stayed up too late almost every night and slept in the next morning, I kept to myself, and most of all, I never looked right at Al because I was sure if she saw my eyes she would know. I knew she was upset that I did not seem to be working, since she was always short of money and could have used my contribution, which was supposed to be a fairly pathetic $300 a month. Every so often she would try to talk to me about the fact that I had no job, and that I wasn't doing anything with my life, and that she was concerned about me, etc. I felt terrible when I saw that she wasn't at all worried about the money but was genuinely only worried about me. Even though she was walking around in these ratty skirts that she had worn since college.

This just made me feel even more guilty, and the more guilty I felt, the better it seemed to go out and score just a little bit of dope, not enough so I was really strung out, I thought, but just enough to take the edge off. Then I would go to work.

Yes, the fact was, I did have a job, which accounted for my being out at about the same time every day. I worked as a telemarketer selling lightbulbs to churches and old people, a scam I hooked up with through some of my drug cronies. Every afternoon from about noon to three, four, or five, depending on how I felt, I would sit in a room full of addicts, most of whom were wearing just their boxer shorts, because the room was about a hundred degrees, and we would call the people on our list and try to sell them lightbulbs that they didn't need. The best approach, which I learned from a guy named Nick, was to call a church and say, "Let me talk to Bill." They would say, we have no one here by that name, and you'd say, "You know, the guy who orders your lightbulbs." "Oh, you mean Ed," they'd say like idiots. "Of course, Ed," I'd rasp exasperatedly. "Come on, now, hurry, I haven't got all day." Some nice old church lady would fluff around looking for the lightbulb guy, some deadbeat custodian who never did any real work anyway, and when he got on

the phone I would say, "How ya doing, Ed (or Sam, whatever), I
just wanted you to know that I'm shipping your order now." Ed
or Sam would say "What order?" and I would say in a weary,
long-suffering voice, "Your lightbulb order, man," like he was a
moron and had forgotten. Most of the time Ed or Sam would
just say okay. Sometimes, however, he wanted to know all about
the lightbulbs, how much they were (a mere $700—we marked
them up a billion percent), whether any of them were fluores-
cent (of course), or how long they'd last (forever). Then, eventually, he would agree to take the shipment. If he refused, I'd say,
"Tell you what I'm gonna do Ed, or Sam, I'm gonna ship these
lightbulbs to you on a trial basis. No obligation on your part. If
you like them, just send me the seven hundred clams. If not,
ship the whole box back to me, no questions asked." Ed or Sam
would agree to this—how could he refuse?—and I would take a
box from our warehouse, drop it on the floor, and kick it around
a little, until I heard a bunch of breaking glass. Then I would call
UPS and have them pick it up, insuring the whole thing, which
was really only worth about fifty bucks, for the $700. When Ed
or Sam received it, he would send it back to me, saying it was
broken, and I would collect the insurance money and turn it
over to the head guy, Sergio. He would give me fifteen percent,
and then I would go out and score some drugs and feel better
for a little while.

So this was the life the Little Chick was horning in on. It
was all I needed, I thought as I saw her and Puffin glued to the
tube, another damn person to get in my way and interfere with
my business. That's how I thought of myself, as a business.
There was a kind of economics to my daily life—output, input,
regulated by the Invisible Hand. (I know about economics—I
went to college, at least for a while.) I left the house at about
eleven each day, which was when the runners began to hit the

street, regular as clockwork, like scoring was my real job. Most days, the buy went smoothly, though every so often my regular guy did not show up and I had to go out looking for someone else. A few times I had to get all the way down to D.C. and back before work, but luckily the public transportation here is good, and I always just about made it.

When I got to my job every day at about noon, give or take, I was in good shape. I never wanted Alice to know that I had a job, and as far as I know she never had any suspicion at all. I mean, it was the last thing on earth you'd think I'd be doing. I figure she thought I just slept late, puttered around the house for a while, then went to hang out in town, since I made a point of being there, sitting in Sonny's Kitchen with a bunch of scuzzy guys, when she walked past on her way home from the Metro station. For a while, I collected unemployment, since I had in fact been gainfully employed as a file clerk in a law firm when I moved in with Alice, or she might not have suggested it— though knowing her, my lack of funds wouldn't have stopped her. The telemarketing gig was all under the table—I was paid in cash daily so I never had any telltale check stubs lying around, and I spent almost all of it every day, so there was no telltale money lying around either. Alice used to give me five bills every so often and she probably figured that was keeping me in coffee.

So this was all fine with me. Life was good, at least I didn't seem to mind it as long as I stayed well, as they say. The few times I screwed up and missed the runner, I did get pretty sick, and was pale and sweating when I took the Metro to D.C. and walked around till I was able to score. But I was always fine by the time I got home, and Alice never knew. When she asked me if I was okay, which she sometimes did, I just told her I was tired.

But the Little Chick changed all this somehow. It was like

she threw everything off balance. One of my pals from town, Zeke, was heavy into astrology, and sometimes I wondered if the Little Chick had disrupted our Zodiac. See, while Puffin and I were water signs—she was Cancer, I was Pisces—Alice was a Sagittarius, a fire sign. Things were okay when water outnumbered fire. But when Alice got another Sag to move in, things started to shift. It was some kind of natural process, like the weather. I began to feel myself drying up, boiling, evaporating.

The Little Chick was always in everybody's face, cooking and cleaning and just generally being helpful. She asked a lot of questions, and she paid attention to what everybody said. And she just seemed so damn dumb. She stared at things like she'd never seen a can opener before, or a Cuisinart, or a man without a job. I couldn't sit down for five minutes without her asking me some goddamn annoying question about whatever the hell it was. She asked me my age (36), and my favorite color (black), and what kind of cake I liked best (I don't like cake). She asked what I thought about the issues of the day, though she seemed never to have heard of abortion, and she didn't understand the basic facts about the Monica Lewinsky scandal. I must admit I was tempted to set her straight but it would have been too much trouble. I kept expecting her to ask me about my drug of choice, and how long I had been using it, but she didn't seem to have heard of drugs either. It was all she could do to comprehend wine with dinner.

I basically found all this terribly annoying, though most of the time I stayed too mellow to care. I would take a hit in the bathroom just before leaving work, so by the time I got home, I was feeling good, and I would hang out and joke around a little before I went upstairs and did another hit or two before dinner. I was just snorting it because when I started, the guy who gave it to me—we were in a bar on Capitol Hill after work, and I was completely bored with life—said that you couldn't get strung out if you just did it that way. As it turned out, he was misinformed. Anyway, I would come down to dinner and have to sit at the table, which the Little Chick had spruced up in the most ridiculous ways, with origami and weeds from the garden, and party hats. I was used to eating in the living room in front of the TV, where no one could check out my eyes, and at first I had a hard time sitting right across from the Little Chick with her staring into my face and jabbering at me. I made a point of never sitting across from Alice, so she couldn't see into my soul. Though I actually had no real reason to worry, since Alice wouldn't have realized what was going on around her if someone had sent her a telegram that said, "Your ex-husband is a shit, your daughter is a brat, your little brother is a junkie, and by the way, have a nice day."

So we went on this way for weeks, then months. I sat at the table with the three of them and joked around, and after a while the Little Chick, who at first didn't seem to understand jokes at all, started joking back, and pretty soon we were laughing over dinner and somehow, though I don't know when or even how this happened, it got to the point where I actually looked forward to coming home. I tried to be just a little less loaded when I came in so I could appreciate my surroundings some, see what new wacked-out thing she had made into a centerpiece (my favorite was when she and Puffin made pink papier-mâché pigs one night when we were having pork chops). I wouldn't say I did less heroin at that point, but I did it more judiciously, in more frequent, smaller doses during the day so I would be on an even keel all the time. I noticed that when I did that, I made even more money on lightbulbs, and at one point I did start to think, hey, if I wasn't spending fifty bucks a day on drugs, I could be pulling in $350 a week and would be able to give Alice rent money and still have a bunch left over. I didn't act on this realization or anything, but I thought it.

It's probably some time in August when I walk into the living room and find a beautiful model standing there. Then when I look again, I realize that it's the Little Chick, and that Puffin has dolled her up in that hoochie-mama way she admires. The Little Chick looks like she's stepped out of one of those horrible magazines that Puffin reads, or a rock video. Her eyes look like someone has punched her, and I know this is what Puffin thinks girls should look like. Despite all that, the Little Chick is gorgeous, I have to admit it, and when I see her, my eyes bug out just a little bit, though then I catch myself and make some kind of sarcastic remark, which is what anyone would expect of me and I try not to disappoint them.

But this was not the first time that the Little Chick had seemed beautiful to me. It was a few days after Puffin got back from Paris, and the Little Chick was so great about that, doing welcoming things that Al and I would never have thought of, and turning the whole occasion into a big party. Well, I was sitting at the dinner table across from her a few nights later and suddenly when I looked at her, I saw a golden glow all around her, like one of those auras that my crazy neighbor Paula talks about. She was sitting there shining like a lamppost or something. A flashlight. A camping lantern. Okay, I was high, but I'm sure it was nothing to do with that. There was this shininess in her that I had never seen before in anyone else, and as I sat there, it just radiated all over me, dripping down on me like honey, or some kind of magic golden nectar.

Now, I don't want anyone to think that I was in love with the Little Chick. First of all, that would make me technically a pedophile, which I am not. I am a normal American hetero-sexual man, though at that time it had been years since I had had a girlfriend and women were the furthest thing from my mind. Second, the Little Chick was not someone you wanted to go out with or marry or anything. Or God forbid, sleep with. No, you just wanted to sit there looking at her and feel-ing that whatever it was that I suddenly felt radiating from her.

So I did that. Night after night, we just sat there at the din-ner table, and in the living room, and I watched her as the year went on and after a while she seemed to lose some of what Puffin always called dorkiness and became more graceful, more golden. I didn't know much about her history, but it started to come out around then that she had been raised in some kind of weird religious sect, which accounted for her seeming like she was from another planet, and she evidently had some kind of obsession with imminent doom. Later, Alice told me the details about what the Little Chick called the Big Cat, which just seemed crazy to me.

"I get it," I said to her one night. "You're Chicken Little. You think the sky is falling down, am I right?"

"Why, no, Uncle Roy," she said. That was what she called me. "It's nothing to do with the sky falling down." She was al-ways so literal, and I realized as she was talking that she had never heard of Chicken Little, since the only bedtime stories she'd ever heard were about Jesus or Zoroaster or whoever.

"Chicken Little," I said. "That's what I'm going to call you from now on." The next day at dinner, there was a little plastic chicken sitting next to my plate. When I asked her if she had put it there, she looked astonished and said, "Put a chicken next to your plate? Uncle Roy, why on earth would I put a chicken next to your plate? What a strange thing to do. Must have been some kind of burglar. We're going to have to start being more careful around here." She went on like this with a totally straight face, a trick she had learned from me. There was such a thin line between joking and lying that I was amazed she could do it. Finally she said, "I guess it probably fell out of the sky," and winked at me. She was a good little winker.

So I just sat there, watching her. I started to feel all sorts of complicated things, things that made my stomach hurt, and I'd make a run upstairs for some more heroin but even that didn't help. One night I found myself looking out the window and saying, out loud, "There is beauty in the world." I couldn't see anything out there but the darkness, since it was late at night, and the sound of my own voice startled me. I'm finally going nuts now, I said under my breath. It was November, and the breeze was cold through my window, which was supposed to be closed, but air still wafted through it and blew the curtains around lightly. I asked myself why I was sitting up late at night talking to no one, and what it had to do with the Little Chick. However, I did not receive an answer, so finally I did enough dope that I actually went into a nod, something I tried to avoid normally, and the next morning I did some more and felt better.

When I had those feelings, I stayed away from the Little Chick for a while, sometimes for a few days at a time. I'd sit in my room, or I'd get home late and miss dinner, but eventually I would come back and find myself at the dinner table again, across from her. Just before Christmas, the three of them were bustling around the house, with decorations and all, but I began to realize that the Little Chick was starting to act kind of weird and moody. I could tell she was upset about something, maybe some religious thing or missing her family, I didn't know. When she first came to stay with us, I really didn't notice or for that matter care, but about this time I started to see that though she was always cheerful, in fact annoyingly perky, there was often something beneath the surface that seemed to be hurting her. This began to affect me, and all I wanted to do was make her feel better, so I would kid around with her until the shadow would seem to lift. But as Christmas got closer and closer, nothing seemed to help—I came home earlier every day and joked more, but it didn't seem to take the edge off her face, like the darkness of the world was finally going to catch up with her and turn her into one of us.

This was how I got roped into spending Christmas at home with Alice, more or less. As it happens, the lucrative lightbulb business closes down for the holidays anyway, so I would have had nowhere to go and would have had to actually sit in Sonny's Kitchen all day talking to my creepy pals and ordering just enough seaweed soup to keep from getting thrown out. Puffin really wanted the Little Chick to go with her to her dad's stupid Christmas party. I can't stand Puffin's father, though I do a pretty good job of not showing it. I mean, he was okay when he was married to Alice and was just a self-centered moron, but when he proved that he was evil incarnate by dumping Alice, the nicest, sweetest, best woman he could ever have hoped to find, I started to dislike him in a big way. I was just about to tell Puffin to go by herself or not go at all, so the Little Chick could be with Al, and I could leave and do my thing, whatever my thing happened to be. But the next thing I knew, I found myself volunteering to spend Christmas at home so Puffin wouldn't have to go to her father's alone, and Alice would have some company on Christmas Eve. The truth is, I thought the Little Chick could use some cheering up. She was looking kind of pale and miserable at that point. She hadn't joked with me in days, her centerpiece output had fallen off, and though the house still shone with all her cleaning and tidying and was crowded with tacky Christmas crap, I could tell her heart wasn't in it. Now, I didn't really think that idiot's yuppie party would cheer anyone up, but I thought it might be good for both Puffin and the Little Chick to go there together and do some girly stuff beforehand, like get all decked out in red and green or whatever and slather makeup on each other, and I damn sure didn't want Al to be home alone brooding on what the party would have been like if she had still been married to Peter and would have been able to invite the kinds of people Alice would have invited: a bunch of mentally challenged homeless people, some psychic healers, some incontinent old men, you get the idea.

So when I stayed home, you've got to understand that this was probably the first act of altruism I had performed since I was a kid. I was a nice boy, and I did fairly thoughtful stuff for people on a regular basis, though my parents didn't seem to notice or appreciate it, being too wrapped up in their own problems most of the time, my dad's illness or later, after his death, my mom and her complicated love life. At some point, I don't know when, I must have realized that samaritanism didn't pay, and that I was better off looking out for number one. It was probably during the eighties, when selfishness became fashionable—anyway, as far as I recall, I hadn't done a single nice thing for anyone since, oh, probably since the day Reagan took office.

But suddenly, there I am, singing "Frosty the Snow Man" with Alice, trapped in the house with no excuse to go out and only enough dope to last me through Christmas. Al and I sat in the living room all night chatting, as she calls it, and drinking eggnog (mine laced with whiskey, which just made me feel sick), and watching *White Christmas* on TV. Every so often I would go upstairs to the bathroom and do another hit, so I was okay all night, but I have to say that I felt panicky being trapped indoors, and not going out to the corner to score, even though I had thought to buy twice as much the day before. My whole routine was interrupted and I had trouble with that, in general.

The day after Christmas, I slept too late, and by the time I got up to Oak Street, my runner had gone. Maybe he had had a big holiday sale and gone home to his family. I rushed past the hardware store, the liquor store, the dollar store, all of which were padlocked shut, like it was still a holiday, though it wasn't. I couldn't see my runner anywhere, and I began to get a sick feeling in my stomach. He usually loitered near the theater that was now a church with religious writing on the marquee in Spanish. I stood in front of the theater, looking for him, for about an hour, but finally it was clear to me that he was not going to show. I walked up to the next block but there was nobody else there, at least nobody who looked right.

There was nothing to do but jump on the Metro and go down to D.C. I spent the next three hours walking around some scary part of Southeast, waiting for somebody to walk past me saying "I'm on, baby boy," and offer me some of his latest shipment of Mike Tyson, or Body Bag, or Sudden Death. It seemed like the more ominous the name, the better the stuff was supposed to be, and the biggest selling point of all was if someone had actually OD'd on it. So I saw a couple of guys who I was sure were runners, but they didn't say anything to me as I passed. I went up to them and asked them if they had anything, but they just said no and looked at me coolly. As I walked up to the next street, I saw my reflection in the window of a hairweave salon and I realized that I was still wearing the white button-down shirt I had foolishly put on in a burst of holiday enthusiasm, and that my hair was combed, my coat was this preppy-looking coat that Al had bought me last

Christmas, and I basically looked like some idiot who was going to get everybody busted, or maybe actually a narc. I went into an alley and put some dirt on my cheek, and messed up my hair, dirtied up my shirt collar a little (I couldn't touch the coat, or Al would have been upset), and before I knew it, guys were coming up to me and saying the magic words, I'm on, baby boy, I'm on, and soon I was back on the Metro, heading home, well again.

When Christmas finally blew over, I went back to my routine, and everything seemed fine. A lot of people in our community were worried about the Y2K problem. I figured, we had a lot of wood, we had some tuna fish, and as long as the Y2K didn't interfere with heroin production, I was okay with whatever happened. Some of the wackier people in the neighborhood had predicted that we were headed for some kind of nuclear-winter-like thing, and they were actually looking forward to it, since it would cause society as we know it to grind to a halt, which would be better for the environment. They thought that what happened to people was not nearly as important as what happened to the bald eagle or the wild bluebell, or something like that. It was all the same to me, people, eagles, whatever.

So this was the buzz in Sonny's Kitchen on New Year's Eve, where I sat with a bunch of my buddies, Zeke and Dave and Tom and a few guys I didn't know. Zeke was strung out too, so we had a kind of special relationship, but Dave and Tom were not addicts and didn't seem to realize that we were. Dave was married to some lawyer who paid all his bills, and he hung around in town with a pad of paper pretending he was working on a novel, while Tom was a plumber who specialized in stuff like Jacuzzis and bidets, so he made good money and didn't work much. We sat at the counter at Sonny's, drinking coffee, watching people come in and out, stocking up on

Korean dumplings just in case all the power went out at midnight. Every so often, Zeke would go into the bathroom, then me, and we'd come out sniffling a little, like we had colds. Zeke was a big dude who was missing some of his teeth, and when he'd come back, he'd wipe his nose on his sleeve. We were a gorgeous bunch of fellows, and women took one gander at us and ran away. The waitresses in Sonny's all looked like lumberjacks, and they weren't afraid of us, but I thought we were pretty scary.

"I got a case of water, I got two cords of wood, I got about a million cans of vegetarian chili, I figure I'm ready to roll," Dave was saying.

"Same with me, but Marla won't eat chili. She went to Sutton Place Gourmet and bought cans of all kinds of French stuff. Evian water. Canned chestnuts. That kind of shit," Tom said. He had a big face like a rump roast, with a little fringe of curls sticking out from beneath his bald, spotty dome, and it was hard to figure what Marla was doing with him, especially since he ran around on her.

"I tried to get Alice to buy me some Spam but she wouldn't do it," I said. Then I felt all creepy because it sounded like she was my wife or girlfriend or something instead of my sister.

"Nitrates," Zeke said. He was very into health, not counting the drugs. "She did the right thing."

"Well, whatever happens, I'm going to have a good New Year's Eve anyway," Tom said, winking. He had a new girlfriend, about his twenty-seventh one this year. He met a lot of women through plumbing, and Marla never found out about most of them. His eyes drifted to the plate glass window at the front of the restaurant. "Hey, will you take a look at that."

I looked out the window and saw Puffin and Mary Fred walking by. "Hey, asshole, that's my niece."

"Not Puffin, man, the other one. The blonde. She's—" Tom happened to meet my eyes in that moment and his voice just died in his throat. He must have figured out instantaneously that if he said one lecherous thing about the Little Chick I was going to take his bottle of organic root beer and jam it right up his snout.

"That's Mary Fred," I said. "She lives with us." I said it like I was just daring any of them to say anything about her, but no one did.

That night when I got home, everyone was out. The girls had gone to some dumb teen party, and Al was already next door at Paula's, helping her (him?) set up for her (his?) Y2K bash. Al wanted me to go to Paula's with her, but I had bigger fish to fry. I was going to sit home and get high all night, and that's what I did. (I had bought a large amount just in case the runners' computers went out and shut down operations.) In the morning, when I finally got up, the power was still on, and everything was normal. Of course, the lightbulb business took New Year's Day off, so I went to Sonny's, where I found a bunch of tree-huggers sitting around complaining that western civilization had not ground to a halt. I thought of telling them about the Little Chick's gloomy predictions for January 7, since that might have made them feel better, but I didn't feel like talking about it. I had told Zeke about what the Little Chick had said, and he had been unimpressed. "Like some teenybopper Nostradamus," he said. I told him to shut up. "Bunch of wackos," he said, dismissing it. I was sure he was right, but I felt disloyal to the Little Chick making any jokes about the whole thing, so I just kept it to myself.

But the fact was, the whole January 7 thing was a big problem for me. Alice was insisting that I go along, and this presented me with a logistical dilemma. I mean, I'm in the car with them for three and a half hours, then we're at some religious compound with a bunch of lunatics, then the world ends and we get blown to kingdom come—when do I get high? I didn't think I could just bring a bunch of dope in my pocket and every now and then sneak some up my nose. Alice wasn't very observant, owing to living in her own little world of clouds all the time, but she would surely notice that.

I was dreading the day, just dreading it, but I didn't see any way around it. I could see that everyone else around me was dreading it too, the Little Chick because she thought it would be our last day on earth, Puffin because she was missing a chemistry test and there would be hell to pay, and Alice because she didn't like driving in Virginia because the roads were tricky and the weather wasn't very good so conditions might be treacherous. I was dreading it the most, but the way Alice put it to me, I could either come with them or she was going to throttle me till I was dead anyway, so it was pretty much a lose-lose proposition. The truth was, I'd have joined them regardless because I could see that the Little Chick really wanted me to come just in case I was going to get to go to heaven or whatever just by being in the right place at the right time—it was certainly clear to all of us that my behavior in my earthly life was not going to get me a good placement in the other world. And I wanted the Little Chick to be happy, especially just in case she turned out to be right and it was our final moment on earth. I wanted the last thing I saw to be her smiling face—and then I felt like a big jerk for thinking that.

Mostly, I felt worried. When I got up the morning of the seventh, I went into the bathroom and snorted a little, like I always did. Then I went downstairs, had some coffee, went back up, snorted some more, then I went downstairs, pretended I forgot something, went back in the bathroom, snorted as much as I possibly could without passing out, then somehow managed to get myself to the car.

The next thing I knew, we were out in the middle of Fucking Nowhere, Virginia, trying to break into what looked to me like some kind of prison camp. The Little Chick actually knew the password to the gate, and we drove into this creepy, empty, frozen landscape, a bunch of cabins at the foot of a big frosty mountain, and a weird little white church in the center. The place looked totally deserted. I didn't know much about the predictions for this event, but I was under the impression that it was supposed to be well attended. As it was, there was no one in sight, and the only person I was expecting to see at this point was David Duchovny.

So when Al and the girls got out of the car and started toward the church, I had time to take a capsule out of my pocket, break it open, roll up a dollar bill, place a little dope on the dashboard, and snort it up before they turned around to ask where I was. I walked toward the church—I almost floated there, filled with the light, delight, the holy fire, just so relieved and happy and serene, and let me say relieved again, that when I walked through the church doors behind the three of them I genuinely expected to be met by a choir of angels, by the heavenly host, by God Himself, or Jesus, or Buddha, or whoever was in charge. But instead, of course, there was no one there, and the next thing I know, the Little Chick is crying her eyes out. She sits down in the front pew sobbing and will not get up, even though the church is so cold that we can see our breath, and Al and Puffin are trying to comfort her but she cannot be comforted. I stand there watching, and all I want to do is put my arms around her and rock her, just rock her, till she feels as well as I feel, till everything in that sad moment is healed for her. But of course I don't do anything at all, since what could I possibly do, and finally they help her into the car and we go home.

The first thing I do when we get home is run to the bathroom. When I come out, feeling okay again, recharged, I find Al and Puffin in the living room with the lights out, and the Little Chick is upstairs in her bed, still crying, I guess, and there's not a damn thing any of us can say. Instead of feeling glad that we were not all liquidated into nothingness by the Final Judgment, I think we're all wishing that for her sake, the Little Chick had been right, and that the end of the world had come instead of us having to sit here listening to the sobbing noise we can hear every so often coming from upstairs.

The next few days were horrible, just horrible. We all wandered around the house like ghosts. I kept getting this weird, familiar feeling, like I had seen this before, maybe in a movie. I couldn't think of what movie it was, and it was driving me crazy, and I thought about it for days and days until finally, one day, I came home from work and I saw that the Little Chick was sitting in the living room with Puffin, watching *Jerry Springer,* looking perfectly normal, like nothing bad had happened, like nothing bad had *ever* happened, to *anyone,* and when I saw her little heart-shaped face, even though her hair was the wrong color, and in fact it was all pulled back in a clip that Puffin made her wear sometimes so she would look hip, though it never really worked, I knew instantly what movie it was: *Snow White.* I realized that for the past few days, I had felt like one of those dwarves, probably Grumpy, when Snow White was lying there in that glass coffin. Later, I thought of this as the Snow White Epiphany, because I had managed to understand *exactly* what my feelings for the Little Chick were: they were exactly like those of Grumpy for Snow White. It was a relief to me to realize this because once I put them in this context, I could be sure that there was no funny business about my relationship with her, nothing I should be ashamed of except possibly that I had all the emotional depth and maturity of a cartoon character.

We were all so relieved that for the next week, everything seemed to go back to normal. In fact, the next week was about the most normal one of our whole lives, looking back on it, the last week I remember where everything was just as plain, straightforward, and familiar as Velveeta cheese, Jell-O, Skippy peanut butter and Welch's grape jelly, all the ordinary things of the world. We got up, we went to school and work, we did our heroin, we came home, we had dinner, and everything was fine. When I think about that week now, it seems all lit up, with gold around its rim, a series of moments that you don't know at the time you should be treasuring. That seems like a funny word for me to use, treasuring, since I had always been the kind of person who didn't believe in treasure of any kind, not material or spiritual or metaphorical, nothing. But I see now that there are times in your life when just the fact that there is a stillness is enough that you should go grab a camera and take a picture so you can remember it forever exactly as it was.

I came home that Friday around three, and no one was there. It had been a good day in the lightbulb business—I had kept some old church janitor on the phone for forty minutes while I promised him free flashlights, hunting knives, and incandescent bulbs in return for his business. "Don't forget," I told him, "check all your Exit signs. It's only a little bulb, but it makes a big difference." The guy had thanked me profusely, and hadn't whimpered when I asked him for his purchase order number, assuring him a twenty-percent markdown because of his patronage. I went upstairs and got high, I came downstairs again, I sat around for a while whistling, I put on the stereo and listened to some Miles Davis, which I couldn't do normally because Puffin would scream at me, I finally

turned Miles off and wondered where everyone was, I wondered what was for dinner, since I was a little bit hungry, I
turned on the TV to wait for Oprah, just in case she was doing
a show on single moms with drug-addict brothers, but before I
could even find out what was happening on *General Hospital,*
I saw that there was a special news report. I hunkered down to
see what new war had been declared or what celebrity had
died in a fiery plane crash, but instead I saw a bunch of reporters standing outside of a school that looked very familiar,
and the word "Live" at the bottom of the screen. As I stared at
the screen to see where in America this latest school tragedy in
a series of school tragedies had occurred, the camera panned a
row of people who stood crying next to a bunch of ambulances. Then it zoomed in close on one of their faces, and it
took me a minute to realize that it was Puffin. I stared stupidly
at Puffin's tear-soaked face on the TV, right where Oprah's
would have been. Then I grabbed my coat and started running.

By the time I reached the school, which took about ten minutes, the same reporters I had seen on TV were standing before me in the flesh. This was one of the weirdest moments of
the whole thing, I later thought, because all of my life I guess
part of me had believed that the things that happened on TV
were not real. But here they were, the same tiny faces that had
been on my screen moments ago were now life-sized people
that I recognized from my living room. A bunch of cops hus-
tled me away from the front of the building, where a team of
ambulances were, and I staggered through the crowd that had
gathered, looking for someone I recognized. Everyone looked
vaguely familiar, probably because I had seen them all at one
time or another in Sonny's Kitchen.

When Alice saw me, she hurled herself into my arms. She
was shaking and breathing very hard, and I tried to hold her

tightly, stroking her back so she would calm down, but it
didn't help much. When she could talk, which took a moment,
she told me she had just gotten there—the school had called
her. I told her that I knew Puffin was okay, because I had just
seen her on TV a few minutes ago, but for some reason my
mouth could not form the words "Mary Fred." I put my arm
around Alice and led her to the edge of the police line, near the
ambulances, and we stood in a crowd of hysterical parents and
curious bystanders, everyone making a noise like a flock of
birds, geese maybe, as if we were all going to take off into the
sky, and I thought the noise was going to drive me crazy and I
began to wonder if it was inside my head. Alice and I stood not
saying anything, holding hands, which we hadn't done since I
was about six and she was nine, until we saw Puffin running
toward us, the mascara Alice always told her not to wear to
school streaked all over her face, her mouth open but no
sounds coming out of it. We both grabbed her and Alice said,
"Oh, Puff, oh, Puff, what happened? Is she—" She was taking
little dog-like breaths between syllables. Puffin's face crumpled and she pointed to the ambulances and shook her head.
As I stood there, the school, the ambulances, the crowd
started spinning around me. I tried to grab onto Alice for support, but she too seemed to be falling, and the two of us just
floated in this vortex, whirling around.

As the ambulances started to pull away, we tried to get close
to see if Mary Fred was really in one of them, and if so, where
they were taking her, but the police kept us back as if we were
trying to riot. "But my daughter is in there," Alice yelled to the
cop in front of us, who said he was sorry but that the victims
were all being taken to the Trauma Center at the nearby hospital and that we would have to check there. "Were they all—?"
Alice asked him, but he didn't seem to hear her, and in the dis-

tance, we saw a guy in a medical-looking uniform carrying two black plastic bags and disappearing into one of the ambulances. Alice clutched my arm and started to say something, but I just told her to take Puffin home and said I would go to the Trauma Center and see if Mary Fred ended up there. "I'm sure she's okay," I said, more for my own benefit than for Alice's, probably. Puffin was still wild-eyed and hysterical, so I didn't have to do much to convince Alice to take her home. She offered me a ride, but I said I would walk, that it wasn't far, though it was actually a lot farther than I had imagined, since I had been in a car the other times I'd gone there—when Puffin cut herself on a piece of broken glass, and when Alice went into anaphylactic shock after being stung by a wasp. I ran most of the way. It was cold out, and my breath felt jagged, going in and out of my lungs like crushed ice. When I got to the hospital, there were ambulances parked in front of the Emergency entrance and a small crowd of people milling around the front, including some of the same reporters I had seen earlier. I took a side door, since I was clever like that, and ended up in the Emergency Room at the head of the line.

"I'm inquiring about a patient," I said. "Mary Fred Anderson. From the school. Blond, sixteen—"

"We don't have anyone ID'd yet," the woman behind the desk told me. "You can wait over there." She pointed to a bunch of vinyl couches next to a rack of magazines and a TV that was blaring coverage of the local school tragedy, as they were calling it, though I still hadn't figured out exactly what had happened. I sat down and started watching. They were showing a yearbook photo of some scruffy, creepy-looking kid, the one who evidently had been driving a car that had somehow plunged into a bunch of students, as some reporter blabbed on about him, how he was a member of the National

Honor Society or some shit like that. There were photos of a few of the victims, and none of them were of Mary Fred. I sat clutching my stomach, rocking back and forth, and after a while I noticed that I was praying that she would be okay. I had remembered scraps of the Beautiful Prayer that she used to say before dinner, and I seemed to be reciting it.

I stayed there like this for about twenty minutes, my arms crossed around my waist, hunching over, rocking, praying, and after a while I started to notice that I wasn't feeling very well. Holy shit, I thought. I had totally forgotten about my dope. I hadn't brought any with me, and it had been several hours since I had had any, though luckily I had done a little extra while battling boredom.

I decided that I had better call Alice. She was relieved to hear from me, since she'd been sitting by the phone hoping for some information about Mary Fred, and even though I had absolutely no news for her, she seemed to feel better receiving word from the front. I asked her how Puffin was, and she said Puffin was okay, she was wrapped in a blanket in front of the TV. Alice had tried to talk her out of watching the news coverage, but she refused to move, so Alice was giving her hot chocolate and cookies and keeping her warm. "She's still shaking a lot," she said.

I contemplated telling Al to take Puffin to the Emergency Room, but it was such a big mess there I thought better of it. Finally, I suggested that we trade places in a while, since she was probably in a better position legally to get information about Mary Fred, since she was her guardian and I was just her guardian's crappy brother. Alice said that was a good point, and that she would drive over soon. I told her to ask Paula to take care of Puffin so we weren't leaving her alone at all, and Al thought that was a good idea. I could tell that Al was going all fluffy in the head from stress and panic, and that someone needed to tell her what to do, including reminding her to put shoes on before she left the house, since it was winter and all.

But I wasn't in such good shape myself. I sat in the corner feeling worse and worse, and by the time Al finally showed up, I had gone into a sweat and was shaking. She didn't even seem to notice that there was anything wrong with me, though. I told her I would go home and check on Puffin and then come back. She handed me the car keys and I made my way through the jumble of people outside and drove home. It was just late enough in the day that the rain, which had just started, was really ice, and when I got out of the car it felt like little needles were driving into my face. But the cold against my face felt good, and when I walked into the house, I looked more frosty than sweaty.

Paula was sitting on the couch next to Puffin, and they were watching *Father Knows Best* on one of those retro cable channels. "There you are," Paula said, as if I was somehow late, though I wasn't. "We're catching up on the nineteen-fifties. That was all Auntie Paula could handle right now." She (or he, whatever) looked up at me through a lock of fake ginger hair that fell in the path of her right eye.

"How's my little Puffin?" I asked in a voice that was so tender it surprised me. Puffin looked up at me with woeful eyes and nodded, as if she was too tired to speak.

"I gave her some Xanax," Paula whispered. "I think it's helping. She was a little bit stressed." She was wearing an oversized Garfield T-shirt, and I found myself trying not to glance at her body.

"Yeah." I walked over to Puffin and gave her a hug. When I stood up again, Paula was looking at me strangely. "Can you stay here with her for a while, Paula? I'd like to go back over to the hospital."

She said she would, and then added, "Have you been running? You're all sweaty."

I nodded. "I've just got to dash upstairs for a minute." I ran into my room, grabbed two capsules of dope, went into the bathroom, snorted some, peed, snorted some more, and went back downstairs again. When I glanced at Paula, she was still looking at me funny, but I didn't care, since everything seemed fine now.

I found Alice in the lobby, parked in front of the TV with a bunch of other parents. She was talking to some of them, since she knew everybody from the PTA or whatever they called it these days, and every so often she and some other woman or man would hug and cry a little bit together. I almost hated to bust in on her, but when she saw me, she jumped up and ran to hug me, and started introducing me to people and telling me that I remembered them from something or other ten years ago, though I didn't. I had never understood why Alice insisted on staying in this goofy neighborhood, but I guess she felt it supported her in some way. I don't know. Myself, I didn't feel like talking to anyone, and I could barely manage to say hi.

Suddenly, a man in a little green outfit—scrubs, I guess they're called—came out and started reading a list of names. Parents leaped up, ran over to him, and started shouting. A few were shouting in Spanish, and I couldn't understand what they were saying, but some lawyers in the group were saying, in English, that they demanded to know where their sons or daughters were, in tones that threatened litigation. I could barely hear any of the names, but finally he said, "Mary Fred Anderson," and Alice and I rushed forward. He pointed to a woman in a green sweater, and we followed her to a cubicle. "Are you the parents?" she asked. Alice explained that we were Mary Fred's guardians. The woman wanted to know all about her insurance coverage. This made me feel like punching her, but Alice just sat there calmly giving her all the necessary information. Evidently Mary Fred was on Alice's policy, which was lucky as they would certainly have thrown her out in the cold otherwise.

"Can we see her?" Alice asked when they had finished. The woman told us to go with the nurse. We looked for a nurse and finally saw a little Hispanic guy in a white coat looking at us impatiently. I found myself running over to him and grabbing him by the arm. "How is she? Is she okay?" asked a hysterical voice that was coming from my mouth. The man told us that she was scheduled for emergency surgery, that they were just waiting for an OR to open up, that the doctor would explain everything to us, and that we were to follow him. He led us into another waiting room and left us there. This was evidently the elite waiting room—it was quieter, and had a better TV. Some of the parents Alice knew had already been sent there, and when they saw her, they hugged all over again, and I sat down and watched *Jeopardy!* Every so often, I would go into the bathroom for a hit. I was ready to highly recommend heroin to everyone else in the waiting room, but I didn't think that would be advisable.

After what seemed like a million years but couldn't have been, since they were only in the Double Jeopardy round, a doctor came in and called Alice's name. He was a short, bald guy with a paunch, and was probably only in his twenties. He started walking down the hallway, and we followed him. I had trouble keeping up with them and only heard snatches of what he was saying, but I could make out the word "surgery" again, and also "internal injuries," "extensive bleeding," "perforated," and "concussion."

"Can we see her?" Alice asked. The doctor led us into a curtained-off section of the Emergency Room, and there was poor old Mary Fred, lying on a cart with a board on it, tubes up her cute little nose, wires in her arm, a heavy collar around her neck, and a monitor beeping next to her. Her eyes were closed, but she was stirring slightly, like someone having a bad dream. Just like on TV, I thought. We rushed to her side but then were afraid to go too near. Alice reached out and brushed a little bit of blond hair out of her face, and said, "We're here, honey. Uncle Roy and I are here." Alice's face was pale and squished up like she was going to either cry or start screaming, and I put an arm around her to keep her from doing either. She leaned her head on my shoulder and we stood there for a moment. Then a nurse burst through the curtains, grabbed the cart, and barreled away before we could even ask what was going on.

For the next few hours, we sat in the waiting room—the nice one—with a bunch of other parents whose kids were in surgery. I kept thinking of us as "other" parents, like we were Mary Fred's folks. Whatever the hell we were, we all sat there, taking turns using the pay phone to call home and check on the siblings. Paula said that Puffin had fallen asleep in front of the TV. She told us to take our time, that she could sleep on the couch, she would just dash home and get her jammies. The thought of Paula in her jammies was kind of scary, but I have to say it was damn nice of her to stay. The lawyers were all on their cell phones, trying to figure out who to sue. When Alice had seen the picture of the Lone Teen Driver (as they were calling him) on TV, she had cried out, "Oh, God, it's Dylan Magnuson, I know his mom." Apparently his mother worked for Greenpeace, and his father was dead. (He had killed himself, according to Alice, though no one mentioned that on the news. I didn't know how they could have missed that tidbit.) "Oh, poor Grace," Alice sighed, her face in her hands. She just sat there sighing for everyone.

It must have been two in the morning when yet another

doctor called Alice into the hallway. He was a tall, solid-looking guy with dark, wavy hair, a little too long in the back and too thin on the top. He introduced himself as Dr. Greenberg and said that he had just completed the surgery, that it had been a success, they had stopped the bleeding, so there had not been much damage to the internal organs. They had had to repair her intestine, but her condition was fair. Her concussion wasn't a severe one. "So she's fine?" Alice said in that idiotic way she has. The doctor looked gloomy and said that the bad news was, she had bled internally, due to the nature of the injury, and that there had been some pretty serious intestinal leakage. They were giving her broad-spectrum antibiotics but as soon as the culture came back, they could give her something specific to the organism, or something like that, to prevent sepsis. "She'll be okay, though, right?" I found myself saying, sounding exactly like Alice.

"We hope so," the doctor said. He seemed really sad, as if he had known Mary Fred for years and wanted nothing but the best for her. He told us that they were moving her to ICU and that as soon as they had a room for her, we could go sit with her, though she wouldn't wake up for some time. I guess he figured we knew all the acronyms from watching *Chicago Hope* or *ER,* and the truth was, we did. We went back to the waiting room, which by now I totally hated and never wanted to see again, and sat there until someone got us. The orderly, or whatever he was, led us down a bunch of halls, up an elevator, down some more halls, and into one of the scariest places I could imagine, a hospital wing. It smelled bad, and the hallway was lined with lots of small dark rooms full of equipment. The guy pointed us to one of the rooms, and when we walked in, we found Mary Fred lying there, still with the tubes all over the place and the big machines hooked up to her.

Al and I decided to take turns sitting there. By this time, it was about 4 A.M., so I told Alice to go home first, since I wasn't tired, and I knew she felt bad about leaving Puffin. Al said she would be back in a while, and she gave me a big hug and left. When I was sure she was gone, I pulled my chair over to Mary Fred's side and started talking. I told her she would have to be all right, that we all needed her, and that she had to pull through, and all that kind of crap. She just lay there, breathing through her tubes, the machine next to me beeping regularly, which I guessed was her heartbeat, so I was glad about that, and though every so often I thought she was about to wake up, she didn't. I tried to hold her hand, but it had needles in it, so I just sat there whispering to her. I said as much of the Beautiful Prayer as I could remember, which wasn't much, in case she was listening, and then maybe I fell asleep, I don't know. In my dreams, she and Puffin were running around yakking, like everything was normal.

When I woke up, Alice was standing over me. She had washed her hair and changed her clothes but she still looked horrible, pale and drawn, her lips in a stressed-out little line. She pulled up a chair next to me and we sat there, not saying anything, for a while. I could see the sun peeking out from behind the closed venetian blind. After a while, Dr. Greenberg came back in. He talked to Alice for a while about Mary Fred's condition, and asked her some other questions too, and I sat there wishing he would go away, since he was making me feel even more tired. He had a deep, peppy voice. I didn't really listen to what they were talking about, but when he left, Alice looked like she felt a bit comforted, and it annoyed me that I couldn't manage to comfort her like that.

Alice told me to go home and get some sleep, take a shower, check on Puffin, and said she would stay at the hospital. She said she needed to be available in case she had to sign anything, but that she was worried about Puffin, who was still in a kind of shock, and was afraid Paula had something else to do but was too nice to say so. On the way home, I found my runner right where he was supposed to be, so I got enough dope to last me through till Monday. I would have liked to get some more, but that was all the money I had for the moment, so it would have to do.

Puffin was in front of the TV when I got there, still asleep, a little pocket of drool in the corner of her mouth. Paula was sitting on the couch, wrapped in Alice's moon and star blanket, watching a show about dolphins on the Discovery Channel. I thanked her and told her I would stay with Puffin for a while, and that she was free to leave. Paula said that she really didn't have much to do this weekend and could just as easily sit around our house as her own, and that I could go clean up and go back to the hospital if I wanted to. She had given Puffin more Xanax and expected her to sleep a lot. I told Paula to watch it on the Xanax, but she said she knew what she was doing and not to worry. I privately thought that one drug addict in the family was enough, but I had to admit Xanax sounded pretty good to me too. I went up and took a shower, paced around my room for a little bit, thinking about whether I ought to stay or go, decided that I really couldn't stand being away from the hospital, went downstairs, thanked Paula again, averting my eyes from her enormous Garfield T-shirt, and left.

When I got to the hospital, Alice was still sitting next to the bed in ICU. "Has she woken up yet?" I asked.

Alice gave me a weird look.

"What's wrong?"

"Well, I think she's in one of those coma things," she said, mumbling like she didn't even want to say it out loud.

"A coma?" I hissed at her. "I thought everything was supposed to be fine."

"She's sick, Roy. She has some kind of bacteria in her blood."

"I thought she was supposed to be getting better. That's
what your pal the doctor said."

"She will get better, Roy." She raised a finger to her lips,
and I remembered that supposedly, people in comas could
hear everything you said.

"Oh, God." The Smiths song "Girlfriend in a Coma" began
playing in my head. "I didn't know people really went into
comas."

"Of course they do, Roy. People have all kinds of bad things
happen to them." There was something incredibly ludicrous
about Alice of all people lecturing me about reality.

"I'll be right back. I have to go to the bathroom." I was
starting to get that freaky, not-quite-enough-heroin feeling.
When I came back, I was calmer. After Alice had gone home to
check on Puffin, I sat close to the Little Chick and talked to
her some more, telling her about all the wonderful things in
life she had to wake up and do, and reminding her of some of
our happier moments. "Remember when you put that chicken
next to my plate?" I asked. She just lay there, and the thought
of her running around the house with Puffin, just being a
goofy teen, in contrast with her lying here, caused my chest to
tighten. For a moment I was sure I was having a heart attack,
and I thought, well, what better place. But it passed, and I realized that I was just incredibly worried and also very, very
sad. I wasn't sure I had ever been aware of sadness before. It
felt like I was wearing it, like a shirt or something. It just
seemed so strange and awful to me that Mary Fred could be
standing there waiting for a bus one moment and lying here
the next, and it made me hurt, not just for her but for every-

one. Normally I would have done anything to get rid of any bad feeling I might have, but it seemed appropriate now, so I just sat there in my gloom and felt pity for the human race for a while.

Toward late afternoon, something about the Little Chick changed. I didn't know what it was, exactly, but she looked different, even though she still hadn't moved at all. When the nurse came in, I asked her to check everything, which of course she was going to do anyway, and sure enough, her fever was pretty high. The nurse asked me to leave, and a bunch of other people started running in and out of the room. I went and called Alice and told her that I thought something was wrong and she ought to come. I guess I was afraid that the Little Chick would actually die or something before Alice could get there. I knew that people died in hospitals because our father had died in one, in fact I had not been on a hospital wing since then, come to think of it. Maybe that was why I hated it there so much, especially the smell, though what I hated most was that there were so many people there who were suffering. It made me mad, and I wished I could be the guy who saved everybody, who just put a stop to all of it, sickness, death, school violence, drug abuse (yeah, sure), and the other bad things that you see on television. Though I had always thought of Alice as overly bleeding-hearted and credulous, it began to occur to me that I was apparently cut from the same cloth. This was a weird thing to find about yourself at my age, but I sort of liked it.

I stood in the hall outside the Little Chick's room, swaying back and forth, until Alice arrived. When Dr. Greenberg appeared, he told us that they were changing Mary Fred's antibiotic, that she wasn't responding to the previous one so they were trying something new. Alice broke down sobbing and before I could get close enough to console her, Dr. Greenberg put his arm around her and let her cry all over his white shoulder. I found this annoying, but it seemed to make Alice feel better.

After a while, the medical staff let us back into the room, and we sat there, holding hands, not talking, staring at the Little Chick like we were going to heal her with the power of our minds. Alice left a few times, to call Paula, or Diane, who I guess was going to notify Mary Fred's real parents, but mostly we just stayed there. At about seven, I told Alice to go home and take care of Puffin, and that I would take the night shift. I promised to call her if anything changed, but the nurse had said that Mary Fred seemed to be stabilizing. It wasn't too hard to convince Al, since she was worried about leaving Puffin for too long, so she went home, and I spent the whole night in the chair next to the bed. Every so often I would lay my head down on the bed and fall asleep. Medical personnel wandered in and out all night, like that was their favorite time of day to work, and sometimes they threw me out of the room so they could do things I didn't want to know about. I got a fair amount of sleep, though, and when I woke up in the morning, I looked at the Little Chick hopefully, like I was going to find her awake and smiling at me, but she was still just lying there.

By the middle of that afternoon, I was pretty scared. Alice had come in the morning and gone again, and all anyone could tell her was that nothing had changed. When Alice came back in late that afternoon, she was wearing a big bandage on her arm. I asked her what had happened and she said she had gone to give blood, since some of the injured kids had lost a lot of blood. "Roy, you ought to go give some too. They really need it."

I told her I was scared of needles, which was true (and a good thing, or I would probably have been mainlining by now), but she told me that was ridiculous. We went to the hospital cafeteria and had dinner, and she kept bugging me the whole time, saying that Dr. Greenberg had told her that the hospital might end up with a serious blood crisis, and blah blah blah like that. She went home to Puffin again after that and I was left in peace, but she came back again at ten and told me that all the other parents were giving blood, etc., etc.

"Alice, I can't," I said.

"Of course you can, Roy. I did it."

"No, Alice, I *really* can't."

"Everyone can, Roy. It's easy."

"No, Alice, I *really, really* can't."

"Roy, don't be such a wimp. Think about all those poor kids who need transfusions. You can help them."

"If you want to help so much, then you go give them some more blood."

"I only have so much blood, Roy."

"I already told you, I'm scared of needles."

"That's not a real reason. Give me one good reason."

She kept on hammering at me until finally there was only one thing I could do: I took a deep breath and told her that I was a heroin addict, and that my blood would probably kill anyone they gave it to, though it might make them feel a whole lot better in the short term. Alice just stared at me for a minute. Then she put her face in her hands and started sobbing. I tried to put my arm around her, but she shook it off and went on crying. Plenty of people in ICU were crying so it's not like we were conspicuous. Finally, Alice lifted her head and without looking at me, said in an icy voice that didn't sound like hers, "What are you going to do about it, Roy?"

"What do you mean what am I going to do?"

"You have to do something."

"There's nothing to do, Alice."

"I have a lot of questions about this, Roy."

"What kind of questions? It's simple, really, I just—"

"Roy, how could you—? How could you—" Her mouth was flapping open and closed, and I put my hand on her shoulder but she knocked it off and stood up, turning toward me, with her hand up, palm facing me, like she was about to sing "Stop in the Name of Love." "Roy, what is it you want? What more can anyone do for you? I've given you a home, I've taken care of you, like Dad asked me to do—"

"Dad asked you to take care of me?"

"Of course he did, Roy, and of Mom. I'm supposed to be the, the—"

"Person who takes care?"

"Roy, how could you do this?" She lowered her voice so her words came out all funny, a cross between a hiss and a growl, and she clenched her fist. For a moment I thought she was actually going to punch me. "Think of all the people in the world who have real problems. Think about Mary Fred in there. And here you are, poisoning yourself. *Tainting* yourself. Your blood. What were you thinking, Roy? What were you—"

"Alice, I wasn't—"

"I know, I know. It's just all about you. It's about whatever you want."

"That's the thing, Alice," I said, sniffling a little, like I was turning into a four-year-old. "It's not like I wanted that. It just happened."

"No, Roy, it didn't just happen. You did it. *You*. We make choices in life and you made them."

"I didn't know I was making one, Alice. All I knew was—"

"I don't want to hear about it, Roy." She gave me this strange look, like she didn't know who I was, and said, "I can't do this now. I'm going home for a while. Will you be all right here?"

"What do you mean, will I be all right?"

"You're not going to, I don't know, Roy, what do I know about these things, I mean, you're not going to OD or anything, right?"

"Hey, this is a hospital. Don't worry, Al, I'll be fine."

"Oh, sure, yeah, you'll be fine, you'll just be so fucking fine."

"Really, Al, go home, get some sleep, we'll talk about this later." I wanted to add, "And don't swear at me, you're freaking me out," but I was afraid she'd just do it some more.

When she was gone, I went into the bathroom and did another hit, but it didn't make me feel well enough, so I did some more, making sure to save myself a little bit for the morning. Then I went back into Mary Fred's room, laid my head down on my arms on the side of her bed, and fell asleep.

When I woke up, it was morning, and I could tell she was worse. Her breathing was rough and the beep of her heartbeat sounded funny. I got a nurse to check on her, and she seemed worried. She called a doctor—it wasn't Dr. Greenberg, which I was glad about, since I was sick of him—who came in and said they needed to run some more tests, that she wasn't responding to treatment. I ran and called Alice. When she arrived, she spoke to me in an exaggeratedly polite voice and never met my eyes. We sat in the hall for a while, not talking, just watching TV. It was Monday, and the hospital seemed a lot busier, which seemed weird to me since it wasn't like sick people got better all weekend so the hospital staff could take off. All the usual shows were on, and we watched some soap opera with people running around pretending to be doctors.

At noon, there was a news update, some Happy Talk about the School Accident, as they were calling it. Apparently the kid who did it, this Dylan kid, the Lone Teen Driver, had been showing signs of schizophrenia, hearing voices in his head, that kind of thing, but it was still not clear whether he had driven into the crowd by accident—he had only had his license for six months—or on purpose. He was now locked up in the loony bin under observation. There had been a total of two kids killed, twelve more injured, and seven of those were out of intensive care. Two were home. The Redskins had lost to Dallas, but we still had hopes for the Super Bowl.

As the news was ending, I suddenly had a horrible realization. It was 12:30, and I was supposed to be at work. Worse still, my runner was always gone by noon, and I had used up my entire supply of dope. I was just about to tell Alice that I had to go home and clean up, that I needed a shower, or a facial, or a manicure, but before the words were out of my mouth, the doctor came back in. He said that they were trying a new antibiotic but they weren't sure it would work, and that we had better go sit with Mary Fred. The words "and say good-bye" were not said, but I heard them. Alice wanted to go call Puffin, but I told her not to bother her, though what I was really afraid of was that there wasn't time. We went into Mary Fred's room quietly, practically on tiptoe. People in white or green were still crowding around her, fiddling with all the machines and tubes and bags. Mary Fred lay there, her face very pale, and again I thought of Snow White.

I sat there for as long as I could, but even as I looked at the Little Chick's poor pale face, I found myself thinking that I was going to have to leave. My head was starting to ache, and I was getting dizzy. I held on to the metal rail of the bed for a while to steady myself, but my arm started to hurt, and then all my joints. I don't know how much time passed then—it seemed like ages, but maybe it wasn't. At some point, I stood up and said, "I'll be right back. Can I take your car?" Alice handed me the keys without asking me where I was going. If she'd been thinking straight, I think she would have realized what I was up to, but she was watching Mary Fred's face like something was written on it, and trying to hold her hand, despite the IV in it, talking to her in a low, soothing voice. She barely seemed to notice when I left.

When I got home, Puffin was sitting on the couch, watching a game show. I said hello to her and gave her a quick hug. She looked miserable and lonely, and I felt sorry for her, but I had important things to do. I ran upstairs and rooted around in Alice's sock drawer where I knew she kept money. I found a bunch of twenties so I grabbed them, vowing of course that I would pay her back before she missed them, and rushed back out again.

Heroin was a daytime drug, who knows why. On Oak Street, the day shift was already gone, and the night shift, who specialized in cocaine, had not arrived yet. I walked up and down the street, not searching for my guy, since he was long gone, but hoping for some shifty-looking little bastard to run out and find me something. If someone looked like he had just escaped from a maximum-security lockup, I went up to him like he was my oldest friend, but no one said anything to me, and I was scared to approach them in case they were narcs. Maybe because it was Monday, everyone seemed to be rushing off somewhere, and no one was loitering, muttering the magic words.

As I wandered around frantically, I started making deals with myself. By this time, I had totally forgotten about Mary Fred, and could think only about my own little problem. The whole time I'd been doing heroin, I had managed never to land myself in this situation, since I'd been very prudent and well organized, you might say, but now I found that I was being completely overtaken by my physical need to get well. I was like someone dying of thirst, and every time I saw some thug coming toward me, it was like one of those mirages in the desert. "Okay," I finally said to myself out loud, "it won't take long, I'll just drive down to the District and find somebody and I'll be back here before Alice even misses me or her car." I jumped back into her disgusting old Volvo and started rattling down Pine Avenue, which turned into Thirteenth Street as I got into the city. I followed the road as if I was being divinely led to my oasis, and ended up in a promising part of town, walking down a street full of boarded-up houses. People stood on the corners, stomping their feet, since it was cold, and no one even looked at me funny, since it was pretty clear what I was doing there. Finally I saw a group of men on a distant corner, and they looked beautiful to me, like a choir of angels, and as I walked up to them, it was as if I was walking in slow motion, and I waited to hear the heavenly words come from their mouths like music, "Poison's in," or "Murder's in," or "Terminator's in," or "Body Bag," or "Mike Tyson," or "Tango and Cash," or "Liquid Steel," or "China White," or "Body and Soul," or "Mob Deep," or "John Gotti" or "Deathtrap" or "Charles Manson" or "Genghis Khan" or "Jerry Lee Lewis" or "Search and Destroy" or "Leopold and Loeb" or "Bozo the Clown" . . .

By the time I pulled into the hospital parking lot, I felt fine. Just fine. But the weird thing was, when I looked at the clock, hours had passed. I had left at around one in the afternoon and it was just past six. It occurred to me to worry about what Alice might say to me, but I felt so calm now I was sure I could deal with it. I went up in the elevator with a couple of doctors and a geezer on a stretcher who looked like he was dead. I felt so hallowed that I could just about bless the old guy back into life. It wasn't until I got off on the fourth floor and walked down the hall that I started feeling afraid.

Alice looked up at me when I came in the room. She didn't even ask me where I had been, just gave me this look of absolute disgust. I was probably a little messy and glassy-eyed, and when I opened my mouth to say hi, my voice was all low and raspy. "How is she?" I asked, trying and failing to sound normal. "The same," Alice said without looking at me. "I need to go now. Puffin's been home alone all afternoon." Her words landed on me like little poison darts.

I handed her the car keys. She snatched them out of my hand and went out into the hall, where I could see her talking to Dr. Greenberg. As I saw him coming toward me, I thought, oh, *great,* and I tried to look invisible, but he came in looking like he wanted to chat. He asked how I was, and said that Mary Fred was still febrile, which I guess meant feverish, but that they were doing everything they could. Then he asked how I was and said that he was glad I'd come back, that Alice had been concerned. I opened my mouth to say something but all I could think of saying was how outraged I was that Al had been discussing me with him. "Your sister is worried about you," he said in a gentle voice. Asshole! I thought to myself. I was sure there was no way Alice could possibly have told him anything about me and my problem, but if she hadn't, then what the fuck was he talking about?

"I'm fine," I said. Which was true. I felt great. "She shouldn't worry so much. But that's Al, always worrying about everyone, always trying to save every flea-bitten old dog that limps her way." I gave him an evil, pointed look but he didn't seem insulted, just patted me on the shoulder and said he'd be back in a bit to check on Mary Fred.

I sat there for a while feeling indignant. I wanted to go into the bathroom and do another line, but I was a little nervous about Greenberg checking up on me, so I waited until it looked like he was nowhere around. As I sat next to Mary Fred, I found myself talking to her, like I was explaining the whole thing to her. "I just want to be happy," I said. "Is that too much to ask? I need to feel well. Things in this world are just too complicated. I want them to be simple." She didn't answer me, just kept lying there, breathing with this rough sound that scared me. "Mary Fred, I wish you'd wake up," I said to her after a while. "The truth is, I really miss you. We all need you. We're used to you now. You have to come back to us." She just lay there, and nothing changed. I sat and watched her.

A few hours later, Alice came back and sat down next to Mary Fred on the other side of the bed. "How's Puffin?" I asked.

"Not too good," she said. "Dr. Greenberg gave me a sedative for her. Paula is with her." Alice didn't look too good herself. When she was tense, she held her lips differently, so they disappeared, and her eyes got all pinched up like she was squinting into the sun. Her hair had obviously not been washed and looked grayer than usual, messy and dull. I suddenly remembered Puffin and Mary Fred offering her a makeover—it seemed like a million years ago, though it had probably only been last week. "Ve vill dye les chevaux—quel couleur do you crois, Marie Fred?" Puffin said.

"You're going to dye my horses?" Alice asked. We were all laughing, and she had danced across the room toward them as if she was a teenager too.

I put my arms across my stomach and started to rock back and forth. Then, to my surprise, big bark-like sobs started to wrench themselves from my body. Alice turned around and looked at me, and I could tell she wanted to comfort me but was stopping herself, like someone had told her to practice Tough Love. I wanted to talk to her, but I couldn't seem to form any words, all I could do was go on making this horrible barking noise and rocking. As I cried, I looked at Alice every so often, hoping that her face would melt and that she would put her arms around me and hold me, but she just sat there, though her mouth was twitching like this was pretty hard for her to watch. I remembered how when I was a little kid, I had cried in my room until I made myself sick, I'd be choking on the snot that poured from my nose and mouth till I felt like vomiting, until one of my parents would come in and tell me to shut up, and that only made it worse. When I saw that I had gotten a rise out of them, I would begin crying louder and louder, till I was standing in the doorway shrieking, and all I really wanted was for someone to come and comfort me, but no one ever did.

I was inclined to cry louder and louder now, until Alice felt sorry for me and went back to being my sister, but instead I found another way of upping the ante. "Al, you've got to help me," I said. "I need to go into rehab."

This was clearly music to her ears, though I have to say that I didn't mean a word of it. "Oh, Roy," she said. I even thought she was going to call me Binky, which was what everyone had called me until I was five. "Of course I'll help you. I've already talked to Diane about it and she says she can get you into a good program. It's hard because you don't have health insurance, but she knows a few places she can pull strings. Oh, Roy, you're making the right decision."

"You *talked to Diane?*" I came out of my crying for a moment and snapped at her. "Alice, what were you thinking? Do you want everyone in town to know about this?"

"Roy, she's an incredible resource. And Bob—Dr. Greenberg—wants to help too."

"Oh my God, Alice. Did you place an ad in the *Mount Pleasant Gazette?*"

"Roy, you're a person who needs help. People are willing to help you. But it has to begin with you."

"Oh, for Christ's sweet sake," I rasped, though I was still crying. Alice stood up and walked to the doorway. "Where the hell are you going?"

"I'm going to go call Diane. She said she can get you in somewhere immediately. I don't think we can afford to wait."

"But Alice, I—"

She was out the door before I could stop her. I sat there shaking my head, still sniffling, though now I was feeling as pissed off as I was sad, in fact I felt furious about everything, everything in the world, I just wanted to scream at how unfair it was that things were so fucked up, and Mary Fred was lying here, maybe dying, while every other idiot in the world was running around in the pink of health. I thought of all the other people I would rather see lying there: Lyndon Larouche; Oliver North; Newt Gingrich; Regis and Kathie Lee; the kid who drove into Mary Fred. It's not fair, it's just not fair, I said out loud, and I started crying again. I lay my head down on the bed next to Mary Fred's IV tube and sobbed until the bed shook.

As I cried, I thought about how poor Alice had gone to set up some big rescue or intervention for me, and how it was not going to work because I had absolutely no intention of going into rehab, and how poor old Mary Fred was just lying there and she didn't seem any better—then I thought, wait. Wait. Maybe I can make a deal. What if the whole problem here was that I was strung out, and God was punishing me? It was just the sort of thing that God as I understood God would do. He was up there on a cloud in His mustard-stained undershirt, lying in a deck chair drinking a vodka collins and wondering exactly what He could do to fuck with people down here on earth. He had seen the whole car accident thing as a way to get to me—of course—and had rigged it up to bring me to my knees. And I was, in fact, literally on my knees, beside the bed. "Are You happy now?" I sniveled out loud. "Is this what You wanted?" I wiped my nose on my sleeve. "Okay," I said, "okay, here it is. This is a test—this is just a test. I'm going to make a deal with You. You wake her up now, You make her well again, and I'll go into rehab like Alice wants me to. You do this for me now and I'll say I'm sorry. Not that I doubted You, because I will continue to doubt You, but I'm sorry that I thought you were just a sadistic slob whose only pleasure was tormenting the poor human beings on this stupid planet. And I'm sorry I made fun of Your undershirt. You wake her up right now, do You hear me?" I sat waiting, looking at Mary Fred, but her face didn't change. She just lay there, breathing quietly, still pale and ghostly. I kept waiting, like an idiot, and getting sadder and sadder, like I was spinning in the center of all the tragedy of the world. I spun down and down into it, into the void, the total sorrow and pointlessness of all of it. After a while, I laid my head down on the bed and sobbed some more until I fell asleep.

When I woke up, I raised my head and found her eyes on me.

REVELATIONS

"What isn't fair?" I think I said. It didn't feel like I had opened my eyes, but now I was looking at different things than I had seen a moment ago. I had been in a meadow with my brothers, and now I was looking at Uncle Roy, who was staring back at me like he was seeing the heavenly host. He was kneeling on the floor like he was saying his prayers, and at first I didn't know where we were, but wherever it was, it seemed perfectly normal to me. It wasn't until later that I realized that I was in a hospital, of all places, and there was nothing normal about Uncle Roy praying. "Did you say something wasn't fair, Uncle Roy?" I guess I must have closed my eyes then, because suddenly I was in the vegetable garden at the Compound, and Little Freddie was helping me weed.

When I opened my eyes again, Uncle Roy was still there, but he was standing next to the bed I was lying in, and Alice stood next to him. A big man with glasses and a white coat leaned over me, holding my wrist and talking. "Can you hear me?" he kept saying. I could hear him just fine, but I couldn't seem to answer.

"She said something a minute ago," Uncle Roy said to Alice. His voice was all excited. "I heard her."

"What did she say?" Alice asked. Her throat sounded tight, like she was choking.

"I don't know, I couldn't really hear. But she definitely said something." I closed my eyes again, and when I opened them, Uncle Roy had his arm around Alice, and it looked like they were crying. The big man was still hovering over me. "You're in Intensive Care," he said. "You've had an accident, but you're going to be just fine."

Then I was in the church at the Outpost, and the Reverend Thigpen was there, and he was preaching a sermon about Lackers, about how we couldn't trust them because they hadn't truly repented of their sin, and then suddenly he started singing a song and dancing around the church, though when I woke up later and remembered it, I knew he would never sing "We Like to Party," a song that I had heard a lot at the bowling alley, and he certainly wouldn't have been wearing a big straw hat. Then I was back in the vegetable garden, surrounded by giant tomatoes, green peppers, and cucumbers that were bigger than I was. They were closing in on me, and I had to hack them all down with a machete. Little Freddie was running up ahead of me, and I tried to run after him, but my feet wouldn't move. There was some kind of golden light in front of me, and I tried to cast myself into its arms, like the Reverend Smith always said to do when the time came, but then it turned into a bus and I was on the way to school with Heather. Suddenly, we were standing at the bus stop waiting to go home, and then I was falling down a well, down and down, and just before I was about to splash into the water, I opened my eyes and saw Alice sitting there beside me.

"Oh, Bob, look, her eyes are open again," she said. The big man in the white coat came back and put his arm around her, and the two of them smiled down at me like they had just given birth to me.

"Hurts," I said. Then I thought for a minute and said "Hurts" again.

"Oh, Bob, she's talking. Mary Fred, what did you say?"

"It's okay, Mary Fred, you're in the hospital. We're taking good care of you, and you'll be fine. You're going to be just fine," he said again, in case I hadn't believed him the first time.

I tried to get up, but I couldn't move, it was like my whole body had turned to jelly, and there were all kinds of tubes hooked up to me, coming out of my hand and my nose. I tried to brush the nose one away, but the big man gently put it back and patted my hand kindly like a grandmother. "Alice," I said, looking at her. She looked very beautiful, her face pulled all tight and her hair standing out around it. It was good to see her. I was hoping to find everyone I knew standing behind her, like we had all gone to the World Beyond and everything was the holiest of holies, but all I could see in the background was a nurse. I could feel her poking my legs, so I was sure they were still attached to me, and I was glad about that since I had always liked them. I hadn't remembered yet about what had happened to me—it was like my mind was giving the rest of me a little vacation before we had to get back to work.

"Oh, Mary Fred," Alice said, her eyes tearing up. "Oh, Mary Fred." That was evidently all she could say for the moment, but it seemed like enough.

I must have fallen asleep then, because when I opened my eyes, Uncle Roy was sitting next to me again. "Uncle Roy," I said, though it came out as kind of a mumble.

"Hey, honey." He leaned over to me. There was a weird smile on his face, like he had borrowed it from someone else. "Are you back with us?"

"Mmmn," I said.

"Oh, Mary Fred, thank God." That seemed like such a

strange thing for Uncle Roy to say that I thought I must be in another dream, but then he said, "Do you remember the chicken? The chicken you put by my plate?"

I nodded.

He looked relieved, like he was afraid I had forgotten everything that had ever happened to me. I hadn't.

"Do you need anything?" he asked. "Are you hungry? Thirsty? Can I get you something?"

"Coke," I said.

"You want a Coke?"

I nodded. I don't think I'd ever had Coke before, but it had always looked like it would taste good. Uncle Roy ran out the door and came back a minute later with a red can and a glass. I tried to sit up to drink but I could only lie flat, so he poured a little of it into my mouth. It tasted like something you'd wash your horse with, but it made me feel better. Then before I knew it, Alice and the big man were back, Uncle Roy was gone, and some people in green jackets were sticking me with needles. Then Heather was there, then she wasn't.

I don't know how many days passed like this. Sometimes there was light outside my window, sometimes it was dark. Each time I came back to the hospital room from wherever I'd been, the Outpost, the Compound, the garden, the school, I found someone else sitting beside me smiling and trying to get me to talk. I began staying awake for longer periods of time, though I still felt all weird and gooey, like I was made out of mush. At one point when I woke up, a nurse was saying, "Your cousins are here." I looked up expecting to see Bobby and Linda from the Anderson side, but it was Jack and Todd, my bowling partners. The nurse was looking at me funny like she was wondering why my cousins were brown and I wasn't.

"We had to say we were your cousins," Todd said. "They

won't let anyone in but relatives." They told me they had missed me and that they had brought me a present. I couldn't raise my arms or anything but they held out a black canvas bag and opened it. Jack took a big pink bowling ball out of the bag. "This is for when you get better," he said, winking at me. He kissed my hand, the one that didn't have wires in it, like he was some kind of prince, and then when I opened my eyes again, Uncle Roy was sitting there. He was holding the same hand Jack had just kissed, though maybe that had been hours before, or even days, I had no way of knowing.

"Mary Fred," he was saying. Maybe he had been saying it over and over for some time. "Oh, there you are. Listen, honey, I have to tell you something. I'm, uh, I have to go away for a little while. I'll be gone for about a month, maybe more. It's really important or I wouldn't leave while you're still in here, but I have to do it, and I just wanted to make sure you understood. Do you understand?"

"Mmmn," I said, though I meant to say yes. I wasn't sure I understood what he was saying, but I could tell it mattered to him so I tried to look like I got it. "Have a good trip," I tried to say.

"What?"

I said it again, and this time I think he heard me. "Oh, thanks, honey. Listen, I just want you to know—" I waited to see what he wanted me to know, but he never finished the sentence, just bent over and kissed me on the forehead. When I thought about it later, it seemed to me that this was not a very Roy-like thing to do.

It might have been the next day when they moved me into a bigger room with fewer machines in it. Every few hours someone would come in and try to get me to eat something. They would explain to me that if I would eat, they would take the thing out of my hand, and they would give me some dessert.

But I was never hungry. So I just lay there as people came in and out. This room had a TV and even though I knew I shouldn't watch it—I mean, I had no excuse since it wasn't as if Heather was there insisting—I didn't turn it off. Once I saw pictures of some kids I recognized from school on the news, but the rest of the time it was the same old shows I had watched at Alice's. I flipped from channel to channel, looking for things like *Judge Judy* and even *Jenny Jones*. When I found them, it made me feel safer somehow, like nothing had changed.

I started staying awake for most of the day, and Heather began showing up every afternoon. She said she wasn't back in school yet, that somebody or other wouldn't let her go back because it was too dramatic, or something like that, and she was taking medicine so she would feel better. We didn't talk much. She would pull a chair next to my bed, or sometimes she would curl up on the bed with me, and we would watch TV just like we used to.

Finally one day, the big man in the white coat, whose name was Dr. Greenberg, said I was so much better that they were going to send me home. For a moment when he said the word "home" I wasn't sure where he meant, but it turned out he meant Alice's house. The next day, Alice and Heather packed up the little toys and cards and balloons and flower pots and Beanie Babies that were all over the room, and we got into Alice's car and drove home.

Dr. Greenberg stopped by that evening to see how I was. Someone, I had no idea who, had given me a big pink stuffed dog, and since I was told to stay in bed, I just lay there and held him. (Later I found out the dog was a present from Roy.) Alice asked me if I wanted her to put a TV in my room, but I knew she would have had to go out and buy one, since the one in the living room was too big to move, so I said no, though the truth was, I would have liked it. Instead, I tried to read from the Book for a while, but there was something about it that made me feel sad and afraid. Maybe it was because there was a whole chapter in it about the Big Cat, and I didn't want to think about that. According to the Book, I was supposed to be in the World Beyond right now, not lying here in Alice's guest room surrounded by Beanie Babies. I don't know if I was mad, exactly, but I felt like accusing someone of something, but I didn't know who or what.

I started reading books from the bookshelf instead, picture books about lost dogs, and one called *Green Eggs and Ham* that I liked a lot, and then some longer stories about a place called Oz. I liked the Oz books the best. At night when I slept, I began to dream about Dorothy, and about Jack Pumpkin-head, Ozma, and Billina the chicken, who reminded me of one of the chickens we'd had at the Compound. I guess the books were supposed to go in a certain order, but I didn't know what it was, so I read them all the wrong way round. It didn't seem to matter though. I also read some books about a girl named Nancy Drew, and I liked those too, especially one about gypsies. I had never realized that books were just like people's dreams, and once I found myself wondering if that was all *The Book of Fred* was, a big dream that somebody had had once and written down.

Finally one morning, I knew I was well enough to get out of bed. I wasn't up to cooking and cleaning, I could tell, but I knew I could walk, so I stood up, went to the bathroom (I hated using a bedpan), and made my way down the stairs. When Heather saw me, she burst into tears, and I had to spend the next half hour comforting her. I told her I hadn't meant to upset her, and she said she was sorry to be such a big dork about it, but it still took her a long time to stop crying. Alice came home right then. Dr. Greenberg was with her, and they made me lie on the sofa, and Alice bundled the moon and star blanket around me and fixed me tea and toast like all I had was a bad cold.

It was weird being there without Uncle Roy, but Dr. Greenberg came to dinner almost every night and sat in Roy's seat. I asked Alice one time exactly where Uncle Roy had gone and it was only later that I realized that she hadn't really answered me. Heather told me he had gone to some kind of camp to get better. I asked what was wrong with him and she said she didn't know, but that Alice said not to be concerned, that it was no big deal, so I let it go at that and tried not to feel worried. I found myself thinking about the Littles a lot, too, since they had been in my dreams most of the time, and wondering where they were and how they were doing. I decided that as soon as I was well, I would figure out a way to go visit them, and that gave me something to look forward to. In general, I felt better every day, and pretty soon I was walking around easily, though my innards still hurt a lot, and I wanted to get back to doing some chores, but Alice wouldn't hear of it. I noticed that the house had gotten a little messier but I guessed there was nothing I could do about it, since everyone yelled at me if I so much as picked up a feather duster.

So Heather and I just sat around doing nothing. She seemed to like that, since it was what she was used to, but it was hard for me. I was always thinking of reasons I needed to leap up and get something, but I still couldn't move very fast, and if I bent the wrong way, I would get a big stab of hurt somewhere inside, so mostly I lay on the sofa, and she relaxed in her favorite chair, and all the shows we had ever watched on TV paraded in front of us like they were our old friends and had come to visit.

This went on for probably two or three whole weeks, maybe longer. With no real schedule besides the TV guide, I'd lost track of time. Then one day, everything changed. I remember it was a Tuesday and it was exactly four o'clock in the afternoon. The phone rang and Heather picked it up, talked for a minute, said, "She's still at work," and hung up. "That was Diane," she said. "She said it was important." A second later the phone rang again. "It's for you," Heather said, handing it to me and giving me a funny look. I said hello into the phone and someone said hello back to me. It was Mama.

Talking to Mama was the weirdest thing. It had been so long since I had heard her voice that she sounded like someone . I didn't know instead of the most familiar person in the world. I felt so excited to hear her that I put my hand on my chest to stop my heart from beating right through it. She sounded tired, sad, even a little mad, and she had a dry crackle in her voice like a fire that was just starting. She'd never had a very joyous voice, but now she sounded flat, like something had happened that made her all gray inside. We talked for a while and I listened to her voice as if it was music, so when I hung up and Heather asked me what she had wanted, I wasn't entirely sure. "I think she said she's coming to get me," I said.

"She's what?" Heather burst into tears again. Whatever medicine they were giving her, I didn't think it was working very well. "Oh, God, M.F., no, no, she can't. You live here. With us."

I didn't say anything for a while, just went over and sat on the edge of Heather's chair and held her hand, patted her head, and whatever else I could think of.

"Tell me you're not going," Heather said, looking up at me with big sad wet eyes.

"Heather, she's my mama. I have to go."

"But isn't she in jail?"

I tried hard to recall everything Mama had said. "She got off with probation. She said Papa's still in jail but she's free as a bird." I remembered those words, that she was free as a bird.

"Are the Littles with her?"

"No, but she says we're going to get them back somehow."

"But where would you go?"

"I don't know, Heather. If she said, I don't remember. The Outpost I guess. It looked like the Compound was, uh, was not, you know . . ."

"But what about school? What about the soup kitchen, and bowling?"

I told her I didn't think we'd be doing any of those things very soon anyway, since neither of us was feeling very well.

"But what will I do without you?"

She started crying again, and I put my arms around her till luckily Alice came home and started fussing about, making her lie down and giving her some kind of pill. When Heather had calmed down a little, Alice sat next to me on the couch. "I talked to Diane," she said, a real serious, anxious look on her face. "Did your mother call you?"

"Yes, ma'am." After just talking to Mama for a few minutes, I had already gone back to behaving how I knew she was going to want me to behave.

"Diane says it's up to you. You can stay here with us—and of course, Mary Fred, we'd like that more than anything in the world—or you can go back with your mother."

I told her I had made a decision and that I was going back with Mama. She looked really sad then, and I hated to be the one that made her look like that, but she said she understood completely but that she wanted me to know that I always had a home with them, that as far as she was concerned I was part of her family and always would be. I said I knew that, and that

I felt the same way, but I had to go. She gave me a hug, then went into the kitchen, and I think she was trying not to let me see her cry because when she came back out her eyes were all red but she was smiling and talking about what we were going to have for dinner. She had gone to the store and bought all the stuff I liked.

I was just taking a big bite of red snapper when the doorbell rang. Alice went over to the front door and opened it, and when I looked up, Mama was standing in the living room, her head moving from side to side like she was scanning the horizon. Her face was all screwed up and she looked like she smelled something bad. I knew what she was thinking because I remembered how weird the house had looked to me when I first saw it, with no brown and no Book and nothing but a bunch of fiddle-dee-dee—this was what Mama was thinking, and I knew it. Her hair had gone grayer, and she had cut it, or maybe they had made her cut it in jail. She was wearing it loose around her shoulders, and it made her face look older and more tired.

Alice introduced her to Dr. Greenberg, and I was afraid Mama wasn't going to shake hands with him, since he was a doctor and all, but she did, though she looked like she was going to go scrub her hand afterwards. I was standing up next to my chair, and when she got finished meeting everyone, I went over to her and put my arms around her waist, like I had done a million times. I had forgotten how she smelled, sort of like gingerbread and soap and lemon. She patted my head, like everything was okay now, and she was going to stand by me and protect me from all of these Lackers. She looked at me and shook her head, like I had turned into some kind of hootchie-kootchie woman while her back was turned.

Alice asked her to join us at the table, but she said she had eaten on the road—which seemed odd since Mama would

never eat fast food or anything like that—and that we needed
to get going because we still had a long drive in front of us. I
was still in the middle of my fish, and it had been tasting
mighty good, but suddenly I wasn't hungry anymore. Mama
told me to go pack up my belongings, so I went upstairs, moving kind of slow, since it still hurt sometimes when I walked,
especially climbing stairs. I went into my room and took my
suitcase out from under the bed where it had lain since last
June. I started putting things in it like my Beanie Babies and
my pink stuffed dog, but just as quickly I realized that Mama
was not going to like that, so I took them out again and
propped them all back up on the bookcase. I opened up the
closet and saw a bunch of the pink shirts and dresses Alice and
Heather had bought me. I knew I didn't need them either, so I
just took out everything that was black or brown and folded it
up real neat. I took *The Book of Fred* from the shelf where I
had set it, and I really wanted to take *Ozma of Oz* with me too,
but I knew better. I left my bowling ball in the corner in its carrying case, since I didn't figure I'd be bowling where we were
going.

   I went into the bathroom and started gathering up my toiletries. I had all kinds of little bottles of stuff that Heather and
I had gotten as free samples at Bloomingdale's one time, and I
knew Mama wouldn't approve, so I was going to leave them
behind but then I thought well, maybe she won't know if I just
take one small one, so I took a little tube of Princess Borghese
moisturizer. I grabbed my toothbrush and my hairbrush. I
wanted to take the deodorant but I knew Mama wouldn't like
that either. I stood there looking at everything on the shelves
and in the medicine cabinet, and there was really nothing else
I could take that she wouldn't mind somehow.

   As I started to grab my pills out of the medicine cabinet, I had a terrible feeling, almost like the way it must feel to be standing on the earth somewhere when a comet falls out of the sky and lands right on your head. I realized that all these weeks I had been taking all kinds of medicine, antibiotics and painkillers and whatever else they'd been giving me, and I hadn't even stopped to think about what that meant. The nurses had been sticking needles in me and thrusting pills down my throat for days before I was even really awake, and it occurred to me that this was exactly what Mama and Papa had gone to jail about. That was how important it was to them. But by the time this thought even began to flicker in the back of my mind, I was in the hospital, I'd had surgery, and it seemed I might as well be hung for a sheep as for a lamb.

Now here I was in the bathroom with this comet-feeling crashing down on my head. I suddenly saw myself and my new life through my old eyes—my body had been invaded by doctors, I had been poisoned with pills, I had not trusted enough in the One but had been a coward and let Evil triumph within me. But then I thought, wait, I was unconscious when Dr. Greenberg did my surgery, I was in a coma, I did not have a say in any of it. For a second I felt outraged about this. But then I had an even more horrible realization: I was glad. I was so glad. I was so, *so* glad. I looked around me and suddenly the bathroom looked like a vision from Beyond—the little white octagonal floor tiles glistened at my feet, and my face in the mirror sparkled, the bottles of shampoo on the edge of the bathtub were all different colors. This strange feeling, like of all the blood in my veins popping like popcorn, came over me and a voice in my head was saying, "I'm alive, I'm alive, I'm alive." I felt like I was falling, and I grabbed on to the edge of the sink. I looked in the mirror. There I was, and I knew that if it hadn't been for Dr. Greenberg, I wouldn't be. Yes, I would be in the World Beyond with my brothers, but the truth was, I wanted to be here on earth.

I reached into the medicine cabinet and took out the bottle of pills Dr. Greenberg had given me. I held the bottle for a minute or two and just looked at it. Then I stuck it under my shirt and went back into my room and closed the door. I found a Swiss army knife in a desk drawer and with it, I made a little hole in the inside lining of the suitcase and dropped the bottle in there. Then I finished putting my clothes in, packing them tight so the bottle wouldn't rattle around, closed up the suitcase, and carried it downstairs. Mama was standing there in the sitting room, still looking around her like she was seeing Evil coming at her from every which way. I put the suitcase down and told her I was ready to go.

It felt so strange and so bad to drive away from Alice's house and know that I would probably never see it again, and I had to steel my mind and just not think about it. It had been hard to say good-bye to Alice and Heather, and I had done it quickly, though I'd had to kind of peel Heather off me as she was clinging to my arm and crying. I told her I'd be seeing her again soon, but the truth was, I was just saying that to make her feel better. I didn't think Mama would like it if we kept in touch, and even though I had only been with her for half an hour or so, I was already switching back to the way I was before and was ready to do whatever Mama wanted, because of course that was how she brought me up to be.

I looked out the window and watched as the little streets that had become so familiar to me turned back into the strange streets they had been when I first saw them. We drove onto the Beltway and I expected Mama to head north toward Frederick, and the Outpost, but she went the other way. She hadn't said much so far, and I could tell she was concentrating on the road, since I knew she hated to drive and hadn't done it much in the past, since Papa was always the one behind the wheel if we went anywhere, or else we went on a big bus, but I couldn't help asking her where we were heading. She said we were going to the new place. I asked her where that was and she said North Carolina, and didn't even tell me that I shouldn't be asking questions of a grown-up. I asked weren't we going to the Outpost and she said no, that everyone had left there. I thought I ought to tell her that Alice had taken me to the Compound and that no one had been there either, but for some reason the words just wouldn't come out. It wasn't like I was lying to Mama if I didn't tell her something, was it? I just didn't think she would like that I had showed Alice and Roy and Heather where the Compound was and that I had tried to go there with a bunch of Lackers, and on such a holy day— though then when I remembered how the Big Cat had turned out, it didn't seem like a holy day anyway, and my mind started getting all confused so I just let it go.

I tried talking to Mama for a while, since I wanted to hear about what she had been doing, but she didn't seem to want to say anything about it, and soon she told me to go to sleep and when I woke up we would be there, so I did. It was still dark out when we stopped driving, just after two, according to the clock on the dashboard, though it was such an old, beat-up car that for all I knew the time was wrong. We got out and I started to lug my suitcase, but when Mama saw me struggling with it, trying to ignore the pain in my insides, she took it and carried it, and said I shouldn't lift anything heavy until the One had healed me up.

In the darkness, I could see that we were walking past a group of log cabins, and all their lights were out. Mama opened the front door to the fourth cabin we came to. She didn't use a key, and that seemed strange for a minute, but then I remembered that of course we never used keys at the Compound either. She brought my suitcase into a little room and set it on the floor. There was nothing in the room but a bed with a brown bedspread, a small brown dresser, and a straight-backed chair. On the wall was a mirror, which seemed odd to me, since I knew Mama didn't approve of mirrors. She told me to go to sleep, that I could unpack in the morning, and she gave me a kiss on the top of my head like she always used to, and said a prayer over me, though not a long one. When she was gone, I opened up my suitcase and took out my pajamas. Alice had bought them for me and they were flannel with cows on them. I liked them because they reminded me of the cows that Diane and all them had sent to that foreign country, and since the cows were brown I figured Mama might not mind them. I reached into the lining of my suitcase and pulled out my pill bottle, being careful not to shake it because Mama had incredibly powerful hearing, and I worked up a bunch of spit in my mouth, took a pill out, and swallowed it.

When I climbed into bed, I was tired and sore from riding for so long, but I couldn't fall sleep, maybe because I had slept in the car. The sheets felt cold and strange, and outside I could hear weird, spooky noises. I wished I could have brought Pinky, my stuffed dog, with me. I could have put my arms around him and fallen right to sleep instead of just lying awake, trying not to think about anything, trying so hard that all the things I didn't want to think about got to be a loud noise in my brain, and when I woke up in the morning, I still had my hands over my ears, as if that was going to help.

Mama came in while I still was lying there and told me to get up, that we had to go to breakfast, since there was no kitchen in the cabin. She pursed her lips a little when she saw my pajamas, but she didn't say anything about them, just helped me to take them off and to put on my old brown dress. She didn't look too happy about my underwear, either, since it was a little bit fancy, with some lace on it, but at least I had left all the pink panties and bras behind, much as it had pained me to do so. "You've grown," she said, and she shook her head like she didn't approve. She brushed my hair back hard and put it in a ponytail that was so tight it hurt my face. I went into the bathroom and washed up, then returned to my room for a minute and while Mama wasn't looking, I took another one of my pills. Then we put on our coats and walked out the door. Now that it was light out, I could see we were surrounded by mountains like at the Compound, though they were taller and darker green, and there were a bunch of cabins just like ours, not in rows but sprinkled around like someone had just dropped them there from the sky. It was a sunny day, though chilly. "I guess spring is on its way, huh, Mama," I said, making conversation as we walked. I hadn't remembered that she was this quiet, although I had never really been alone with her before, come to think of it, there was always the whole bunch of us, and Papa.

"Did you have any boyfriends while you were up there?" she asked, as if I hadn't said anything about spring.

"Oh, no, Mama."

"Why not? You're a pretty young woman now." She glanced over at me, then went back to looking down at the path as we walked.

"Just didn't have any, I guess. I had some friends who were boys, but we just went bowling."

"You never let any of them touch you, did you?"

"Oh, no, ma'am. Of course not."

She looked at me again, to see if I was lying. I remembered this look from my whole life, how Mama had a way of knowing everything you were thinking, so you had to keep your mind pure and clear. Then she made a little noise in her throat, and we turned onto a dirt road that led us up to a square one-story building. It was gray concrete with almost no windows, like an office complex or a police station, with a high wall all around it. There was a man at the front gate holding a long-barreled gun. Mama introduced me to him, telling him that I didn't have my ID card yet, and he let us pass. We walked through some glass doors and down a long hallway to the back of the building, where we came into a huge kitchen full of people in white jackets and little white paper hats. "This is where we'll be working during the week," she said. "We've got today off though. You hungry?"

I told her I was starving, though the truth was, I wasn't hungry at all. Maybe it was from taking a big pill on an empty stomach, but I felt a little queasy. She led me out of the kitchen and into a long cafeteria line, where she loaded up two plates for us with eggs and grits and pancakes and potatoes and sausages. There was no fish to be seen, and that seemed odd, since Mama generally made fish for breakfast, and she never did like sausage, said it was too heavy and would slow us down. I didn't think I was going to be able to eat anything, but we sat down at a long table and I did my best. The whole time we were sitting there, folks kept coming up to us and saying hello. Sometimes their faces were familiar from the Outpost or the Compound, though mostly I didn't know them. "Where did all these people come from, Mama?" I asked her. "There's so many of them here."

"We joined up with some other like-minded fellowships," she said. "They have chosen to share in our gospel."

"Oh," I said, and added, "that's nice."

I did the best I could with all the food, and then Mama let me give up, though normally she'd have made me eat every bite. We stood up and took our trays over to a conveyor belt. As we were heading to the front door, I saw the Reverend Thigpen coming in, and I have to admit that my heart sank. I was surprised at myself for this, but that was how I felt. I guess maybe in part of my mind I blamed him for the Big Cat not taking place. But the truth was, I had had to admit to myself that I was glad it hadn't happened, and I felt all mixed up and angry about that, like I didn't know what to think about anything anymore. And it was the Reverend Thigpen who had stood up there at the pulpit and yelled all those things about the terrible fates of the Lackers, how they were going to stand in the flames of justice, and their bodies would catch fire and their skin would burn right off until they were screaming all the names of the One but it would be too late for them, they would never be able to stop the eternal lake of fire that would consume them forever and a day. When I imagined those things happening to the people I knew, instead of making me feel all safe and happy like it had all my life because I wasn't going to have to burn up like that, it made me feel sick and angry and mean.

"So this is our young sheep," he said, stroking the side of his long face, "back to the fold."

"And not a moment too soon," Mama said darkly, looking at me like I had just returned from a visit to the Evil One himself.

"Living among those who lack," he said in his Sunday morning voice. "Oh, what a trial that must have been."

"And there was a doctor," Mama whispered. "A *Greenberg.*"

"Do tell," he said, his hand on his heart. He turned to me and said, "I understand you were also in a hospital."

"Yes sir," I said, hoping that was all anyone would ask me to give in the way of commentary.

He shook his head and sighed, then turned back to Mama. "And the others?"

"Still with Lackers. But we're working on getting them back."

The Reverend Thigpen offered Mama his condolences. He picked up my hand and held it for a minute, and I was glad when he let it go because his hand was fat and damp. I looked up at his huge square bald head, into his beady eyes that peered over his square wire-rimmed glasses, and it occurred to me that the truth was, I had just never liked the Reverend Thigpen. When we had been at the Compound, the Reverend Smith had been our main preacher and he used to talk about nice things, how golden it would be in the World Beyond, and how we would spend eternity without a care, instead of all the horrible, grisly things Reverend Thigpen mentioned like people's skin burning off and stuff like that.

"Where is the Reverend Smith?" I asked them, just to make conversation.

Neither of them answered at first, then Mama said, "The Lackers got him."

"I'm afraid he's in the penitentiary," the Reverend Thigpen said in a kind of snooty voice, it seemed to me. "There were some irregularities with his finances."

"Well, then I guess we'll hear you preach on Sunday," I said to the Reverend Thigpen as we started walking away. He didn't answer, and the smiling parts of his long cheeks seemed to droop.

"He's not our preacher anymore," Mama said, chiding me as we got out of earshot. "We've got a new one. He's the head of this whole operation." Mama led me over to a little wooden bench and sat me down, though it was kind of chilly out to be lollygagging around outside. Though the sunlight was bright and clear, there was a mean little wind in the air. Mama turned to me and looked into my eyes, her face all serious. "I need to talk to you about this, and there's no time like the present. Things aren't the same here, Mary Fred, and you need to understand the new ways. I'm sure you've already noticed some differences."

"A few. Like at breakfast. How there was sausage and stuff. And no fish."

"That was turkey sausage," Mama said in kind of a weird voice. "The Book led us to the fish, but here in this fellowship, why, they eat the turkey."

"The turkey? How come?"

"The turkey is a sacred bird," Mama said, looking away. I couldn't believe she was letting me ask so many questions. "This place is a big turkey farm."

"Oh, those must have been the noises I heard."

"Noises?"

"Last night, while I was trying to sleep. It must have been gobbling. I thought maybe it was ghosts or something."

"Now, Mary Fred," Mama said, turning to me and absentmindedly smacking my hand, like she always had. We weren't supposed to believe in ghosts. "Anyhow," she said, still holding on to my hand, "there are other differences."

"And the people here don't wear brown, do they?" I said, though Mama was still wearing brown, and so were some of the people we'd seen that I'd known from before. "They wear a lot of purple, don't they?"

"Only certain ones," Mama murmured. "But you're right about the brown."

"But we wear brown because of Fred Brown," I said, starting to feel so confused that I forgot to trace an *F* and a *B* in the

air. Mama didn't do it either. "How can people in our fellowship not wear brown?"

"You see, Mary Fred," Mama said, suddenly sounding a little testy, like she was finally getting tired of my questions.
"Here in this place, there are other prophets. Ours is not the
only one. That's why the Reverend Thigpen is not our
preacher. There is someone else now, and he's the one we follow. I need you to understand about that. Do you understand?"

"Of course I do, Mama," I said, but the fact was that I
didn't, not at all.

Mama seemed to relax a little. She smiled at me some, and
touched my hair, catching a few strands that had fallen out of
my ponytail and tucking them behind my ears. She stood up,
so I stood up too, and we started walking. I didn't ask her
where we were going. I didn't think I wanted to ask Mama any
more questions—I would just see what happened, and try to
travel hopefully in the One. I figured that whatever else happened here on earth, the One still had to be the same, at least
I hoped so.

We walked past the concrete building, along the dirt road
and onto a path that led through some trees and up a hill.
When we got to the top of it, we could see a white house, big
as a mansion on TV, with six tall white pillars in front of it and
a huge front door. I had never been in a house that size and I
couldn't imagine who lived there, while everyone else was
stuck in little cabins. I figured that if it was the big preacher,
maybe he had a lot of relations.

At the side of the front door was another man with a gun. I
didn't like guns much—I had grown up with them, but ever
since the one time I had shot a deer, they made me feel sick
and frightened. Mama showed the man an ID card and explained who I was, and he let us in. Some more men with guns

were in the hallway as we entered, and yet another one stood
at the foot of a long circular staircase. Mama and I went past
him up the stairs and through some double doors into an enormous room with wood paneling on all the walls, and a bunch
of mirrors, and dark purple curtains on all the windows. At
the end of the room was a big purple chair, and a man was sitting in it like it was a throne. Mama took my hand and led me
over to him.

"This is my daughter, Mary Fred," Mama said to him. She
was smiling in this weird way I had never seen before, like we
were on TV and she wasn't sure she was dressed right.

I almost felt like I should curtsy, but I held out my hand in
case he wanted to shake it. He stood up and I looked at him.
He was a tall man with colorless hair that covered his head like
fuzz. It was cut very short except for a long braid that hung
over his left shoulder. He had round wire-rimmed glasses that
made his eyes look big and blurry, and he was wearing a purple
shirt with little red and gold stripes in it that made the fabric
look like gift wrap, and blue jeans. He didn't have a scrap of
brown on, and I wondered just what kind of preacher he could
possibly be.

"Mary Fred, this is Cyrus," Mama said.

Cyrus took my hand in his and held it for a moment, then
put both arms around me and drew me close to him. As I was
pressed against his chest, I could smell him, a combination of
sweat and what must have been deodorant, even though no
one I knew was supposed to wear chemical smells because
they weren't natural. He held me tight, and I began to feel
strange. I noticed that having his arms wrapped around me felt
nice. It felt *really* nice. No man had ever held me close, unless
you counted Papa, but Papa wouldn't have held me like that,
not so tight and not in such a warm way, a way that made me

feel almost like I was burning. Things started to hurt inside me, not because he was squeezing too tight, although he was, but because they were shifting around somehow.

Then, just as suddenly as this embrace had felt good, it began to feel suffocating, like my face was pressed so close against the shiny purple shirt and the hard chest inside it that I couldn't breathe, but then I realized that I couldn't breathe because of something else. All the hair on my arms and on the back of my neck began to stand up, like when you see a copperhead in the grass and you have to stay real still so it won't panic and strike you. I stopped breathing and just didn't move, as I waited for the whole thing to end.

The man put his arms on my shoulders and held me away from him, looking me over. "Catherine," he said.

"Pardon?"

"We're going to call you Catherine from now on."

"But my name—"

"I sense that you're a Catherine." He turned to Mama and said, "She's a beauty, Susan. Just like her mother."

Mama was no beauty, and she didn't look much like me, either, since I look just like Papa, and of course her name wasn't Susan, it was Ellen, but she got the weird face again and smiled at him shyly, like a girl.

I thanked him and tried to step away, but he kept his hands on my shoulders. "We'll be seeing a lot of you up here, Catherine," he said, smiling at me and rubbing my shoulder with his hand. "I understand you're still recovering from an injury."

"Yes, sir."

"All better now, though, I can see that." He took his hand away from my shoulder and laid it across my abdomen, as if he knew right where it hurt and was going to fix it. His hand felt warm, and once again I felt things moving around in me, things that made me feel uncomfortable.

"It still hurts some," I said.

"Well, don't worry, Catherine, you've come to just the right place for healing."

"Yes, sir," I said, wanting him to take his hand away but at the same time, not wanting him to. Just as I felt I couldn't stand another second of it, he dropped both his hands and sat back down on his throne. We backed away from him, and Mama gave a little bow, so I did too. He said something weird then, something like "Bukulahara," and Mama said it back to him, so I tried to do the same. Then we said a regular good-bye, and Mama led me away again. As we walked back down the hill through the trees, Mama said, "I think he liked you." I couldn't tell if she was happy about that or not.

We spent the whole day tidying up the cabin, sweeping it out and scrubbing everything, even the front stoop. We took breaks for lunch and dinner up at the cafeteria in the concrete building. Mama called it the Bunker. As we worked, we didn't talk much, but every so often I asked her a question, like how the Littles were. I could tell she didn't want to talk about them, but she said they were as well as could be expected, given that the Social Services had placed them with Lackers, even though our own people had been more than willing to take them. She said that we would get them back soon. I asked her how Papa was, but she didn't seem too eager to discuss him either. She said he had received a long sentence. I asked if we could go visit him and she said it wasn't allowed. I said I thought everyone was allowed to have visitors in jail, unless they were in solitary confinement (I knew this from TV, though I didn't tell her that), but she said Papa didn't want any visitors. I said, I thought you said it wasn't allowed, and she told me not to get smart with her or she was going to use the discipline stick on me when I was well. So right then I got the idea that there was something funny about her and Papa, but I put it out of my mind.

The next morning at 6 A.M., I started work in the cafeteria. Mama took me to meet a woman named Angela in the back office. When I first saw her, she was smoking a cigarette, and that really shocked me, since I thought only Lackers smoked. She stubbed it out when she saw us and handed me a plastic card with my name and a number typed on it. She had wrinkled gray hair that was trying to climb out of a little bun she had tied it in, and her cheeks were fat like a baby's. A purple scarf was tied around her neck in a big bow. "You'll be on the grill for a while," she said. "Susan, will you take her and show her where to go?"

Answering to the name "Susan" like it was her own, Mama led me down the hall to the kitchen and parked me in front of a big flat stove-like thing. "You'll be working with Jeff," she said, pointing to a plump man in a white apron. "He'll tell you what to do. I'm over there prepping." She gestured toward a long wooden counter on the other side of the room.

Jeff, or whatever his name really was, seemed nice enough. He told me how to scrape the grill, and said that I didn't need to flip anything unless he was busy, that he would do all the cooking and I was there to act as his assistant. He said we needed to make sure that the grill was clean, that we had to put new grease on it, and that we had to be careful not to mix up the meat and the eggs too much because some people didn't like that. He told me that we always cooked turkey meat, not beef, and that it burned easily so I had to watch out for that. I told him I liked cooking and he said that this wasn't exactly cooking but that it was an important job, and I should be glad that everyone was trusting me to do it.

After a while, another girl showed up. Jeff said her name was Sarah and that she was late. Sarah said she was sorry but that her alarm clock hadn't gone off. She looked like she was a few years older than me, maybe nineteen, and after a few days I found out that her alarm clock didn't work very well in general. Sarah was in charge of handing the food to Jeff for him to put on the grill, like they were in surgery and she was his nurse. By now it was nearly seven and people were already showing up on the line for breakfast, so we went into production. It was a mad rush, with Jeff flipping and Sarah handing and me scraping, but it went quickly and by the time breakfast was over, about ten or so, I felt kind of glad to have something that occupied my mind so totally, though my insides were hurting from standing for so long.

"So you're one of the Fredians," Sarah said when we were finished and were washing up in the women's bathroom. I could see her in the mirror. She had a round face with spotty red cheeks, and two of her side teeth were missing.

"I guess so."

"Yeah, a bunch of your people showed up here a while back. I guess this place is a bit strange for you."

"I don't know. I mean, I haven't been here long enough to tell."

"Well, we do things different around here. I grew up in another church too and I can tell you right now, some things go on around here that will surprise you."

"Like what?"

"You'll see." Sarah dried her hands on her apron. The door opened and another woman came in and started washing her hands. "We can take an hour break now as long as we're back by eleven-fifteen to start lunch," Sarah said, opening the door for me and walking with me out into the hall.

I asked her what I should do for an hour and she said I

should go home and take a nap, that was what she was going
to do. We started walking and it turned out that her cabin was
not too far past mine, so she walked me home. As we neared
my cabin, she said, "Wait, are you that girl whose father is in
jail?"

"Maybe. I mean, there must be others."

"The one whose mother copped a plea and blamed everything on her husband?" Sarah's brown eyes bored into me
hopefully, like she was just dying for details.

"No, no, that's not us," I said. I told her I'd see her later and I
went into the cabin. I sat down in a hard chair in the front room
and put my hands over my abdomen, which was hurting pretty
bad now. I rocked back and forth for a little bit, though that
didn't make it feel any better. It was like everything hurt from
way deep inside. Mama came in just then and asked me how I
had liked my first day of work and I said I had liked it just fine.

For the next few days, Mama and I spent most of our time
in the cafeteria, taking breaks between meals and then going
back. We'd walk back and forth, not saying anything. There
were still a lot of questions I wanted to ask her, but I didn't
think it was a good idea. Often she seemed to be pondering
something, maybe about Papa or the Littles, and when she got
that sad, dreamy look on her face, I wanted to know what she
was thinking about, but she never said anything that gave her
thoughts away. Sometimes I felt surprised when I looked at
her, because she looked so familiar to me, but she had started
to have a face all her own, as if in the past she had been just
my Mama but was now turning into a separate person. Her
strangeness made me feel lost and nervous, like all the other
new turns things were taking.

I got so I knew every step of the path from our cabin to the
Bunker. After that first day at work, I tried to avoid talking to

Sarah or anyone else, since if there was anything unpleasant to
be said, I didn't want to hear it. Luckily, no one was very talk-
ative. We all had our little jobs and we did them. There must
have been seventy-five people in the kitchen, and it reminded
me of how Fred and I used to watch ant colonies. We'd lie on
the ground outside their hills and feed them crumbs of bread,
and they would come out in lines and take the big heavy
crumbs away like they knew exactly what to do, like they knew
what do to every minute of their lives.

On Sunday morning, I got up at the usual time and worked
breakfast, but after that, it was time for church. Mama and I ran
back home and put on our dresses. She was still wearing brown,
and I felt relieved about that, since it was at least one thing that
was the same as it had always been. Everything seemed so different that I had begun to feel jittery all the time, like the ground
was going to disappear from beneath my feet as I walked.

It was easy to figure out where the church was because
everyone was heading there, streaming down the dirt roads
like flocks of geese. Just beyond the Bunker was a big red brick
building with a round stained glass window above the entrance, and as we neared the front door and the path nar-
rowed, I felt bodies press against me on all sides. Being
wedged between so many strangers reminded me of school,
and how I used to think it was exciting to be around so many
people and to wonder what the new day was going to bring.
But having that feeling now just made me afraid, like a car
might suddenly plow into me at any time. It didn't help that
there were men standing on either side of the front door with
great big machine guns in their hands.

Mama led me to a pew as close to the pulpit as we could
get. The place was packed. People were lined up on all sides of
the room, and I was glad we had gotten to sit, since I was tired

out from being on my feet all week, and my innards still hurt
some. We were probably ten or twelve pews back from the
front row, which was empty, like the seats were being saved for
someone. I wondered who, but then finally a dozen or so girls
around my age or maybe a little older, all of them with big
round stomachs sticking out in front of them, pushed their
way to the front of the room and sat there.

Then the choir at the side of the room began to sing. They
had a little band accompanying them, with an electric guitar
and some drums. I was expecting to hear one of the songs I
knew, like "The Temple of the One," but they were playing
what sounded like the kind of music I used to hear at the bowling alley, and the choir sang something about seven angels
with seven trumpets. When they sang the part about the trumpets, the guitarist took out a horn and started to blow. He
didn't play very well, but it still sent shivers down my spine. As
the trumpet sounded, Cyrus came out from behind a curtain
on the side of the church, and everyone started to shout things
like "Praise the Lord" and "Amen." I had never heard people
shout in church before, though I had seen it on TV, and I
started to feel strange, as strange as I had felt at the church
Alice took me to.

Cyrus walked to the front of the choir, in a long white robe
with red and purple embroidery on the front. When he
reached the pulpit, suddenly the band stopped and everyone
hushed. He leaned into a microphone and said, "It's morning,
my brethren." It had gotten so quiet in the room that his voice
was as startling as a gunshot.

"It's morning," everyone called back to him, like this was
some kind of greeting.

"My children," he went on, his voice getting louder as he
raised his arms in the air. "We have come to the end of time.

The great controversy is about to end, and we will be anew in the world victorious. We have unlocked the secrets of Daniel, Isaiah, and Joe, and we are ready to begin the millennial order. Are you with me, hallelujah?" And everybody shouted some more.

Cyrus started talking again, and some of the things he said sounded familiar to me. He talked for a while about the seven seals, and of course I knew all about them, though when I was little I had thought for a while that they were seals like the animal, which we had learned about from Mama. He talked about angels, hail, and locusts, things I had grown up hearing about, and I started to feel a little more at home. Then he said that no one had ever made it past the fifth seal, that even his great predecessors had not managed to crack the sixth one, but that we were on the verge of it. We knew when the earthquake would come—it would come on April 15, just as predicted through the ages. I listened to this feeling just a little bit sad about all the predictions I had heard in the past and how sure everyone had been about them. "The sun will be black as sackcloth, the full moon will be like blood, and the turkeys will cry out to the heavens," Cyrus said, raising his arms again. I found myself hoping that for once someone would be right about something.

The sermon went on like that for a while, and then the choir sang a few more songs. Then Cyrus asked us to come down and receive the sacred seal. Row by row, we filed down to the front, where Cyrus put a dab of something red on our foreheads. I thought it was probably wine, but later someone told me it was turkey blood. When he saw me, he smiled like he remembered who I was.

As we walked out of the church, a few of the girls with big stomachs squeezed past me, giggling and looking important. I asked Mama why there were so many pregnant women around, but she didn't answer me. We went down to the Bunker and made everybody a late lunch, since by now it was nearly two. Cyrus had gone on talking about the seals for a long time, though he never really got to the seventh one. I figured he'd talk about it some other time.

As I worked, I thought about how odd it had felt being in church again. I thought of all the times I had wished I could be in church, and now that I was there, it was both familiar and terribly foreign. All the colors were wrong, and there were too many people, but some of the words were the ones I knew, words I had been hearing all my life. I used to love them, but now I had to admit that they sounded different to me. Maybe because I had actually been in my own accident, now suddenly all those things, earthquakes and mountains of fire and eagles crying "Woe, woe," seemed real. They seemed like they would hurt. I had always thought of death as a beautiful thing, but now I knew something I had not known when my brothers died, I knew how your body just goes dark inside as death starts to spread through you. It wasn't even the pain that I found scary, but that darkness. I thought of Dr. Greenberg in his white coat, and it was the first time I had thought about anyone from back there in some days, because I generally wouldn't let myself. But today I could just about see Dr. Greenberg in my mind like he was standing right in front of me, with his arm around Alice and a little smile because I was doing so well. Right then it came to me that I wanted to grow up and be a doctor like him, but then I thought no, of course I can't do that, I'm not even in school anymore.

As I considered this, my mind started to get all confused. Whenever I thought about what I was doing now, or what I might do for the rest of my life, I felt like I was trying to see the future in a crystal ball like the witch had in the video of *The Wizard of Oz* that Heather and I had rented. But whenever I looked, it was all cloudy, and if I tried too hard, all I would see was those winged monkeys carrying Dorothy through the sky.

For the next few days, time passed in a blur while I was running around in the kitchen, and I liked the blurriness, it made me feel like I was spinning and couldn't see anything, like my brothers and I used to do when we were little, just turn around and around and then fall down on the floor while everything kept on whirling in circles. On Thursday, Mama and I finished lunch but instead of going back to our cabin, she said she was supposed to take me back up to see Cyrus again. I went into the ladies' room and washed my hands and splashed water on my face, which had a tendency to get a bit greasy from the grill. My hair looked all flat from being inside a hair net but I fluffed it up a little the way Heather used to do for me. I looked in the mirror and saw that I still looked grubby and dull, but I figured there was nothing I could do about it, so I came back out and found Mama talking to some tall man with a mustache. I waited for her to introduce me to him, but she didn't, and we walked up through the trees to Cyrus's house.

When we walked in the front door, I looked off to the side and noticed a living room with a bunch of the same pregnant girls I had seen at church sitting around on couches, drinking Cokes. Mama led me up the stairs and through the double doors, and there was Cyrus, on his throne. This time he was wearing a long white shirt that was almost like a robe, and when I got close enough, I could see that there were tiny purple stars all over it. I stepped up to him and said hello. He looked over at Mama, and she nodded at him and left the room. I just stood there waiting for him to say something.

"I wanted to know how you were getting on," he said,

standing up and leading me over to a leather couch on the side of the room.

"I'm very well, thank you," I said. We sat down, and he picked up one of my hands and held it.

"I know you've been through a lot of trials, little girl, and we want to make everything easier for you here. We want you to be comfortable in your mind so you can do the holy work."

"Oh, I like it here just fine," I said. "I'm working hard in the kitchen, and everything is just fine. Just fine," I said again. I noticed that my palm was starting to sweat and I wanted to take it back from him and wipe it off on my leg, but I couldn't figure out how to do that without just yanking it away and seeming rude. He started stroking my arm, and that just made it sweat worse. Then he leaned over and kissed me right on the mouth, grabbing my shoulders, as if to keep me from getting up and running away.

I was so shocked, I didn't know what to do. I just sat there with my mouth hanging open like a fish, not really kissing back, since I didn't really know how, though I had seen it enough on TV, but just letting him rub his tongue all around my teeth and the insides of my lips. One of his hands was rubbing my arm, up and down, making a wider motion that seemed to take in my whole body at once, and then his other hand landed on my knee. I was wearing heavy black tights, and his hand slid along my leg smoothly, like an ice skater. I started to relax into the whole thing, and in my mind I was seeing how we would throw grease and margarine on the grill and it would melt and start swirling around, and that was how I felt, like melting grease. But then suddenly, he stopped and pulled his face away. I was still sitting there with my mouth open, too surprised to do anything but gape.

"Has a man ever done that to you before, Catherine?" Cyrus asked, smiling at me. His wire-rimmed glasses had gotten a little steamed up, and it made his eyes look like they were far away.

For a second I wondered who he was talking to, but then I said, "No, sir."

"Or a boy," he added, like he was correcting himself.

"No one. Sir."

"You can call me Cyrus." He ran his hand through my hair, greasy though it was, and smiled at me some more.

Now that just beats all, I thought, a preacher who kisses people and has them call him by his first name.

"How are your injuries now?" he asked.

"My injuries?"

"From your accident. How are your insides? Healing well?"

I was about to say that I felt fine, but that wasn't quite true, especially now, since being here next to Cyrus was churning things up again, and then something clicked in my mind, something that was much smarter than I felt at the moment, and I said, "It hurts a lot inside. In my female parts. Cyrus."

He drew back a little, patted me on the head, and said, "Well, we'd better give you time to heal, then." He stood up, took my hand, and pulled me to my feet. "I want you to come back and see me soon. When you're better."

"Oh, I will," I said, feeling giddy.

"Bukulahara," he said.

"Bukulahara," I said back to him, or something like that anyway.

He opened the door and led me to the staircase, where a man with a gun came and walked me down to the living room. I found Mama sitting there waiting for me next to all the pregnant girls. They were wearing frilly flowered dresses, and some of them had their hair tied up in purple hair ribbons. As we walked down the hill through the trees, Mama didn't ask me anything about what Cyrus and I had talked about, but she seemed sad, and I thought well, jumping Jehosophat, she knows.

From that moment on, everything seemed all funny, like when Cyrus kissed me my brain began to melt and just stayed that way, oily and slow, and the oil spread over everything the way it would on a window, so you couldn't quite see out of it anymore. I walked around looking as normal as a piece of pie, but on the inside, I was lurching around, bumping into a million things, all of them different. I would stand behind the grill, scraping it every now and then, and find myself thinking about the kiss, and it would seem to pierce me all the way from my mouth to my toes, passing through a lot of places in between, and then I'd feel like I couldn't wait until Sunday when I would sit in the pew again and watch Cyrus, and maybe have him splash whatever that was on my forehead again. But then other parts of me were angry. I was angry at my mother for bringing me there and leaving me alone with him, knowing what might happen. I was angry at Cyrus, and at myself for feeling the way I felt when he kissed me. I even felt angry at Alice for letting me go away to a place like this, where everything seemed inside-out and upside-down. I found myself being angry at Dylan Magnuson for driving his car into me, though I had tried hard to turn the other cheek, since I saw on the news that he was probably crazy and couldn't help himself, but still, one day when I was standing at the grill I found myself scraping it extra hard, clenching my teeth and pounding on it until Jeff said, "Hey, honey, ease up on that thing."

Well, days passed like this, and then Sunday rolled around again. I put on the prettiest dress I could find, though I wished I'd had one of the really nice ones Alice had bought me, and Mama and I went off to church. It was a beautiful sunny day, truly spring now, and the mountains around us were all waking up with green, and the air smelled good, like there was suddenly life in it. We arrived early enough to get a seat pretty close to Cyrus, and at one point during the sermon I thought he saw me. I smiled at him just in case, but then I felt stupid.

This time he was talking about the seventh seal. He talked about the silence of heaven, the hail, fire, and blood, and the stars dropping down from the sky, and the turkeys crying out for justice. He said, "Fallen, fallen is Babylon the great," and again he mentioned April 15. I liked it when he talked about things that were familiar and I jumped on those things when I heard them and tried to feel like everything was the same as it had always been. But this April 15 business sounded just like the Big Cat to me, and we all know how that turned out. I was still hoping for life to go back to normal, and the last thing in the world I needed was another false apocalypse.

On the way out of church, Mama took me to the side door and we said hello to Cyrus. It seemed funny to see him after having been alone with him. In church he was like a different person—he seemed much taller and grander, like a rock star or the president. I said hello and he put his hand on my shoulder again. I didn't want him to remove it, but he did, and we left, and afterward, while I was frying a bunch of lunch stuff on the grill, I felt all grumpy and bad, like now I was going to have to wait another whole week before life became interesting again. At the same time, part of me hoped that Mama would not get it into her head to take me up to see him again during the week, since who knows what might happen.

But the week just dragged on, and we didn't visit Cyrus. I was partly relieved and partly irritated. Everything seemed flat and ordinary. Sometimes I'd see Cyrus's car drive past, a brown Mercedes, and I would look up and feel excited for a moment, but then I wouldn't even wave at him like everybody else was doing, since what was the point, he was going away in a car. I found myself imagining that he would pull up beside me, stop, open the door, and ask me to get in with him, and we would drive away somewhere, but he didn't. I'd watch his car wind away down the road, past fields full of turkeys with the hazy purple mountains behind them.

Finally it was Sunday, and I made Mama leave for church even earlier than usual so we would be closer to the front. We made it into the fourth row, not too far behind all the pregnant girls, who were still whispering and giggling together. Cyrus came out from behind the curtain and started talking, but this time it wasn't so much a sermon as a meeting. Some other men got up and started talking about what was going to happen on the fifteenth.

Unlike Cyrus, who made the day seem dreamlike and glorious, they made it sound like it was going to be hard, and there wasn't going to be much fun in it. One man held up a big map of the whole property. The Bunker was circled in red, and he said that was where we were going to have the standoff. He said we had enough supplies for a year stored in the warehouses. I had been to the warehouses in the second cellar beneath the kitchen and I knew this was true. He said we were hoping it wouldn't take a whole year, but it might, and we had to be prepared to live that way the whole time. He said the Bunker was just about readied up, and now we just had to wait.

Cyrus thanked him and then got up and said a bunch more stuff about olive trees and lampstands, lions and dragons, moons and serpents. Then we all went down and he put the seal on our foreheads, and this time he was so busy blessing everybody and laying his hands on them that when he put his hands on my shoulders, he didn't even seem to recognize me and just stared right through me. As we walked away up the aisle, I found myself looking back at him and thinking how weird it was that I had ever been close to him, that his tongue had hunted all around my mouth like it was looking for something. I felt sad and backwards, like I was going in the wrong direction, and I had to practically drag myself out of the church and away from him. Mama and I walked over to the kitchen and went back to work, and I tried to think about other things for a while.

When lunch was over, I noticed Mama talking to the man with the mustache again, so I started walking home alone. Sarah caught up with me and started chattering away about this and that. She said she was excited about the fifteenth, and that everyone was, it was what we had all been waiting on for so long. I guessed that her former church had never had to go through any Big Cats. She asked if I was all packed up, and I said no, and she said I had better get my suitcase together, that we were only allowed one, and that I should remember to bring a lot of underwear because we weren't going to get to wash much. I thought to myself that not washing was not going to be good for Sarah's pimples, but I held my tongue.

"Your mama has a new boyfriend," she said. "That mustache man."

"No she doesn't," I said, trying to walk faster to get away from her.

As we reached my cabin, she gave me a sideways look and asked me if I had met Cyrus yet. I said I had, and asked why. She said he always wanted to meet the new girls, especially if they were blond. I said I wasn't really blond, that my hair was more of a light brown, but she said I was blond enough for Cyrus. "They say it's a divine gift if you have relations with him," she said, giving me a sly smile like she was checking to see if I already had. I didn't say anything. "I went to meet him one day, but nothing happened," she said. We were standing outside my cabin, and she kicked a little stone with her shoe. "I think he's really good-looking, don't you?" I still didn't say anything, and she laughed a bit, like she had discovered my secret, and she tapped me on the shoulder and said, "You be careful now. When we're all in the Bunker, why, I guess you'll find out then what it's all about."

"What what is all about?" I asked, but she skipped away like a six-year-old. I felt an awful lot older than that all of a sudden. I went into the cabin, sat down in the straight chair in the living room, and sank my head in my hands. My head felt as heavy as a boulder, and my hands felt little and weak like I could barely hold them up. Mama came in then and I had to pull myself together and act normal, but it wasn't easy. I just felt strange and miserable, and I didn't know why.

"We need to get ready," Mama said. She bustled around the cabin as if it was going to take hours to pack everything up when the fact was, neither of us had much stuff. I didn't know where the rest of her belongings were, but alls I had was the suitcase I'd brought from Alice's, and I didn't really care about anything except for my cow pajamas. All the other things I'd really liked, my new clothes and my stuffed dog and my bowling ball and the Oz books, I had left behind. I had finished my medicine two weeks ago. There was truly nothing I wanted, but I went into the bedroom and filled the suitcase back up again. It looked exactly as it had when I arrived.

For next few days, we cleaned the cabin so much that even the walls glittered, and we washed our clothes down in the laundry room in the Bunker, though they were already clean. We made everything just so, in between working three meals a day, and when we were finished, we did it all again. It seemed like we needed to stay busy, maybe to keep from being nervous. You could tell something was going to happen, and happen soon. Everyone in the cafeteria seemed edgy and keyed-up, and when someone said something funny, everybody laughed extra hard, loud laughs that sounded like machine gun fire to me, but then I was sensitive about loud noises ever since the accident, which still roared in my head sometimes. "I guess we won't be paying no taxes this year," somebody said, and everyone laughed some more.

The moment I opened my eyes on the morning of April 14, things felt different. Mama and I got up and went to work in the kitchen, and while the same amount of cooking went on, the whole time we were serving up the food, men were carrying big boxes past us and going down into the lower floors to the warehouses, and the cafeteria seemed more crowded and frantic than ever. People were wolfing down turkey sausage and eggs like it was their last meal, and men were strolling around with machine guns cradled in their arms like babies. In the corner at a long table, some women were teaching a group of children to duck under the table when they gave the signal. Most of the children were ducking like it was a really fun game, but some of the littler ones looked frightened.

Lunch was pretty much the same way as breakfast, but there were even more men with boxes. Truckloads of supplies were going into the cellars, and by midafternoon, it seemed like every man had a gun, and even some of the older boys. As I was walking back to the cabin alone, I saw the brown Mercedes coming up the road from the front gate. I neatened my hair a little and sucked in my cheeks the way Heather had told me models do. As the car passed me, it slowed to a stop and the back window rolled down. "Catherine, isn't it?" Cyrus said. I nodded. I felt like I couldn't speak. "Are you ready for the great day, little girl?" I nodded again. His face looked big in the window, almost like a dog's. "I want you to come to me tonight. Tell Ed at the front to let you in." He wrote something on a scrap of paper and handed it to me. It just said, "Permission granted, Cyrus." I said I would, and he drove off without even saying good-bye, or "Bukulahara." I still had no idea what that meant and decided I would have to ask someone.

When I got back to the cabin, I put the piece of paper in my suitcase and sat down. I felt a little weak, maybe from working so hard without eating much. We always had our meals at the end of the shift, and sometimes by then I was so tired of the sight of whatever we had been serving, turkey chili or turkey burgers or turkey tetrazzini, that I didn't want any. While I was sitting there, Mama came in, and I debated whether to tell her about Cyrus or not. Then I thought, well, I better let her know, since things could get pretty complicated around here soon. I took the paper out of my suitcase again and showed it to her. She looked at it and leaned against the cabinet, like Cyrus's message had blown her over, then shook her head. "Do you understand all this, Mary Fred?" she asked. She still called me Mary Fred, though a lot of people had started calling me Catherine. Her face looked serious and kind of gray. "You understand what he wants from you?"

"I think so, ma'am," I said. "But I always thought—"

"This is one of the differences—" She stopped as if uncertain about how to continue.

I waited, not saying anything.

"It's not that they don't accept the teachings of Fred here," she went on, not looking at me, almost like she was just talking to herself. "They accept that Fred was a true prophet. But they believe that there were other prophets that came after him. Cyrus is just the last one in a long line. So they believe—"

"I know," I said. "Someone told me. I understand."

"If Cyrus is really a prophet," she said, walking over to the window and looking out, "then it's true what they say. His physical, uh, love is divine."

Neither of us said the words "but what if he isn't." They just hung in the air.

Mama walked over to me and put her hands on my shoulders, just where Cyrus had put his, though of course they felt much different. "I don't know what to tell you, Mary Fred. You're a big girl now. You're sixteen. I wasn't much older than that when I married your father. I guess this is a decision you have to make for yourself."

Mama had never said anything like this to me before. All my life everyone had told me what to do, and now when I really needed them to, no one was telling me anything, except Cyrus. I was holding the piece of paper in my curled fingers like it was something precious, and then I knew exactly what I was going to do, I was going to go and do whatever it was he wanted, because I guessed he was the head of our church now, and it seemed like people thought he was more important than Fred himself, so that meant I ought to do whatever he said. Besides, all the warm parts of me were whooshing around, sending me there like a wind.

"We need to get ready and take our things to the Bunker," Mama said, walking away and changing the subject. "We need to settle in there tonight. It all begins tomorrow morning and they want everyone to be ready." She looked back at me and said in a soft voice that didn't sound like her own, "You might want to have a bath first."

As I lay in the bathtub, I looked over my body. It was long and blue-white under the water. The scar from my surgery curved like a lightning bolt across my abdomen. It was still red in the middle and white along the edges, and the skin was still puckered. I ran my hand along it, then lightly touched myself below there, where my hair floated on the surface of the water. I sank under the water until it covered my face, then rose up again. I washed my hair with baby shampoo, rinsed it under water, soaped my whole body extra hard, rinsed, and stepped out on the bathmat. There was a mirror on the wall, which still seemed odd to me. It was clouded with steam, and all I could see in it was a strange blurred naked woman, someone I didn't know.

Mama and I walked to the Bunker without saying much, carrying our suitcases. After a little while, I asked her what "Bukulahara" meant, and she said she didn't know, exactly, but that Cyrus had heard it in a vision, and everyone here said it instead of good-bye. "He says it's Chinese," she told me. There were other questions I wanted to ask her, but she seemed to be in her fog again, and I didn't know how to ask them anyway. They all seemed to be the biggest questions in the world, but I guessed that I was just going to have to find out the answers for myself.

When we got to the Bunker, men with guns directed us to a huge room in the first cellar. It was already packed with women, and there were a lot of cots, though it was clear that most people were going to have to sleep on the floor on mats and in sleeping bags. There were a bunch of little kids, too— evidently this was a room just for women and children. I had seen the men getting everything ready on the other end of the floor, past the first warehouse, when I went for supplies, and I guessed that their rooms were down there.

Everyone was making themselves at home in their little corners, putting dolls on the cots, which seemed odd, since I had never been allowed to have dolls, and tacking up photographs of Cyrus. Some of the little kids had drawn pictures of turkeys, and they were putting those up too. People were hanging bunches of turkey feathers tied together with purple yarn in the corners of the room, for good luck. I put my suitcase down, and Mama and I went up to the kitchen and worked the dinner shift. She stayed and had some stew, but I couldn't eat a bite. I was carrying the note from Cyrus in the pocket of my dress. My stomach was all in knots, and I didn't know what to do, or even where to go, since I didn't know where Cyrus was.

At about nine, a man with a gun started to send everybody downstairs. He said it would be lights out soon, and we needed to hurry. I stood there for a moment. Then I took the note out of my pocket and showed it to him. He gave me a look that I didn't much like and called on another man. "She goes to Cyrus," he said, and the other man gave me the same look, then led me down a long corridor toward the back of the building and up some stairs to a part of the Bunker I had not known was there. Another man with a gun was standing outside a heavy wooden door, and I showed him the note. He opened the door and motioned me to go through it. I hesitated, and for a moment I wanted to turn around and run, but then I felt myself entering the doorway as if I had suddenly sprouted wings on my heels and they were bearing me away.

When I got inside, it looked as if I wasn't in the Bunker anymore, but in a fancy hotel, or maybe even a palace. I wandered through a small waiting area, with new-looking red velvet couches on either side, and entered through some wooden double doors that led into a larger room with purple fabric on all the walls, and no windows. There was no furniture except for Cyrus's throne at the back of the room, but he wasn't in it. Another man with a gun leaned against the back wall, and I started to show him my note, but he waved me into another room to the left. It was smaller, but full of people, a few more armed men but mostly a lot of girls, blondes, lounging on leather couches that lined the walls, and chatting. Some of them were the pregnant girls I had seen in the church. No one even looked at me as I entered.

I stopped walking and just stood there, and suddenly I was terribly afraid. I turned around and looked behind me, wondering how I could leave without anybody knowing I'd been there, but at that moment, Cyrus appeared. A blond girl followed behind him, but I barely noticed her, since I was just looking at him. His braid hung over his shoulder, and he was wearing a purple T-shirt and blue jeans. His feet were bare. He saw me and started walking in my direction, and when his eyes landed on me, blurry behind his wire-rimmed glasses, they froze me to that spot. I stood there wanting to move, maybe even to run, but was unable to do anything but stare back at him. "Catherine," he said, and the way he said my name, or whosever name it was, made me feel grand and important. He came forward and took my hand, and began to lead me back into the room he had just come from. I followed him past the blond girls, who barely seemed to take any notice of me, and through the doorway. He turned around and closed the door. I stopped breathing, in fact I tried to take a breath but my lungs had locked up and were just tiny little things that no air would fit in.

In front of me was the most enormous bed I had ever seen. It took up half of the room, and was covered with messy purple sheets. On either side of the bed were couches. They were orange brocade, and they clashed with the draperies, which were purple too. Cyrus, still holding my hand, led me over to the bed and motioned for me to sit down. I kept waiting for him to say something, like that he was glad to see me, but he positioned himself next to me, and started to unzip my dress. It was one of the brown dresses I'd had for years, and the metal zipper didn't work very well, so he had to use both hands and struggle a bit. I was still not breathing. He yanked on my dress and I had to move so he could slide it over my head. He laid it on the edge of the bed, but it slipped down onto the floor. We both watched it fall. Then he looked at me. I was wearing the newest-looking white bra I could find and white panties, and I found myself again wishing I had kept some of my nice pink underwear.

"You understand what your duty to me is, don't you?" he said, looking at my body, not me. I had never felt before that my body and I were two separate beings, but his look made me feel like my head had become completely detached from the rest of me.

"Yes, sir, I think so," I said. But suddenly the head part of me, which hadn't really been operating very well up to now, said loudly to the body part of me, *No, wait, I don't understand, I don't understand at all.*

"This is an important moment in history, Catherine, and you are part of it. We are going to transcend earthly life and begin the world again. We are a race of fresh beings. This is your moment, Catherine. This is the moment your real life begins. Are you ready for that?"

I tried to answer but I couldn't—my voice wouldn't come. I just sat there staring at him as he unfastened my bra. I covered my breasts with my arms, but he moved them away and said, "Very nice," like he was looking at something in a store. He motioned for me to lay my head down on the pillows, and as I moved, he slid my underpants off me so I was lying there stark naked in front of him. In the strange new parts of my mind, I had seen this moment before, but what I hadn't known was that instead of feeling like it was magical or full of glory, as it always was in those glimmers, I was so scared, and so unable to breathe, that there was nothing happy in it at all. I was just cold and revealed and alone.

Cyrus lay on top of me, his clothes still on, and his mouth moved along my neck. His face was scratchy, like he needed a shave, and his body felt big and lumpy. It felt so foreign and unnatural to have such a heavy man on top of me, as heavy as a thousand bricks. From this close up, he looked old. There were tiny wrinkles in his skin, and his braid flapped against my neck like a rope. I kind of hoped that he would kiss me again, since that at least had felt good before, but his mouth just stayed on my neck. Then he rolled off me and ran his hand along my stomach. "You had a nasty wound here, didn't you?" he said, tracing my scar.

"It still hurts," I said. "It hurts a lot. When you lay on me, that hurt."

"I'll try not to hurt you," he said, but as if it didn't really matter to him. There was something about the lack of concern in his voice that made me feel even stranger, like I was dreaming or going crazy.

"And they told me," I said, I don't know why, maybe because I was talking from inside a dream, "they told me I could never have any children. That there was something wrong with my insides. They got sewn up together the wrong way or something."

Cyrus snatched his hand away and stared at my stomach as if there was something completely disgusting about what I had just said. The strangest thing was, I had told him this lie to get him to stop, to go away and leave me be, but when he took his hand away, I just wanted him to put it back. "Is that true?" he said, running his fingertips along my scar again, like he had just noticed it.

"Yes, sir. They said everything had been all ripped up. Like an explosion went through me."

He shook his head and then leaned on one elbow, staring into my face. "That's sad, Catherine, that's just sad." And then he started to talk to me about angels and clowns, about how my problem was that I had been all caught up in the fifth seal, and that now, in the end time, all manner of things would occur like this, unnatural things where the weasel would eat the eagle, and the ocean would be on fire. "I mean, look at that lake in Ohio," he said, and went on about the spirit with the crown and sickle, and the marsh full of onions, and the rainbow made of sobbing clouds. Some of these images were familiar to me, as familiar as bread, but others were weird and unsettling. He talked about snakes hanging from the ceiling, and babies smoking cigars. "Women are whores," he said, in a matter-of-fact voice like he was talking about what he wanted for lunch. "They're all whores in the end time. But someone like you, Catherine, why, you're the bride of the Lamb. You're the golden city. You're pure and undefiled." He seemed more interested in me now, like he was picking up steam. "Nothing can spoil you, girl. You're the crystal jewel." Then he moved over, stood up, and walked out of the room.

I lay there for a while, not even breathing. Everything in me ached, partly because his weight really had hurt me, and partly because I wanted him to come back. It seemed unfair that a body and mind could be so muddy and cloudy like an old pond. I felt incredibly tired, like I had been awake for days, for weeks, and my body sank into the bed like I was falling into the water. As I fell, I soared through wet space. Water surged and lapped around me, and as I looked down to see where I was falling to, way far down below me, I could see the earth, a tiny blue ball in the water that was getting larger and larger. As

I fell closer to it and could see it better, though, I could see that it wasn't a real ball of rock at all, but a bunch of bags of garbage that were all hanging together somehow, plastic sacks of moldy bread, someone's old bags of lunch, and some heads of brown iceberg lettuce, and just as I got really close and was about to land on it, the whole thing exploded, blowing apart into a million pieces. Garbage flew into the air in all directions, flying past me like escaping wild birds.

I opened my eyes. It was dark, and I was still lying in the huge bed with no clothes on. The room had gotten cold, and I had rolled myself into a ball to try to keep warm. As my eyes began to focus, I heard a noise to my right. I turned my head and looked over. A streak of light came in from the door, which was open a crack, and fell across the bed. Two naked people lay beside me, moving together, one on top of the other. I recognized one of the little blond girls I had seen outside, though I couldn't tell which one it was, and on top of her, Cyrus flashed like a running horse, his long bare back curving above her. Sounds were coming from them, slapping and sucking sounds, moans, and breathing. I rolled over sideways so I could get a better look at them. They didn't seem to notice me. I couldn't see Cyrus's face, but the girl's mouth was open and her eyes were closed, and she looked like she was dying, but then her eyes fluttered open for a moment, like butterflies, and she smiled upward a little, then closed them again. This is it, I thought. This is the mystery itself, and I am watching it. I felt very powerful suddenly, like I was looking down from the other world on the little beings here on earth, at how small they were, and how like animals. There was nothing beautiful about it, but it interested me. I waited, watching them, until I was quite sure they had no idea I was there at all.

Then I slid out of the bed. As I crawled along the dark floor and found my dress, I saw their naked bodies in my mind, and it was some days before I was able to make the image go away. I put my dress on silently, not even zipping it in case that made noise, and I crept on my hands and knees to the door. It was still open a crack, and as I got there, I eased it open so I could pass through it. In the living room, the men with guns were asleep on couches, and none of the pregnant girls were there anymore. When I passed the men, I stood up and tiptoed to the door. I smoothed my hair, zipped up my dress, opened the door, and stepped out into the dark hallway.

In the women's room, all the lights were out, and the room was covered from back to front with sleeping bodies, women and kids flopped all over the place. I went to my mat, but someone was on it. Mama was sleeping on a mat right nearby. I wanted to crawl in next to her, but there wouldn't have been room, since there were people on either side of her, so I lay down on a mat I found on the other side of the room and tried to sleep, but whenever I closed my eyes, I saw them, Cyrus and the girl, naked and thrashing like fish beside me.

I guess I must have fallen asleep, finally, because when the lights went on, I couldn't remember where I was. Everyone rose, groaning and wiping their eyes, and soon the little kids were running around the room, all excited because it was finally April 15.

Mama looked surprised to see me. "But Mary Fred," she said. "I thought you were—"

"I had to leave," I said. "Things weren't exactly what I expected."

"They never are," Mama said, which surprised me. She stared down at the floor for a second, then touched my arm and said, "Are you all right?"

I told her I was just fine, and that there was nothing to worry about.

"Did you—"

I shook my head.

Tears filled her eyes and she took my hand. I had never seen Mama cry, not even when my brothers died, and I gave a little gasp of horror. "It just doesn't feel right," she said in a whisper. "I thought it was the right thing, I truly did, but now—"

Just then a man came into the room carrying a machine gun and told us that it was time to assemble in the main hall. Everyone quickly finished getting dressed and we all dashed there, traveling up the stairs in a crush, crowding into the big meeting room in the west wing of the Bunker. At the front of the room was a stage with a pulpit on it, and I saw Cyrus come in from a side entrance. I was far enough toward the back of the room that he couldn't see me, but I could see him. He didn't look like the same person I had been with last night, in fact he didn't look familiar at all. A white robe with red and purple trim covered him, and he had let his braided ponytail loose so his wrinkled hair spread across his shoulders. He raised his hands like he was blessing us and said a little prayer. Then he picked up a cell phone from behind the pulpit and dialed.

"This is the seventh seal," he said into the phone. He was reading off a little index card. "We are armed, and we are ready. We are dreaming of Golgotha. Oh, send us the soldiers of eternity. We are your sons and daughters." He went on talking on the phone, giving directions to where we were, and explaining more about the seals, and turkeys, and the end time, and the next world, and we all crowded toward him, our legs getting tired from standing, listening while he talked. After a while, maybe forty-five minutes, we started to hear sirens, at first just a few and then lots of them. Loud voices began to crackle from outside, and when Cyrus heard them, he raised his arms again, the cell phone still in one hand like it was some kind of magic wand, and smiled like he just couldn't be happier.

The crowd went wild. Everyone started clapping their hands, singing, stomping their feet, and shouting hallelujah and even a few bukulaharas. Some pushed toward the front, as if they were trying to get closer to Cyrus, but men with machine guns formed a line in front of him to keep people from getting too near. I started backing away and let the people surge forward on either side of me. I looked over at Mama and noticed that she was backing away too. She took my hand and pulled me so we were still facing the front but our feet were walking in the wrong direction. "Baby girl," she said, putting an arm around me. "I can't let you do this." I could see that she was starting to cry again. "I just can't watch another one of my children—" I didn't catch the end of the sentence, and it was so loud in the room that I could barely hear her at all, but I knew what she was saying. I felt her put something into my hand, and when I looked at it I saw it was a crumpled bunch of money. She looked at me and started saying something else, but the yelling and singing drowned it out, and I just watched her lips move, and her eyes looked at me all wild and sad, the way they had looked when she stood over each of my brothers, praying. She put her arms around me and pulled me very close, and as she held me, she shouted into my ear, "The second warehouse. Downstairs. There's a door there."

I told her I wasn't going anywhere without her, but she said she couldn't leave yet or someone would notice us, she would get out later and come find me. I tried to ask her how she would get out, and what she would do to find me, but as the crowd broke into a loud chorus of some song I'd never heard before, she gave me a shove and her eyes were begging me to go on and run. I looked back at her for a moment, and then I slid past all the hot bodies pounding against me, and darted into the kitchen. I walked past the wooden counter where Mama had done all her prep work, and through the doorway that led down the stairs into the cellars.

There were no guards at the door to the first cellar—they were all upstairs, I guessed—and I just kept on at a slow, steady pace, like I had all the time in the world. If anyone stopped me, I was going to say I was looking for some turkey sausages for breakfast, that we were out of them upstairs, but no one saw me as I sneaked down the dark hallway and into the huge high-ceilinged room that was full of supplies, brown bags of potatoes and carrots, boxes and boxes of canned vegetables, cases of matches and tanks of propane. I went through a doorway and down some stairs into the second cellar, into another warehouse full of barrels and more boxes, and a whole wall of cases of Coca-Cola. I kept walking until I was sure there was no one else in the room, and then I started running.

At first I couldn't find the door to the outside. It was so dark in that corner of the room that when I did finally get to it, I could barely see it, and I sort of stumbled into the doorway. I pushed on the big metal bar that locked the door, but it wouldn't move. I pushed on it again, but nothing happened. I started struggling with it, getting frantic. I could hear sirens outside, and the loud, crackling voices, and mixed in with them, I thought I could make out some singing. The door still wouldn't open, and I began pounding on it and trying not to scream. Finally as I threw myself against the bar, it slid to the side with a scraping sound. I shoved the door open and looked out through it, but instead of seeing the daylight, I saw nothing but darkness.

I ran back across the warehouse and grabbed a few little boxes of matches, then returned to the dark doorway. I struck a match and held it up until it started to burn my fingers. Through the threshold, I could see a long, black passageway with dirt walls that looked wet and slimy. I couldn't see where it ended, and for a moment I thought about just running back upstairs, but then I thought of Cyrus, and the look on Mama's face, and I figured, well, I guess there's really only one way to go. I stepped through the opening, holding another lit match, and let the big door fall closed. It shut with a dull thump and then I heard the lock catch behind me.

The matches burned my fingertips every few seconds as I inched my way along the tunnel. In the flickering light, I could see that it twisted and sloped downward a bit, and for a moment I was afraid I was going to end up in the center of the earth, and that then it would blow apart like in my dream of the exploding garbage, but after a few minutes the path seemed to right itself and go back up again. I trailed one hand along the muddy wall, holding lit matches in my other hand. The money Mama had given me was still stuffed in my pocket. It was cold in the tunnel, and I wished I had brought a sweater, or put on some tights or something. I moved as fast as I could, but a couple of times I slipped on the wet ground and almost fell. All I could do was move slowly and carefully, one step at a time. After a while, I ran out of matches, and I had to just inch forward, holding on to the wall, taking tiny little steps. I could hear dripping sounds, and I thought again about my dream of all that water. The tunnel had an interesting smell, like the smell of the earth itself, a rich, clay-like smell, like I was inhaling the core of everything.

I guess I must have been crying, because my face felt wet and warm, and every so often I'd make a little sobbing sound. I was getting really tired, and my insides started to ache, and I thought of just lying down on the ground and going to sleep, just staying there for the rest of my life. I didn't know if there was any air in the tunnel, and that seemed okay, since I didn't really need air, did I, I could breathe in water, or at least I could in the dream. I think I was getting a little confused from all the darkness, and just when I thought I wasn't going to be able to go any farther, that I was going to have to lie down right there and melt into the earth, the light in the tunnel started to change—I began to be able to see things, like the outline of the walls, and as I rounded a corner, I saw that there was a little hatch of light coming from above me. My foot bumped into something, a wooden crate I think it was, and I found that if I stood on it, I could reach the ceiling of the tunnel where the light was. I pushed on it and a panel moved aside, and through it I could see the sky. I stood on the box and hoisted myself up. It was hard, since the opening was pretty far above me, but I got a foothold on the side of the wall where there seemed to be some steps, and I kicked and pushed and clawed until I was through the hole and standing in the sunlight.

When I looked around, I found that I had gone a lot farther than I thought. I was in the middle of some woods, and the Bunker was far off in the distance, beyond a huge barbed wire fence, completely surrounded by police cars, their lights all flashing. Men in black suits were climbing up the side of the building on ropes, and loudspeakers were blaring. I stood and watched. I knew Mama was inside, and I wanted to run and try to get her out of there, but I knew I couldn't. It was hard to get myself to do it, but after a few minutes, I turned around and ran straight into the woods, away from the Bunker.

There was a path through the trees, though it was kind of overgrown. I was used to running through the woods, since I had spent my whole life at the Outpost playing with my brothers or hunting with Papa or just wandering around. As I ran, I kept expecting Fred or Rickie or Little Freddie to come running out from behind a tree and shoot me with their fingers, the way they always did, but I didn't see anyone at all, just the people in my mind. I ran as fast as I could, until the path I was on got so narrow and covered over with leaves that I could hardly see it. The farther I got, the more brush I had to push through, but just as the path was about to disappear altogether, I began to see something flickering past in the distance, between the trees. I headed toward the light and the flickering until I found myself on the side of a highway. For a moment I didn't know what to do, but then I stuck out my thumb, like I had seen someone do in a movie on TV. I hadn't stood there for but a few minutes when a car stopped just past where I was standing. I ran to the window and looked in. The car was a blue Ford, and the driver was a middle-aged man with a kind-looking face. He asked me if I was okay, and I said I was. I must have looked like a mess, and I was shaking. He frowned, like he was concerned. I asked him to take me wherever he was going and said that I needed to get to a bus. He said he was going to Greensboro to see his daughter, and that he didn't mind dropping me off at the bus station.

As we drove, he asked me again how I was, and again I said I was fine. He looked like he didn't believe me, but after a while he started talking to me, telling me about his grand-daughter, who was around my age. He said he was worried about her because she wasn't doing very well in school, she was just hanging around with her friends smoking pot all the time. I told him it was just a phase she was going through, and that if her family stood by her, she would be fine in the end, and that seemed to make him feel better. He asked me if I was cold, since I was still shivering, and I said no, but he told me to put on a rain poncho that he had in the backseat in case of emergencies. I put it on and I did feel a lot better. He said he knew right where the bus station was, on Lee Street. When he dropped me off, he told me to take care of myself, and to keep the poncho, and said God bless you. I said thanks, and God bless him too, even though by this time I had no idea who would ever bless anyone again. But that didn't seem to matter, since it made us both feel better, and when I walked away, I turned back to wave at him and found him waving at me too.

As I walked through the lobby of the bus station, I saw a row of tiny little TVs with a bunch of tired-looking people sitting in front of them. When I glanced at them I could see that on most of the TVs was a picture of the Bunker, with all the police cars still outside it. I wanted to go watch and see what was happening, but I had gotten very good at not letting myself think about stuff, especially since I knew there was nothing I could do about the whole situation but hitchhike back to the Bunker and stand outside it with all the police, waiting for the earthquake, or the heavenly thunder, or the seven angels, or turkeys, or the hail, fire, and blood, whatever it turned out to be. And if it turned out that alls that happened was the police broke down the door and arrested everyone, or set fire to the whole building, Mama would be a lot happier if I was on a bus going someplace else.

I bought a ticket to Washington, D.C., pulling the crumpled bills out of my pocket and counting out forty-two dollars. The money was damp, and my hands were muddy. The cashier told me that the next bus was in twenty minutes, so I just had time to go into the bathroom and freshen up. The bathroom was so dirty I didn't want to touch anything, but I washed the mud off my hands and face and tried to get some of it off my clothes with a wet towel. My hair was messy and I didn't have a comb, or for that matter anything else, but I smoothed it down with water and shook out most of the loose dirt that had fallen on me in the tunnel. Then I walked out and asked a man in a uniform where my bus was. He pointed to a gate, and I went and stood there with a bunch of other people. I was glad I still had the poncho because it was cold in the station, and I still felt chilled to the bone, even though it was a nice spring day. As I passed through the doorway to where the buses were parked, I turned and looked behind me. A big TV hung above a row of seats, and there on the screen, the Bunker was still there, and the police and the men in black were still standing outside it, yelling things through loudspeakers and holding a lot of guns. I turned around and got on the bus.

As we drove, I stared out the window for a while. Everything looked the same, since we were on a highway and it was just like all the other highways I had ever been on. After a while I found I was closing my eyes, but I didn't like what I saw when I started to fall asleep—naked bodies, dragons and serpents, explosions like fireworks, smoke and locusts, horses with human faces, crowns of stars, clusters of holy fire. So I kept myself awake by pinching my arm every so often, and I stared out the window some more as we drove past billboards and shopping malls, and through a city, and past more billboards and shopping malls, until finally I saw the green signs for Washington, D.C.

As I climbed down from the bus, I felt kind of weak and woozy, and I realized I hadn't eaten anything all day so I found a fast-food stand and bought a tuna-fish sandwich. I started eating it as I walked out of the station, but it tasted bad to me, like someone had put poison in it, so I dropped it into a garbage can. Outside the station, it was a bit cool out, and I realized that it was evening and that I had no idea where I was. I still had plenty of money with me, so I went over to a taxi that was waiting at the curb and got in. I told the driver that I needed to go to Mount Pleasant, and he said he could take me for twenty dollars, but that I could easily get the Metro from Union Station. Twenty dollars seemed like an awful lot of money to spend, so I chose the Metro. I followed the signs with the big M on them, bought a ticket in the machine, got on the Red Line, and headed north. When the doors chimed open at Mount Pleasant, I got off, took the escalator down into the station, went outside past a bunch of people selling T-shirts at the curb, and started walking down Laurel Avenue. I walked past the stores that Heather and I had been to a million times, the place we rented our videos, the restaurant where we always saw Uncle Roy and his friends, and I kept walking down Willow Street, then Holly Street, then Maple Avenue. I walked until I saw a pink house with purple trim that no longer looked newly painted. Big bushes full of pink and purple flowers spread across the front of the house, flowers I had never seen because I had never been here at this time of year.

I opened the wooden front gate, which still needed a good nail or two, and climbed up the front steps. I stood on the porch for a few minutes, leaning against the door and looking through the pane of beveled glass in the front door. I could feel my breath going in and out of me, and the door was cold beneath my fingers. I could see them all at the table, but it was getting dark out so they couldn't see me. There were two candles burning in the middle of the table. Alice and Dr. Greenberg sat on one side, and across from them sat Uncle Roy and some dark-haired woman I didn't know, and on the end was Heather. There was still room for me at the table, and I knew that.

I stayed there for a while, watching their mouths moving, saying things I couldn't hear. Then I rang the bell. I saw Alice look surprised, then stand up and walk over to the door, coming closer, her image turning into a sea of diamonds because of the beveled glass, just the way it had when I had first stood there that day with Diane. When she looked out the window and saw me, she jerked the door open as fast as she could, and her mouth opened but at first no words came out, she just stood there staring at me. Then she shouted, "Puffin! Roy! Come here! Look who it is!"

Just before I threw myself into her arms, I heard myself say, "I'm back."

It had taken me a while to get warm. Alice had given me a bunch of the sweaters I'd left there, wrapped the moon and star blanket around me, put me in the armchair in the sitting room, and made me drink some hot soup. I finally stopped shivering, but it wasn't until I was actually lying in bed that I began to feel warm again, being in my room, holding my pink stuffed dog and watching the dark air around me.

Everyone had been so surprised to see me that they couldn't stop touching me, patting me on the arm, and giving me hugs. Heather had cried at first, but soon she was making jokes again and seemed more like her old self. She told me that she was back in school, and so was Danny Fox, though he had lost a couple of toes in the accident and couldn't play soccer anymore, and that he would be really glad to see me. It sounded to me like she'd gotten to be pretty good friends with him, and I was glad about that, since there was never anything wrong with Danny Fox that I could see, and I never did think he smelled bad, though Heather was always complaining. She asked me if I was coming back to school with her on Monday, and I said I didn't know. Roy told her to stop badgering me and let me get my breath, and he was right, that was just what I was doing, sitting in the armchair trying to breathe again.

Alice made a lot of phone calls to try to find out what was happening with Mama, and we turned on the TV, though I was scared to watch since I was sure I'd see the whole Bunker going up in flames. Heather put on all the same stupid shows she always watched, and every so often a News Bulletin would come in and tell us about the North Carolina Standoff, as they were calling it. Finally, my eyes started falling shut, and Alice tried to whisk me off to bed, but even though I was afraid of what I might see, I didn't want to leave until I found out what was going on in the Bunker.

Finally, at around midnight, the news teams standing around there got all excited. The front door to the Bunker opened, and a bunch of people began streaming out with their hands up. Most of the ones who came out were women and children, and I guessed that a lot of the men with guns were staying behind. At almost the end of the line, I saw Mama, her hands on her head. She seemed to be looking around nervously, like she was making sure I wasn't there, and she was squinting like the light from all the police cars and cameras bothered her eyes. When I saw her, relief just whooshed right through me, and I finally let Alice talk me into going upstairs and lying down. I didn't have my cow pajamas anymore, since I had left them behind, and I felt sad about that, but Alice found some other pajamas for me, Heather's I guess, and when I got into them I suddenly felt all cozy and sleepy.

When I was lying down in bed, Alice came in and sat next to me. She brushed my hair away from my face and said how glad they all were to see me, and that I could stay there as long as I wanted to, hopefully forever, though she understood if I felt I needed to be with my other family. I noticed that she didn't say "real" family, and I was glad about that, because at that moment, though it surprised me to realize it, Alice and Roy and Heather felt just as real to me as anyone.

"I don't know what's going to happen with Mama," I told her. I could hardly think straight, but it did seem pretty clear that this business with Cyrus and the Bunker was not going to do Mama any good in trying to get the Littles back, and I might have a better chance of seeing them on my own. And the truth was, now that I was sure Mama was okay, and that she was out of the Bunker, I found myself looking back on the whole thing in a different way. I wasn't sure that if I were someone's mama, I would let them go into a big concrete place with a lot of guns, or that I would let them go alone to some old man with a braided ponytail, no matter who he said he was. It wasn't like I was mad at Mama—I understood why she did those things. But it seemed clear to me that I was going to have to start taking care of myself in a new way, that I was going to have to stop relying on people for things as if I was still a child.

When I looked at Alice sitting next to me, her face was kind, and she was looking at me with that hopeful way she had, her eyes all soft and out of focus because she wasn't wearing her glasses, looking like she wanted to give me whatever I needed, at least if she could. But I didn't know what I needed. I suddenly didn't even feel like sleeping anymore—I felt all keyed-up, just lying there thinking about things, and I was kind of afraid to shut my eyes for fear that I'd see myself back in that dark tunnel again. I found myself telling Alice that I would definitely be here for a while. I told her that I wanted to be a doctor like Dr. Greenberg and asked her if she thought I could do that.

"You could do anything you want to, Mary Fred," she said, and I could tell she really believed that.

"Is he—are you—"

"We've been seeing a lot of each other." Her cheeks got a little bit pink, and that made her look younger. "It's all because of you, Mary Fred. When I think back on all the things that have happened because of you, it just amazes me."

"Why, what else?"

"Well, there's Roy."

"What about Uncle Roy? Did he like that camp he went to?"

"I don't know if he liked it, really. Let's just say it did him a lot of good. Doesn't he seem well?"

"He seems really different. He doesn't look so sleepy anymore."

"Did you like Marcy?"

"She seemed nice." Marcy was the dark-haired woman, and I guessed that she was Uncle Roy's new girlfriend. "Did he meet her at camp?"

"That's right."

"So everyone's happy."

"I guess so, Mary Fred. I guess we are. Puffin's still a bit affected by the accident—she has nightmares sometimes, but she's much better. How about you, honey—how are you? I mean really?"

"I'm happy to be here, ma'am." Then I laughed and said, "Alice."

"But how was it where you were?"

"Oh. . . ." I tried to think of a way to tell her about it, but I couldn't think of any words. "Alice, I sort of realized something while I was there."

"What's that?"

"I don't really know. Alls I know is there was this moment when I had to decide if I was going to stay or go. And I decided to go."

"That's called voting with your feet," Alice said. She held my hand and patted it.

"So I guess I did that. And here I am."

"I'm so glad you're here, Mary Fred," she said. She leaned over and kissed my forehead, then stood up. "Get some rest, honey. You've had a rough day."

Alice didn't know the half of it, I thought. I said good night to her, and thanked her, but she laughed and said I didn't need to thank her, that this was home. Then she said thank you to me, and we laughed a little bit, and then she turned out the light and left.

For a while, I lay there in the dark, trying to sleep, but I still didn't feel the least bit tired. When I'd close my eyes, I'd see Cyrus at the front of the room with his cell phone, or next to me with the naked blond girl, or else I'd see Mama and the way she looked at me just before I said good-bye to her. Then I saw myself running through the woods, and at first I felt scared again, but suddenly the Littles were skipping alongside me, playing, and then Alice and Heather and Roy were there too, and all of them were laughing together. Then, just as suddenly, I was back in the tunnel, with Ozma of Oz, and Dorothy, and Billina the chicken, and they were all groping in the darkness with me, trying to get away from the Bunker, holding little matches that burned brightly for about two seconds before going out. The darkness of the room, or maybe it was the tunnel, seemed to sparkle around me, as if it was full of little magic things that I had never seen before, all the things that connected me to the people I knew, as if all around us were fine webs, everywhere we went, threads of gold and silver that flashed in the darkness and showed us where we came from and where we had to go.

About the Author

ABBY BARDI, born and raised in Chicago, has worked as a singing waitress in Washington, D.C.; an English teacher in Japan and England; a performer on England's country-and-western circuit; and, most recently, as a professor at Prince George's Community College. Author of a column called "Sin of the Month" for the *Takoma Voice,* she is married with two children and lives in Ellicott City, Maryland.